BLACK SUN MOON

A SWORD AND SORCERY NOVEL

DYLAN DOOSE

BOOK DESCRIPTION

BLACK SUN MOON

In the beginning there was madness and there was death.

A string of occult murders leads veteran holy-man-with-a-big-sword, Cullum Shrike, to Wardbrook, a treacherous place of pagan practices, corrupt leaders, and sinister sorcery.

Cullum must purge his beliefs as he is forced to face the evil within, for when all light dies, only darkness can kill a shadow.

New heroes join the fray. Are they friend or foe?

Cullum Shrike, warrior priest of the holy Order of Seekers. Haunted by the ghosts of his failures, he clings to his faith even as treachery and insidious betrayal are revealed.

Nyva, the young witch, bound to the black house on the hill. She is stronger than she could imagine, she just needs someone to unlock her latent power.

An unlikely pair, but a pair they do make and when the dancing starts, they might just bring the house down.

Don't miss this thrilling—and terrifying—stand-alone full-length novel in the dark and gritty Sword and Sorcery series!

ALSO BY DYLAN DOOSE

SWORD AND SORCERY SERIES:

Fire and Sword (Volume 1)

Catacombs of Time (Volume 2)

I Remember My First Time (A Sword and Sorcery short story; can
be read at any point in the series)

The Pyres (Volume 3)

Ice and Stone (Volume 4)

As They Burn (Volume 5)

Black Sun Moon (Volume 6)

Embers on the Wind (Volume 7)

RED HARVEST SERIES:

Crow Mountain (Volume 1)

∽

For info, excerpts, contests and more, join Dylan's Reader Group!

Website: www.DylanDooseAuthor.com

BLACK SUN MOON
  e-ISBN 978-1-7752350-1-9
  print ISBN: 978-1-7773245-2-0

www.DylanDooseAuthor.com

PROLOGUE

T he blond-haired, blue-eyed boy sat with his back against his favorite red maple in the courtyard of Wardbrook. The boy's favorite birds, two ravens, were speaking to each other as they hobbled on the branches above him. The boy knew they were talking about him, he knew they were laughing at him too. He didn't mind; he knew he deserved their mockery. Because he had sat here every day since his parents had left, looking down the hill past the trees to the village. He hoped he would see them coming home. Like a fool, like a child, like the faithful, he hoped they would come home. He always smiled as he let the hope swell and persist, he smiled from the thoughts of what was and what could still be.

But now after, all those days, those weeks, those months- —has it been that long?—since they left, the emotions beneath the smile were changing. They were transforming into something terrible, something monstrous, something the boy would need even if he were not sure he wanted it.

"Theron," whispered Chayse as she came up from behind

7

the tree, silent as a cat. Or maybe Theron was just too deep in thought to have heard her coming.

"Hey, Chayse," Theron said without looking up at her.

"What are ya' doing," she asked, just like she did every time she found him out here. She put her back to the tree and slid down next to him. It must have hurt; it must have scraped her skin. She didn't flinch, though.

Theron gave a short laugh.

Chayse was quiet for a time, looking down the hill with him. Then she asked, "Why'd they do it? Where did they go?"

"I've told you this a hundred times," Theron said without irritation. "So has Hakesworth, and Welfric, and how many others?"

"Told me what? That our parents went on a journey? A mission? For a king? That they are sacred monster hunters of a secret royal order that traverses space and time to slay demons and beasts, all for the betterment of mankind?" Chayse laughed and ruffled Theron's hair.

That was what he always did to her. He winced.

"That is a fucking bedtime story, brother," Chayse said, serious now. "I had my first blood last week. I don't want any more bedtime stories. I want the truth."

Theron laughed a deep bitter laugh. It sounded like a man's laugh, one who was filled with hate. He turned to Chayse, still smiling, and in that instant, he knew that his smile was poison. The cynic's smile who can't help but unspin the tethers of purpose until they are just wild strands of absurd jokes.

"You think I know the truth?" He shook his head, baffled.

"You know something I don't," Chayse said.

"Oh yeah? What would that be? That they didn't go on a mission? That they are part of no order and serve no king, no higher power than themselves? Are you too not aware that they were so close when it came to shaping us in their own image, and so far when it came to a parent's love?"

Chayse looked away.

"Don't look away. You asked, so listen," Theron said.

She looked back, and for a moment he thought she might hate him. He didn't stop. She'd asked for the truth as he knew it, and he would give her that because he hated the lies that others had given him.

"Our parents left us because they were bored, Chayse. That is the truth of it. There was a time when they thought they had it all figured out, that they knew their purpose, knew what they wanted. But they were wrong. They were bored from the start, and whatever we are, whatever we have become wasn't enough to make them stay. They aren't coming back. Not ever." There. He'd said it aloud. At last. At last.

Chayse's eyes welled with tears and he almost regretted what he had said. Almost. But if Chayse was to hunt monsters, she would need to be strong. The truth would make her strong.

"At least they left you the sword," she whispered. "They left me with nothing." The tears rolled down Chayse's cheeks. Theron wiped them from her chin.

"They left us with each other." He squeezed Chayse's arm and then he panned his other hand over the vast lands of village, farm, and ravine before them. "They left us with all this. And so we can hate them, but we have to thank them, too. Because they left us with freedom Chayse."

Chayse squinted at him, unsure of what he meant.

"We get to choose. We get to choose who we become, where we go, who we fight, who we love. The battles, the parties, they won't be theirs, they will be ours. We can be the shapers and the makers of our own destiny." All this came to Theron only as he said it, as if his sister's tears had rallied

9

him to find something in the dark to grab onto, to hold up and place on a pedestal, even if it was the dark itself.

"What should we do then?" Chayse asked. "What should we do with our freedom and our destinies?"

"I was in Burnswich yesterday. I saw two contracts on the notice board, small bounties for small prey. One is a Grave Banshee that has been terrorizing farmers on the outskirts of Baytown, and the other is for an old lycanthrope that is believed to be a citizen of Burnswich, changing when the moon is right and eating people's chickens. I think my sword skills and your bow skills are ready for it."

Chayse smiled.

"I think so," she agreed. "Should we tell Welfric to help us?"

"Don't need him."

"Which contract should we take? Baytown, or the old wolf in Burnswich?" Chayse's hands were shaking now with excitement

Theron reached into his pocket and took out a Brynthian Ducat. "Flip a coin?"

Chayse nodded.

"Heads for the Grave Banshee."

"Tails for the wolf."

The blond-haired, blue-eyed boy flipped the coin.

≈

In another place, another time—future, present, past—those who knew the truth danced at the Deadmen's party. Here is the story of the time before the legendary hunter Theron Ward, a time when he was yet to be.

PART I
THE CALLING

$\approx$

*T*his house, this house, this blackened shadow home. The hallways, the floorboards, the walls; I hear them weep, I hear them moan.

In the nighttime when the moonlight leaks its way in through my open window and the wind blows the curtains within, silhouettes dance and call me to sin.

As I shiver in my bedclothes, my eyes shift to the mirror that hangs beneath the painting of Father. I see their red eyes, those of the shadow men.

Even in my waking hours as I walk the estate grounds alone, I see no daylight, only fog that has fallen from the hanging clouds.

As I write this, I lift the knife to my breast and pray for forgiveness for all the things I have done in this black house of Wardbrook, this place that is a gateway to the catacombs that call me closer, ever closer to the Shadow Zone.

$\approx$

CHAPTER ONE

✍

A BAT OUT OF HELL

*E*ight hooves of nocturne-black steeds thundered across the prairie, the torches of their riders setting the sweat on their backs to glistening as they charged a fire-lit cave entrenched in a hillock beyond the moonlit pasture.

A glowing hunter's moon frowned down from above, thousands of frantic flying silhouettes cast upon it. The bats screamed as they flapped from the cave into the night sky.

A girl screamed from within.

The bats dipped low at the riders.

"We're too late," Herres called as the bats shrieked and flapped around them.

"We're not. We can't be." Cullum whacked at the bats with his torch. The faces of the last two victims flashed in his mind's eye. *Not again. I won't fail again.*

As he closed in on the cave and the pagan magic within, his Luminescent-blessed left hand ached with the *Bloodburn* —a gift possessed by all Seekers, an ability to sense sorcery. Every sorcerer, every beast, every incarnate, every single magical thing gave off a signature *Bloodburn*. A good Seeker could differentiate between species of creature, legion of demon, discipline of sorcery, by having a strong awareness of their supernatural sense. Cullum was not merely a good Seeker. He was a gifted Vicar, and not only could he make all these differentiations, but by reading the blood the way a scholar reads a tome, he was able to trace all magical discharge back to its caster. He welcomed the pain in his hand. He always did.

Another shriek echoed from the cave entrance. And then another.

But the second was not that of a human.

The bats dispersed and melded into the darkness, as if even those winged creatures of the night feared the happenings in the cave.

Cullum swung his leg over before his horse had come to a full stop and sprinted up the stony hill toward the cave entrance.

Three rituals.

One to find him...and that girl died—

One to beseech him...and that girl also died—

Cullum threw away his torch, drew his sword in one hand, and took a frost flask from his belt with the other.

And one to bring him unto flesh...

"Don't die. Don't die." Cullum panted the words in rhythm with his leaping strides.

"Cullum, wait!" Herres called from behind. Too far behind. Cullum could not afford to wait. The thirteen-year-old girl had been taken from her home, from her parents while they slept, by people they had once called neighbors.

He would not slow down.

He breached the entrance. He saw what was within, and the fractured, charred, crumbling thing Cullum Shrike called his heart felt like it finally turned to dust.

An ember of rage touched that dust and it caught flame.

He was too late.

The cultists in their red hoods surrounded the girl where she lay bound on the altar. She twitched as she died, true horror carved into her face as the furless, gray-fleshed bat grew, doubling in size as it tore from her abdomen.

If Cullum were a normal soldier in the King of Brynth's army, the fear and the heartbreak would have turned him back. The ugly odds and a mission already failed would have turned him back. The hell-spawn manifesting from a raped virgin's dead flesh would have caused him to lose his faith. *For what sort of god is the Luminescent that he could allow such atrocity to occur among his children?*

Cullum was not a soldier in the king's army. He was a Seeker, the Luminescent's hunter, a soldier in *his* army. *Soldiers of the sun never turn tail; we never run. Our faith—the invulnerable shield that keeps our will to task—does not break, even if the heart of the man who holds it already has.*

"I am Cullum Shrike!" he roared. The cultists turned from their rising demon and faced him. "Vicar of the Church's holy order of the Seekers. And I am here to show you wrath!"

Their red robes wet with the blood of innocence lost, curved, dripping daggers in their hands, they murmured prayers to the dark as they came forth. The demonic bat that had crawled from the dead girl's womb stretched its folded wings and wobbled on its new legs. It was now at its full size, as large as two men.

Cullum maintained his slow advance. The girl was dead. There was no longer any need to hurry. He could take his time and be sure he sent each and every one of them down to the iciest domain at the bottom of hell. He could do his best to make sure it hurt. He could do his best to be certain that, in the end, these vermin felt all the pain and fear of those they victimized and tortured.

None would escape.

"However dark comes the night, the heretics' flesh will

stoke the fires of the Light, and come the morning, the Luminescent will smile on their ashes." Cullum knew he sounded more animal than man as he bellowed the old Seekers' proverb, and he was glad for it. He was the hound dog that always, *always* rooted out the prey.

Cullum hurled the frost flask at the feet of the apostate filth who circled to his left.

It exploded into an orb of righteous blizzard, large enough to engulf four of them and turn the leg of a fifth to solid ice. The man screamed in agony as he collapsed to the ground and dragged himself away from his frozen cohorts across the cave's stone floor, staring at the limb that was so cold he must have thought it to be burning with hell fire.

"That is called *doom*, what you are feeling now, you filth," Cullum shouted. "There is no way out."

In the periphery of his vision, he saw the demon move, his wings lifting and expanding, flicking the coating of afterbirth at the cave's walls.

A cowled figure—a woman—lunged, stabbing out with a weak yell. Cullum's coat billowed as he evaded the assault and swung his saber in a glinting silver flash to sever her head. She collapsed to her knees, her head rolling off to hang in her hood.

A throwing knife whirled by his head, sticking the next foe between the eyes.

Herres.

Then two more blades glinted past, and two more heretics fell dead.

The bat's wings were fully spread now.

"Cullum, don't let the fiend take flight!" Herres yelled.

The wings flapped.

Too far. Cullum was too far away to strike it.

He whipped his shoulder and hurled his saber like a spear.

The blade struck the bat in its chest.

If the creature had a heart, it was apparent that it did not need it to live, for despite the sword buried to the hilt in its chest, it still came forth, smashing two of the cultists aside with its wings.

Cullum rolled his shoulders, reaching to the cauldron in his soul for the power bestowed by the Luminescent and his Order. His focus was complete. He saw the demon, only the demon. It moved as slow as sap running down a tree in early spring.

The back of his left hand throbbed and prickled as if it had been struck by a hammer, as if a thousand fire ants bit at his skin. The *Bloodburn* was speaking to him, and it was telling him this devil in front of him was asking for the Order's chains.

The magic took him and became him, and he became it.

Herres would battle the mortals while Cullum battled this thing of dark magic and death.

"In these shackles, I return you to hell," he yelled, and the sound of his voice traveled as slowly as the hell-spawn moved, each second an eternity.

The bones in his forearms felt like they would split as he raised both arms to the fiend, palms open. From the center of his hands, the arcane blue chains shot free and wrapped around the bat's body and wings. The fiend shrieked and struggled.

In an explosion of high-pitched noise and rapid movement, time again flowed at a raging pace.

But still Cullum could only see the bat.

The more the bat struggled, the tighter the glowing, ephemeral chains became. The thing's flesh began to cook and smolder, the stench of it far more impactful than the pong of burning human flesh. The creature's massive black eyes bulged. The chains touched Cullum's sword where it protruded from the demon's chest, and the blade took on the same arcane glow. The bat choked on its screams as it writhed.

Cullum's state of complete focus collapsed as a blade slashed through cloth and skin and muscle. Agony. Heat. Cold fear.

The chains were broken.

The snarling, gritted teeth of the hooded cultist standing before him greeted his return to the mundane world. The man's knife protruded from Cullum's leather armor, buried deep. Herres came up from behind and stabbed the cultist through the base of the skull and out of the mouth.

Cullum tilted his hat just in time to keep the spray of blood and saliva from getting in his eyes as the man fell away, leaving his blade in Cullum.

"Sorry, Cullum. One of them got me," Herres said quietly, but his eyes were wide with fear. He was sweating hard beneath his wide-brimmed hat, his already pale complexion paler still, with a tint of green, and the glow of his eyes looked dim. Cullum was sure he looked the same, but whereas he was bleeding from the abdomen, Herres was leaking from the low back.

"It's all right. Now we are both got," Cullum said, keeping the anger from his voice. Anger that he was stabbed at all, that the one doing the stabbing had been a heretic peasant. "The sun will rise."

"The sun will rise," Herres agreed, then turned and stumbled at the impaled bat. The fiend met him with a swiping claw, and Herres hacked at the fingers with his long knives.

The murmuring of an apostate turned Cullum's focus. A tall man wielding the same flame-shaped knife as the rest of them took two long steps forward and stabbed downward.

Even with a few inches of blade still stuck in his gut, Cullum caught the attacker by the wrist. If the apostate had known anything about combat, he'd have simply dropped the knife from the ensnared hand into the quick, rising grip of his free hand. He would have opened Cullum's throat an instant later.

But the apostate didn't know a damn thing about combat. He knew how to lie, how to steal, how to kidnap, rape, and murder from the shadows, but there were no shadows close enough for the imp to ply his trade. He was likely a village reject who had bonded with the others over the teachings of the wrong types of books. The evil types. Their kind rarely knew anything about how to survive in a direct fight.

So when Cullum's iron grip—enhanced by *the Ordeal* to join the Order, enhanced by the rage and the hatred that seethed in his arcane depths—closed tight enough to break bone around the apostate's wrist, the knife dropped.

The heretic's dark utterings turned to a tormented cry. It sounded to Cullum much like the singing of angels he had heard in his holiest of dreams. He smiled so widely that he felt his cheeks flexing.

Cullum grabbed hold of the dagger sticking in his side and pulled it out with a wince and a spurt of blood. With a twist of the broken wrist, Cullum sent the cultist to his knees and rammed the sacrificial blade under the man's chin so hard that the tip of the knife emerged from the top of his skull. Cullum tossed the flopping corpse aside and moved to defend Herres, who was now making his own attempt at the chains on the bat demon that wriggled within the tethers. There were only five cultists left, and they were not eager to attack Herres as Cullum placed his back to his partner's. The cultists circled and bayed like starving coyotes preparing to risk all for a big-game meal.

"Darkness breaks before the light...always, heathens," Cullum said, his words steady, his breathing under control. It was nearly over. He would kill them all. "Despite your dark efforts, your demon is going back to hell's pit in the chains of the Church. You will be going to hell with it in chains of wrath and torment."

Two broke off running toward the mouth of the cave.

"And the shadow will never escape the sun!" Cullum pulled the fire flask from his belt. He threw it with perfect aim and hit the fleeing woman in the lead. The glass orb burst on her back, and the mixture within erupted. Magma cooked her as she screamed, a flaming human torch that burst and sent molten blood and fire washing over the second fleeing cultist. Robes blazing, he ran wailing from the cave into the night.

The bat's shriek reached its pinnacle, and then there was a pop, and wet warmth splashed over Cullum's hat and coat.

The bat was no more.

The last three cultists dropped their knives and cowered, knees trembling.

"The sun will rise," Herres said, stepping next to Cullum. Black demonic ichor dripped from the tip of his hat and covered his face. His glowing blue eyes beamed again, the signs of pain from his wound swallowed by the euphoria that came after the destruction of any demon or beast, sorcerer or witch who felt the justice of the chains. It was a kind of drunken bliss.

"The sun will rise," Cullum agreed, and put pressure on the wound in his side, wincing. Then he smiled as he looked at the remaining three cultists. They were on their knees now, praying for mercy, as if they finally understood the wrath of the Luminescent. But they did not understand. Not yet.

≈

It took until sun up to get it done.

It could have taken moments.

But Vicar Cullum Shrike of the Order of Seekers had time to spare. It was his duty to the Church to spare that time. It was his oath to the three dead little girls to spare that time.

The first of the children had been nine, the second girl fifteen, and the last thirteen. Some would claim the latter two were young women. They would be wrong. Cullum understood they were just little girls. And that was why the punishment that came down upon the heretic filth who had harmed them had to be righteous.

The fact that Cullum enjoyed carrying out that righteousness was inconsequential. Or so he told himself.

"As violence will beget violence, so too will sorcery summon the Seeker's wrath," Cullum said.

"Through us, *His* hands, they will suffer," Herres said from beside him, the words broken up by the chattering of his teeth. Herres' wound had been worse than Cullum's. They had washed the gaping slash with water from the stream that ran near the cave, then burned the wound shut and used what medicaments remained from their travels across Brynth.

"Your wound?" Cullum asked. His own throbbed and ached.

"The holy serums will keep me alive," Herres said after a moment, and offered a sickly smile. "The *Ordeal* was worse, *much* worse."

"It was." Cullum stood, turning to the two cultists still with them. One of them lay a few strides behind Herres' horse, tied by his feet to the back of the saddle. Cullum had shattered his spine with a mallet and a flattened spike after he was tied and stretched, fully prostrated, on the ground. The man felt nothing below the waist, but he felt the rest. He was still feeling the rest. He would feel it as they dragged his crippled body all the way back to Aldwick, to the House of Deacons. To where all of Cullum's holy missions began, ended, and, ultimately, began again.

The second remaining man had his arms snapped by Cullum's bare hands. Herres had slit the tendons in the heretic's heels soon after. He was slung over the back of Cullum's horse, drifting in and out of consciousness, screaming for a moment when he came to, only to pass out again as the horse calmly grazed under him in the pasture, the sun rising in the background to complete that perfect picture of punishment.

In the beginning, such a scene would have sickened Cullum. The Cullum of old would not have been able to carry out such atrocity. But this Cullum had seen what they and their kind did to little girls, little boys...even babes stolen from their cradles.

The majority of the blood on Cullum's hands, arms, chest, face—everywhere—was not from these two. It was not from Herres or himself, or even the battle they had fought. It was from the man they had left outside the cave where the girl had died in agony staring up at hooded faces.

Cullum had nailed the last cultist, spread-eagle, to the hill at the cave entrance. He and Herres had buried the mutilated, barely cold remains of the girl while her tormentor screamed to the morning sun. Then Cullum had taken his time with the finest, sharpest blades to flay a most magnificent portrait of a beaming sun into the man's flesh.

It started on his chest and abdomen. To make the circle that was the sun's center, Cullum had skinned a wide radius, just enough layers for the blood to rise from the pores in red beads.

Then came the rays, and they were brilliant.

"The world can be miserable. It can so often be unjust. It certainly can be, but you did this to yourself," Cullum had said, leaning in to look in the man's eyes. "The rats in the cave, they will smell your blood and you will be consumed by what you are, vermin."

The apostate had answered with bestial grunts, his eyes all animal. Pain, horror, and madness twisted his face into a thing hardly human.

"Hail the Luminescent; we have done his work," Herres had said, prying the knife from Cullum's blood-slick fingers. Cullum had let him.

They could still hear the heretic's screams now.

"What a sweet symphony," said Cullum as he tilted his head and let his ears bask in the sound.

With a sidelong glance, Herres raised his hands in prayer to the Luminescent. He did not speak, and this left his gesture's motive in question. Cullum wondered if Herres was afraid of him, just as Mikael had been, and Forrestan, and Vayrus. They had feared him. And they were all dead now. He had a long list of dead partners. Regrettable. Even sad. But he could not change the past now. He did not allow himself to miss them or mourn them. He did not allow himself the bonds of friendship.

Cullum knelt and washed the blood from his hands. He stared at the watery reflection of his own blue eyes, his gaunt, pale, clean-shaven face. The scars of old wounds with their tiny stitch marks lined his brows and cheekbones. They mangled his lips and clawed his nose. Before the scars, perhaps some women would have found him handsome. He smiled at his reflection. He was happy for the scars; he had no need to be handsome, only fearsome. And that he was.

"'Neath the hunter's moon,
The bat's wings spread,
The bat's wings spread,
The bat's wings spread.
The black rats feed
And the Heretics scream.
'Neath the red moon,
The wicker man burns,
The wicker man burns,
The wicker man burns.
The throats are slit,
The bones are split,
And the mother bleeds."

Diana Ward sang to herself as she rode her spotted gray mare through the rolling hills in the dead of night. Such a grand adventure she had just had. Great escapes, heartache, beauty, romance, hatred. Towering black monoliths with thousands of steps. Fishmen, dragon-people, and the sound a world makes when it ends. She had liked the girl, Eona. Such passion, such fight. She had liked her and so had saved her, though she could have let her die. She couldn't save them all.

Wolves howled in the nearby ravine that Diana had always loved so dearly—the budding green in spring, the colors in autumn.

Three years it had been, but she was finally home. Home to her husband, her lands, and her people. Wardbrook. She smiled and sang on.

"'Neath the hunter's moon..."

CHAPTER TWO

❦

MESSENGER

*T*he embers from the burning Golden Goat petals in the wide bowl of the long pipe crackled, the hot smoke scorching Nyva's throat as she filled her lungs. Her eyes went wide and tears formed as she coughed the smoke back out. She doubled over in a fit of coughing and rolled on the dirt floor of Nan's house.

Jeremiah and Franklin only laughed at her suffering. They had already gone through it themselves, and when she looked up, she saw they watched her with absolute glee.

Nyva's heart pounded like she had just run for her life, and run far. For a moment, she was afraid, anxiety building from her toes and rising to her forehead with a wave of nausea, and then...then there was joy, pure and holy. The heat turned to warmth. Her pounding heart sent tingling sensations down her spine, and she shivered.

The hearth fire glowed so brightly that Nyva had to shield her eyes, and she laughed at the brightness as if it were funny. The threads of Nan's dreamcatchers—circles of braided wicker filled with woven net—that hung from the low ceiling vibrated and undulated. The white and red

29

feathers swirled and mingled with the black ones and the gray ones, before re-forming as they had been.

"Ahh," Nyva exclaimed. Jeremiah and Franklin turned their heads up from where they were huddled together on her small sack bed, and they too exclaimed, "Ahh."

The three of them stared at the dreamcatchers, with the glow of the fire blazing by their sides. For how long, Nyva did not know. The dried, crushed Golden Goat petals that they had smoked had removed the comprehension of time from their understanding.

Nan had warned Nyva it would do that. She had warned of this, and she had warned not to do it at all. Nan thought Golden Goat was for spells and rituals. But Nan wasn't here.

"Nyva," Jeremiah said. Nyva did not respond or turn from the rippling dreamcatchers. She was only somewhat aware of her mouth hanging open and the drool forming at her lower lip.

"Nyva," Franklin said, right after, or maybe long after. This time, Nyva looked back at them; they were still in the bed and had taken off their shirts. She did not remember their bodies being so beautiful, so lean and strong. Franklin was smiling, and he patted the bed in the space between he and Jeremiah.

Nyva began to stand, but as her world spun, she opted to remain on her knees and crawl toward the space in her bed between the boys she'd known all her life. But in this moment, she thought she didn't know them at all. They were both dark-haired, tall and tanned, but Franklin was more handsome, so Nyva paid her attention to him first.

She crawled up between them and then touched Franklin's chest. He stroked her arms, his palms rough from farm work. There was something to be said about the caress of rough hands. Franklin kissed her as Jeremiah wrapped his hands around her waist and kissed her shoulder through her dress.

"Take this off," Franklin said, and he and Jeremiah pulled up her hem. A flicker of unease pricked her. Not from the boys she lay with—this activity was not a new one, though the addition of the intoxicating herb was. They had been secretly playing together like this since they were children.

No, something else sent a chill of wariness crawling across her skin. Nyva glanced at the door. She squinted against the dimness and the shadows cast by the hearth fire, but saw no one. Still, she felt unease. She felt as if they were being watched.

Nan's house was but two rooms, the room where Nyva and Nan slept and the room where Nan did her work and saw her visitors. But Nan was out gathering herbs, or so she had said an hour ago, and the herbs she needed were far off.

Had an hour passed already?

"Did you two hear something?" Nyva whispered, and sat up, pushing the boys' hands off her dress. "Nan? Are you back?" Nyva called into the other room, signaling to the boys to be silent. There came no response.

"Nyva, relax. There's nothing and no one here but us," Jeremiah whispered, and ran his hand up Nyva's dress and between her legs. She sighed and lay back down to kiss Franklin hard on the lips as Jeremiah used his strong fingers to stroke her. She closed her eyes and cherished the warmth and taste of Franklin's mouth, only pulling hers away so that she could let them pull her dress over her head.

She gasped when cool lips touched her back and went warm as they sucked her skin. Franklin slid down her front, kissing her breasts and stomach.

Nyva again opened her eyes, and gasped.

Crawling and scuttling from the shadows into the fire's glow was a thing that turned her blood cold and made her skin crawl. Bulging black orb eyes stared at her from a bearded face that was human in feature but not form, for it was smaller than a child's, attached to a rodentlike body with long and dark matted hair instead of fur, its abdomen covered in boils that glowed orange like hot coals. The creature had four arms instead of two, with little humanoid rat hands at the ends.

Nyva tried to cry a warning, but was paralyzed by fear and horror as the thing crept closer to Franklin's back.

It rose on its hind legs.

She held utterly still. Franklin drew back and stared down at her, looking puzzled.

The atrocity smiled to reveal its long, jagged human teeth.

Nyva shoved Franklin and screamed, a shriek so piercing her own ears rang.

As Franklin fell from the bed, he glanced back. All color drained from his face and, with a squeak, he scuttled behind Nyva and a confused Jeremiah to physically put their lives before his own.

"Nyva!" The boil-encrusted, hairy horror was gone, and in the doorway stood Nan, all six girthy feet of her.

Jeremiah's trousers were down, his softening dick out. Nyva was stark naked, not a sheet near enough to cover up. The picture was not a good one. Nan glared with enough rage in her eyes to stare down a bull with a bee stinger in its bollocks near a heifer in heat.

Nan hated everything. She hated her first husband and her second, both of whom beat her. She had hated them until she killed them, and she hated them still. Only Nyva knew that. Nan hated the Enlightened and their god the Luminescent, even though Brynth was not the place to hate the Church. Nan didn't give a damn. She'd been whipped, she'd been exiled time and time again, she'd been blinded in an eye and had lost an ear for her hatred, but she hated on.

Only in the fiefdom of Wardbrook had the lord and lady not sent her on her way when the village people reported her a pagan, and although children threw shit at her and men and women threw insults, they had not come to the door with pitchforks like so many before.

Yes, Nan was hated by nearly all, and she hated all just the same.

All but one: the orphan girl that was her charge.

Nyva.

And that did not bode well for the boys.

This was the first time Nyva had brought the boys here. They usually met in the woods or a barn. But it had been cold that morning, and Nan had been meant to be away. Nyva thought of the time she had spent convincing Franklin and Jeremiah that it was safe. She had been a fool.

Nan already had her pot in her hand and a wide stance at the door; the only way out was through. Jeremiah and Franklin knew Nan from stories—and not from stories Nyva had told them, but from stories their parents and the church father told them. Stories of the big witch woman who lived in the hut past the trees and up the hill on the ravine's edge.

"Oh, you boys wanna fuck, do you?" Nan asked in a deep voice that rumbled from her belly. She lowered her chin and stared blades. "I'll give you a fuckin'. Oh, old Nan will fuck you right and good."

Nyva was too giddy from the smoke of the Golden Goat to react beyond pulling her dress back over herself and staring wide-eyed at Nan. "A rat," she blurted, stumbling over the word as the memory of the rat creature made her shudder.

"It's not how it looks," Jeremiah said, voice cracking, as he fumbled to put his dick away while Nan lumbered forward, grimacing, the pot so tight in her thick fist that her knuckles were white.

Franklin tried to crawl away while Nan's wrath was diverted, but that was what Nan wanted. She was near sixty years, and although she was still built like an ox, she was built like an old one that had no energy to chase or flee from anything. Nan met things head-on, the way a wall does. Franklin crawled just close enough; another few inches and Nan would have probably landed wrong.

Fate had it that she landed right, and she landed heavy as she sprawled onto Franklin's back. The air burst from them both when Franklin hit the dirt floor, all of Nan's mass bearing down on him.

Nyva felt dizzy as she watched, her mouth wide. "The rat," she said again, but no one was listening.

Nan got to her knees and planted her left hand on Franklin's face, using it for balance.

Jeremiah should have waited the extra moment and got his trousers fully up before he tried to escape, but as always, he was premature, and this time it cost him more than it cost Nyva. He fiddled with his buckle, and so he did not have his eyes on Nan when he tried to run past her through the very tight doorway where she mounted the defeated Franklin.

She hit Jeremiah hard in the shin with her pot, dropping him. And like a massive toad, Nan leapt from Franklin's beaten form to mount a much more prepared Jeremiah, who fought with all his fear and vigor against Nan's downpour of strikes with fist and pot.

After a few seconds, Jeremiah's left hand was pinned flat by Nan's knee as she delivered unanswered blows to his face with her right fist, whilst he clung for desperate life to her other hand—the one that brandished the pot, his grip weakening with each blow of Nan's concussive hambone fists.

In the chaos, Nyva watched, horrified, as, from the shadow, again came the man-headed rat thing, an orange glow beneath it. It scurried into the fray and, with its filthy teeth, bit into Jeremiah's left hand.

Nyva screamed.

The storm froze; all elements went completely still but for the rat thing, which again scurried away, melding back into the shadow as fast as it had manifested from it.

"Nan, the rat! It's a rat!" Nyva yelled, and leapt to her feet. "Nan, stop."

Nan lifted her head and stared at Nyva.

Franklin had enough life in him to get back to his feet and stumble on wobbling legs out of Nan's abode.

"Did they 'urt you?" Nan asked, breathing heavily. She held her fist at the ready and kept her dominant mounted position atop the beaten Jeremiah. Nyva could hear him weeping.

"No, Nan," Nyva said. "It was my choice. They are friends."

Nan snorted a laugh as she slowly got to her feet, pushing off Jeremiah's chest to stand.

He crawled toward the door, then scrambled to his feet, a stain on his trousers' bottom. He fled the small home, bloody and afraid, without looking back.

"What have you done, Nan?" Nyva asked, head spinning, gorge rising. She felt like...like she would soon...

Nyva threw up, tea and oats that tasted like Golden Goat.

"What 'ave *I* done?" Nan asked. "What the fuck 'ave *I* done?"

"The rat—" Nyva began.

"Nyva!" Nan yelled. "What did you take? Why were there two Enlightened, church-goin', Luminescent-fearin' farm boys in your bed with their dicks out and your two little sorry excuses for tits out? Eh?" Nan asked, and pulled Nyva upright to look her in the eyes. Nan's eyes were a brown so faded they looked like old parchment that held the wisdom of ancient gods. Sunspots speckled her leather-tanned face, and deep wrinkles and scars told an ancient tale of a woman that hardship had carved from stone.

"The Golden Goat," Nyva said. "I smoked of the pipe."

Nan laughed again and released Nyva's shoulders. "A puff of the Golden Goat 'as put you in such a state? Slutting about and losing your breakfast?" Nan nodded to the throw-up on the ground. "I'll clean it up," Nan said with a sigh, but without any condemnation.

"I'll clean it—" Nyva said quietly.

"You'll shut your mouth and lie down. You're pale and clammy, and your eyes are wide and wild, like you just seen a divil. I'll fill a couple buckets," Nan said, and went out the door.

"Nan, wait. I did see a devil," Nyva whispered, but Nan was already gone. Again filled with fear, Nyva scanned the room for the rat thing with the glowing boils on its belly. It was not there. She walked to where the dirt floor was clearly marked by the conflict between Nan and the boys, but Nyva could see no sign of the creature's paw prints on the ground. She went as far as getting down on her hands and knees to look for them. Nothing. Part of her wanted to run after Nan and go with her for the water, afraid to be alone, but the dizziness was getting worse and she needed to sit down.

That thing was not real. It was only the herb playing cruel tricks on my eyes.

It had been the boys' idea to try one of Nan's herbs to make things more exciting. She felt a fool. Had she just said no, they would have listened, and when Nan walked in like that, Nyva would have had the composure to explain. She knew that would likely be the end of her friendship with those two boys. They'd go to whispering now, like the rest of the townsfolk.

"Idiot," Nyva said to herself. She lay down on her bed and looked up. The ceiling spun and Nyva wept herself asleep.

When she awakened, she was pleasantly surprised to feel quite well. She yawned, stretched, and smiled at the sun washing in through the window.

"How long was I sleeping?" Nyva mumbled through her dry lips, and sat up. "Nan?" she called.

There was no answer.

Nyva stood. Thoughts of the boys and Nan and the rat thing flashed, and for a moment her stomach rose to her throat before she could swallow it back down and get a hold on her anxiety.

Nyva brushed past Nan's gathering of intricate, feather-decorated dreamcatchers as she made her way to the door of the small log house and out into the bright spring day. She smiled when the sun and the wind touched her. She momentarily forgot all her earthly woes and dreads. She looked out down the green hillock at the village of Wardbrook a few miles off. There was a thicket of trees at the bottom of the hill that wrapped around to the back of Nan's house, creating a ravine. It made Nan and Nyva's gap from the inhabitants of the small village feel larger than it was. Past the village, atop another hill, one higher and also rimmed by ravine woods, was the great black house of Wardbrook. Even on a day as beautiful as this one, it looked ominous, too big, too dark, like the shadow of a house rather than a house itself. Nyva had met the lady only once and never the lord, although she had seen the blond beast of a man many times at a distance.

The lady, Diana Ward, had ridden up to Nan's house when Nyva was all of ten summers—six years past. She had been beautiful, tall, with sharp features. Wide shoulders, big breasts, narrow waist, strong hips. She had been wearing leather armor, and her hair was tied up in wonderful and intricate braids. She'd had a sword at her hip and a shield on her back.

Nyva had thought her to be everything that she ever could want to be. When Diana shot Nyva a look, squinted like a hungry wolf, and then smiled and said, "Beautiful child, would you be so kind as to tell me where your nan is?" Nyva had nearly swooned.

Nan had never told Nyva why Diana came that day, but Nyva was no fool. She knew it had to do with spells and potions, and she had sensed in Diana something even stronger than what she felt from Nan. If Nan was a witch, Diana was far more. Nan had told Nyva three years ago that Lady Ward was gone, that she might never be coming back, and although Nyva knew the woman not at all but for that single visit, she remembered being greatly disturbed at Nan's words.

Nyva thought of her beautiful ladyship as she looked at the ominous black house on the high hill far in the distance, beyond the village in the valley.

"Nan?" Nyva called out. Only her echo answered.

She closed her eyes, tasted the fresh air through her mouth and nose, and reached her hands out to run her fingers through the tall green field, then she walked toward the wood, away from the village, and called once more for Nan, to no avail.

The long grass rippled not far off just before the tree line. Nyva followed the movement until it stopped dead at a large stone, about five feet tall, stuck alone like a single tooth on the hill on which Nan's house was built.

Even before it emerged atop the rock, Nyva somehow knew what was about to appear. A memory of the thing's filthy hair pierced her mind's eye. Then it appeared again, not in memory, but before her, there on the spring day in the high grass atop the lonely stone. The rat thing with the old man's head was more hideous in the light of that beautiful day.

Fire and ice twisted into a storm in Nyva's breast as she felt both immense fear of the thing and raging hatred toward it. She could explain neither to the extent she felt them; it was as if she had felt that way for some time. Like she knew that creature from another life, or in her dreams, forgotten. Or both.

It stood atop the rock, upright on its hind legs, and quickly ran its other four paws through its filthy, long beard of human hair, the motions like those of a fly rubbing its lead legs together and stroking its feelers.

Its left eye bulged as if it were about to pop, the skin around it bright red, surrounded by the purple and blackened flesh of infection. The right eye was small and squinty.

It smiled its rotten, jagged smile and spoke. Or it must have, for Nyva heard its high-pitched voice carry to her with the spring breeze. Its mouth did not move; it just kept smiling and staring with its black eyes.

"Born of the beast," it said, and with the words came a pain in Nyva's skull, as if it had been split and hot coals were being poured in. She saw an image of a woman's naked back, clawed bloody and deep. Black hair, blacker than anything Nyva had ever seen, flowed wild, swaying through the air, sending flecks of her blood to the gray stone floor below. The woman's head tilted back at an impossible angle as she screamed in ecstasy and a clawed, golden-moon-furred hand wrapped around her throat. Her eyes glowed a poisonous emerald green.

"And you will love one who becomes a beast of a different sort."

The vision of the woman dissipated and Nyva's focus returned to the present, the beautiful spring day and the creature atop the rock, its beard and long fur swaying with the breeze. "And to the beasts you shall return. What comes next is going to feel much like a horrible dream, my lady. The new night is endless, and you will never wake."

"What does that mean?" Nyva yelled at the filthy little devil, and looked around for something to attack it with. It was grotesque, but it was small, and she would kill it the way she killed chickens if she had to. She'd twist the maddening fiend's head off. "What are you?" she asked, storming toward it, unarmed. "I'll rip your head off by your little devil beard. Speak!"

"I am only Black Brenna, the humble messenger, my lady," said the creature. Its bulging eye twitched and its little rat paws etched symbols into the air, and then it was gone.

"Nyva!" It was Nan; her voice was frantic and coming from the direction of Wardbrook and the village. "They're coming! Run and hide! Run!" she yelled. And then Nyva heard the shouts of the bloodthirsty mob in the distance.

～

Alexander Ward dozed—drunk—in his armchair by the fire. His hounds were at his feet; his host of drinking companions sprawled, snoring, in the once immaculate dining hall of Wardbrook, now filthy with scraps of food and sprawled cups and bowls in the absence of his orderly wife. The servants, the butler, they remained. But Alexander never allowed them to do their jobs.

When Diana abandoned him yet again, he had wept, just as he had done all the times before. But then his woe turned to spite, and that spite turned to cynicism, and so he chose to revel. And all in the House of Wardbrook reveled. And all in the village at the bottom of the hill beyond the trees got on under the rule of their own laws. They grew ever closer to the teachings of the Enlightened beneath the nose of their pagan lord. He knew it, and he couldn't make himself care.

"I don't give a damn what she'll say..." Alexander mumbled, half-asleep.

The doors to the dining hall swept open. A cold wind whooshed out the fire and then howled about the chamber. Rubbing his eyes, Alexander sat up. He stared, disgruntled, at the extinguished fire and felt a shiver at the chill. There was no light but for the moon's tepid beam coming through the stone windows.

And there she was, standing in the open doorway.

There. She. Was.

In the doorway to the dining hall, she stood. Naked, beautiful, beckoning. "Husband, to the bedchamber with you."

Horror filled him, as it always did when he set eyes upon her after she had been long away. It was not just horror he felt, but hate and revulsion and love and a lust that came from the very nameless pits of his instinct. He rose from his chair and moved toward her, just as he had every other time she came back.

41

CHAPTER THREE

❦

THROUGH THE RAT HOLE

*N*yva's heart wrenched and her stomach turned as she stared at Nan, wild-eyed, hair disheveled, sweat drenching her clothes. She caught Nyva's wrist and yelled, "Run! I tried to talk sense into them. I tried to explain it was not our doing."

Nyva matched Nan's pace, and they ran along the flat terrain of the plateau, through the long grass.

"What was not our doing?" Nyva cried as the sounds of the villagers carried from behind them, distant still, but perhaps a little closer than they had been.

"They're coming up the hill," Nan said. "Faster!"

Ahead of them stood Nan's hut, flanked on two sides by the dark woods and on two sides by the long grass. Nan shoved the door open, and Nyva stumbled through after her, gasping for breath as she slammed the door. As if a door would hold them back. "Nan, there is no safety here. We must go."

Nan grabbed baskets and dumped the contents on the hard-packed dirt floor. A silver thimble rolled to Nyva's feet.

"Where are you? Where are you?" Nan said as she grabbed yet another basket.

Nyva watched through the window. She could hear the mob growing closer, but couldn't see them yet.

"Ah, here it is," Nan exclaimed, and spun around with a mad smile on her face, one unlike any Nyva had ever seen. Her eyes were wide and her teeth were clenched in an underbite, so she looked like a beast baring its teeth while still wagging its tail.

"The mob," Nan said, as she snatched something from the floor and slid it up the sleeve of her baggy sack shirt. "The rabble, the fools, the simpletons, the sheep—they come for violence. They come for more woe. They'll get it." Nan nodded in short, quick bobs.

Nan stormed to the fireplace. Producing flint from her pocket, she worked at getting a blaze going.

"Nan, please. We must go."

"One of the boys, he's dead," Nan said as she worked on the fire.

"Which boy?" Nyva whispered. Franklin? Jeremiah? Which one was dead? Which one still lived?

Nan reached up her sleeve and withdrew a stubby black candle on a small brass dish with a curved handle, no larger than Nyva's palm.

She lit it in the fire, and the flame that danced on the wick was a crimson red, dropping embers to the floor. Nyva stared at the dark flame that produced no light.

"They found the boy dead in the ravine. His flesh was black, his lips and tongue a deep blue, and his eyes were rotted and blistered."

"And they blame us?" Nyva whispered.

Nan shrugged and lifted a bottle of her home-brewed spirits before walking back out into the spring day.

The rat creature. The bite. So it was Jeremiah who lay dead. She wished it was neither.

The baying of the mob grew louder. Closer.

Nyva had once looked into a rabbit's eyes as Nan twisted its neck. She thought her own eyes must look like that now.

Witches...cunt...burn...justice...

"Nan, there was a creature. I saw a creature," Nyva called through the open door. "A rat that was no rat. It bit Jeremiah, and it returned today. It spoke to me." Nyva was no longer able to hold back her tears. "Nan, we'll tell them. They'll listen to us if we tell them."

Witches...cunt...burn...justice...

"Will they?" Nan gave an ugly laugh and lifted the light-less black candle of crimson flame. "This creature, did it have a name?"

"Black Brenna," Nyva whispered through trembling lips. "It said its name was Black Brenna."

"Oh no. So soon," Nan said, her eyes growing dull.

Witches...cunt...burn...justice...

Louder now, and so very close.

"Oh, my little Nyva," Nan said. "If I could, I'd kill them all for you, I would. But alas, I can't. You must take my knife. You must enter the woods and you must get to Wardbrook. Our lady has returned. She will protect you, even after her falling out with your mother."

"Diana Ward has returned? Wait...my mother? What falling out with my mother? You never said you knew my mother... Nan?" Nyva's thoughts swirled and twisted.

"Go, child. My knife. Be swift." Nan jutted her chin toward the woods.

"Nan..." Nyva wept.

Nan lurched forward and bumped Nyva with a light head butt, like the crazy old goat she was.

"Go through the woods," Nan commanded her. "Give the

45

village a wide berth. Don't stop moving until Lady Ward stands before you." Nan pulled Nyva close with one powerful arm and kissed her on the forehead.

Nyva's knees were shaking so terribly that she could hardly stand.

"Get," Nan said. "You don't want to see what old Nan is capable of when she has no choices left. You don't want to see that at all." Nan's expression turned to stone. She tilted her head. "The hatred is rising in me, a hatred greater than any you've seen." She pushed Nyva away.

Nan's dagger was where it always was, hanging in its sheath on the wall next to her bed. It was a blade designed with one purpose, and that was killing. Nyva grabbed it and ran from the house as Nan stood in the open doorway yelling, "This old bitch is too tired to run, so come get some, you bastards!"

Nyva ran to the trees, stumbling twice, cursing herself, demanding she find her composure.

"Witch!" a man roared from the direction of Nan's house. Nyva stopped dead, spun round, and dropped flat, thinking they were upon her. But she had not been spotted. They oozed toward Nan's as a single mass. Alone, none of them looked like much, but there was nearly a score of them. Heart slamming against her ribs, Nyva lay still, afraid they would see her if she got up and ran.

"You'll pay. You and that little slut that coaxed my boy will pay!" a man yelled. He was tall and thin, hunched forward, with long, unkempt black hair and a mustache.

Jeremiah's father.

"You killed my boy, you fucking bitch!" he screamed, his voice quaking with emotion. He held a large stone in his hand. Others in the throng held stones and pitchforks and reaping hooks.

Nan stepped out and raised the black candle toward Jeremiah's father and his mob, then said something that Nyva could not hear.

"I isn't afraid of your magic, devil. You can't take nothing from me now!" Jeremiah's father hurled his stone, and it struck Nan hard in the chest. Nyva had to cover her mouth to stifle a scream. Nan held tight to her candle and the bottle of spirits in her hand.

Nan's face...the expression on her face—

The crimson flame twisted and writhed, reaching upward.

Nyva closed her eyes and put her hands to her ears. She still heard the screaming, though. It wasn't Nan's. It was a man dying...dying a horrible death.

For a moment that spun into forever, the mob was silent.

Then a man cried out, "Kill her! Kill the witch before she takes another one of us!"

"Hold her, hold the fucking boar still!" another yelled.

And Nyva knew they would take her beloved Nan, kill her, for Nan was spent. Nyva had seen her guardian do magic before, and she knew what toll the spells and incantations took. Nan had already done her worst to them.

An animal wailing began, a terrible, painful sound, and Nyva closed her fist around the hilt of Nan's knife and bit her lip until she tasted blood. She ached to stand and defend Nan, who had kept her so well all these years. But that would make Nan's sacrifice for nothing. They would both end up dead on the ground. So instead, staying low, Nyva crawled away, her silent tears dripping salt on her lips.

The men grunted and cursed each other, and Nan wailed. She must still be fighting. It ended with a loud crack.

Stone on bone.

"Check the house! Find the other devil-witch!"

Nyva reached the slope that led down into dark woods that stretched for miles. As a small child, she'd loved to tuck her arms tight and roll down this hill. But she felt no love as she rolled now, only fear and loss and pain. At the bottom, she stood tall and ran. They'd not catch her, those drunken filths. Nyva had grown up running these woods. She'd run now, and she'd make certain Nan hadn't given her life for nothing.

Nyva heard the searchers calling out to each other as she ran, their voices growing distant. She let her tears run and her emotions pour through her. The sadness was dull, and Nyva's whole life seemed distant and absurd. Her past life was a faraway dream, and now she was awake to a reality where she was nothing, an orphan, forlorn, from nowhere and entirely without somewhere to go.

No, I have somewhere to go.

Lady Ward. Nan said to go to Lady Ward. And she said to avoid the village.

Numb and desolate, Nyva went deeper into the woods for at least another hour before she turned and went toward Wardbrook.

As hunger grew in her belly and fatigue turned her legs to heavy logs, Nyva felt the first sparks of anger. *Lady Wardbrook knew Nan. They were friends. If she has returned, she will punish those murderers. She will make her husband take off their heads with his massive sword. They will pay for what they did to Nan.*

And what will that bring? What good will that do? a wiser voice, still Nyva's, asked from within, the voice of the girl running now through the woods rather than the girl who had played with the farm boys...was it only yesterday?

The King of Brynth demanded of his citizens by law that they kill those responsible of witchcraft. Eventually more men would come, Seekers perhaps. Then Diana would hang for killing the men who had killed Nan.

No, there would be no justice for Nan.

Nyva's anger halted dead in its tracks at this thought, and so did her march to Wardbrook. Exhausted, despairing, Nyva sank onto her haunches against a tree and wept.

The sound of a chime interrupted her crying. She held back her tears and listened.

The woods were quiet.

Then the scurrying of little paws, so faint it could have been nothing but a trick on her ears... Nyva knew better. He remained unseen, but Nyva felt his black eyes watching her as she scrutinized her surroundings with tear-blurred eyes. He was here, the devil that had killed Jeremiah, the devil that had started all of this.

"Brenna?" Nyva said through clenched teeth, her emotions turning from woe to anger. "Are you out there, demon?" Nyva got to her feet and wiped her nose and eyes with a dirty forearm. "You did this. You bit him. That was why he died, and that was why they killed Nan." The words clogged her throat, and she took a moment to gather herself before she demanded, "Show yourself."

"Here, my lady," came the rasping voice from low to her left. Nyva looked at him for seconds before she fully saw him, so well did he blend with the forest. He was filthy, covered in mud, and he lingered among the exposed roots of a tree. "Wait," Brenna pleaded as Nyva lifted a stone and hurled it at him. She missed, and Brenna only smiled and snickered.

Nyva almost screamed in rage, but she was wiser than that. And she was wiser than running at it again, for it would only disappear.

She turned away and began walking again in the direction of Wardbrook.

"Don't go that way, hehe," Brenna said, and his little paws pattered as he followed Nyva.

"Why? Are they still looking for me?" she asked, then added, "Because of you." Hatred dripped from her words.

"No, I saw them," Brenna said. She turned and flinched, for he sounded as though he were speaking into her left ear, somehow hovering there. He was not, nor was he to her right or below, or above. She stood still, closed her eyes, and listened. His claws scrabbled through the dry leaves.

"They went back to the village," he said. "A few are still out and about, and I heard them talk of raping you, hehe. They won't, though. I saw their fates, hehe. Tonight's a hunter's moon, you know?"

Something rubbed against Nyva's ankle. She jerked her foot away and opened her eyes to see Brenna weaving around her ankles. She kicked the thing hard. He squeaked and flew feet through the air. Right before impacting a tree, he burst into tentacles of black smoke that snaked down to the earth, where the rat devil re-formed.

Nyva stumbled back.

Brenna snickered. "She wasn't as much your friend as you think, that Nan."

"Shut your mouth. I promise I'll gouge out your eyes and cook you alive, rat," Nyva said.

"You won't, hehe," said Brenna and he scurried close to Nyva again but remained out of kicking range. "I've foreseen it. You won't."

"Leave me be," Nyva said, and again began walking toward Wardbrook.

"Don't go that way, my lady. All jests aside, don't go that way."

"Why?" Nyva asked, the crunch of the dry leaves telling her he followed. But she did not stop. She would not stop.

"What do you know of Lady Diana Ward? Eh?" Brenna said.

"Nan said to go to her. So I will, and there is nothing a

filthy, lying devil like you will say to sway me." Nyva glanced back at the thing that followed. "I will kill you."

"Your mother asked for me to bring you back—" Brenna began.

"My mother? What fucking mother? You just got my mother killed." Nyva shook her head and kept moving. She would not listen to his lies. Nan had told her enough of demons, of curses, of the lying fiends that lure and manipulate.

But…just before Nan died, she'd said something to Nyva about her mother.

Nyva's stomach coiled so tight that she thought she might keel over. What had Nan said? That Diana Ward and Nyva's mother had had a falling out…

"You were a hostage, one well enough treated, but that is what you were—"

"You lie—"

"Your mother had to give you up. She had to give you up to Diana. But now the Lady Elyra, the Emerald Queen—"

"Queen—"

"Your mother—"

"My mother is dead—"

"Is alive and would have you back in Romaria. She crossed Diana, nearly defeated her, but the golden whore survived, escaped her imprisonment, and if she gets her hands on you, consider your life forfeit." Brenna spoke quickly, and he cackled not once.

"I don't believe any of it. Your magic is weak, for I feel no pull to follow you to Romaria to meet my *mother* the *Emerald Queen*." It was Nyva who cackled now as she stomped through the woods, and she hoped that Brenna felt some sort of sting for his failure.

"If not for your own sake, then do it for the innocent people of this land," Brenna said. "If you are not returned by your seventeenth birthday, your mother will come for revenge. I don't know when, but she *will* come, and she will join with the darkest powers to have it. This I have foreseen. But that is only one of the possible outcomes. Even my visions can change. You get to choose, my lady."

Nyva stared straight ahead, putting one foot in front of the other, moving forward, only forward. Maybe if she could get to Diana then this nightmare would end.

"You get to choo—" Brenna started, but he came foolishly close, and Nyva stomped him instead of kicking. She felt his thin rat spine under her shoe and put all her weight onto that foot, then grimaced as a shiver ran down her back from the sound of Brenna's spine popping. He let out a squeak that turned to a rasp as Nyva pressed harder, and then he went silent.

She lifted her foot and, without looking at him, stomped on Brenna over and over. She felt his little bones turn to mush, and a repulsive sensation of sadistic glee blazed through her blood.

Turning away, feeling both sick and exhilarated, she kept walking.

Hours later, the brightest hunter's moon Nyva had ever seen hung in the deep azure sky above, so large and beaming that she could see her path even in the woods at night. Thick trees towered all around her, and that meant she was close, for if she had gone this far in any wrong direction, she would have long since been out of the wood.

And then she heard the dogs barking, and a man yell from somewhere behind her, "She's here, she's here!"

Fear rose, a slick, oily surge.

Something howled, something more bestial than a wolf, the sound ratcheting her fear even higher. From the corner of her eye she caught a flash of movement, fur like moonlight, a glint of fang.

Then the dogs yelped and the men behind her screamed.

Whatever had howled was not in their command. Those were death screams.

And whatever had killed them had run right past her. Why? Why let her live? She was not inclined to wait and ask the creature directly.

Nyva stumbled forward a step, and then another, and then she ran. She kept running until she was clear of the trees, until she reached the foot of the hill and stood staring up at the great black house of Wardbrook. Her legs could not move another step, the weight of her own body bearing down on her, crushing her, every breath a struggle.

There was a woman before the house, looking out to the woods, to the screams of the dying men and dogs.

She wore a dress of silver-white, her blond hair tumbling down her back and shining in the moonlight, and she was as beautiful as Nyva remembered.

"Beautiful Nyva, welcome to your new home," Diana said, and extended her arms wide.

"Lady Ward," Nyva whispered.

"You will call me Diana. No formality between us."

With a sob, Nyva ran toward the sorceress' embrace. With every footstep, time seemed to slow, and despite her relief, Nyva could not shake the dreadful feeling that this was a dream from which she could not wake.

*O*n his knees, the young disciple wept as he begged the archdeacon for answers. "What is the difference between me and them, Father? What makes me better? What prevents the magic I wield from being something to be reviled? How am I not the very same monster as they? How? I beg you. I need the answer. The question...it hurts too much."

The dreams hurt too much. They felt so real, the horrible things he saw. He knew it the ultimate sin, but he wished to end his own life.

"Cullum, my child. The difference is you feel shame for what is inside of you. You wish to keep the beast in chains, while others like you, they would set it free. They would unleash the beast and all hell on this world, on the guilty and innocent alike. You answered the call of the Light and followed its incandescent beam; you rejected the dark—" the archdeacon said, in his amazed way of speaking, as if every single moment were a wonderful gift, but Cullum, the young disciple, cut him short.

"No!" The boy shook his head and closed his eyes. "That will not do this time. It will not do, your holiness!" His voice shattered on the final word with sobs, and after a few moments, he gained control of the raging stallion that was his wild emotion and uttered in a whisper, one only the Luminescent would hear, "It will not do."

"Open your eyes, child," the archdeacon said, answering the boy's plea with one of his own. Cullum abided the command. "Do you wish to die, my son?"

Cullum stared at the old man's clean-shaven face. His blue eyes, burning with the arcane, glowed from under the shadow cast by his dark blue hood.

"Do you wish to die, my son?" he asked again.

"Y-y-yes, yes, your holiness. I wish to die. I wish to take my own life. The dreams, the horror of the dreams...the things I see them *do...the things I want to do to them..."* Cullum collapsed and curled into a ball, holding his knees to his chest as he rocked and wept.

"The difference between you and them, my son," the Archdeacon said. *"The only difference is that, like myself and all in our holy order, the dreams that come to you in the night, the thoughts that crawl into your human mind in the day from the black depths of the beast soul within, fill you with fear and shame instead of excitement and pride. And with that fear and that shame and devotion to the Luminescent, we bravely do what the flock that we shepherd cannot."* The archdeacon reached down, grabbed Cullum by the collar of his nightclothes, and ripped him to his feet. His glowing blue eyes became all that Cullum saw.

"Take your own life, or live and slay the beast and the witch, and the heretic and the mutant, until you can slay no more...the choice is yours and it is yours alone. That is the glory of the Luminescent. And it is why we are named the Enlightened. Because even though we know there is a divine plan, we still have a choice to play our part. If my answer will not do this time, as you say, then just end it. There is no shortage of ropes, poisons, and knives in nearly every room of our glorious House of Deacons. Be my guest, Cullum, and help yourself." The archdeacon spoke with no cynicism, no condemnation, only acceptance. He produced a blade from his belt and extended it hilt first to Cullum, who still wept before him. *"Help yourself,"* the Archdeacon said again.

~

CHAPTER FOUR

THE DISORDER

*A*s was habit whenever he entered Archdeacon Lazarus's study, Cullum touched the hilt of the knife the man he named Father had given him when he had wept on his knees as a boy of twelve. It was a reminder of his own mortality and his freedom to do with that mortality as he would. It was the reminder that he stayed walking that thin, righteous path. He walked it fine, that razor line.

He had come straight here, not stopping to bathe or change his travel-stained clothing, or even partake of a meal. He needed to make his report, to let the burden of his guilt spill out.

There were new stained-glass windows that ran nearly from floor to ceiling depicting the *Founders*—the first of the Order of the Seekers—smiting apostate and heretic filth, impaling every manner of demon before them. Cullum felt their stares upon him, and he wondered if they had ever failed as he had. He had heard every story of their successes, but surely there must have been instances where innocents were left unsaved, the guilty unpunished.

Cullum looked away from the windows as the

archdeacon entered. He had been old from Cullum's first memories of him. Now he was ancient. He had more lines and wrinkles than a gnarled oak, and his pale skin looked so thin that the bones of his skull might at any moment poke free.

But as ancient and weathered as the archdeacon was, the glow of his eyes was as strong as ever, gleaming from under the shadow cast by his dark blue hood.

Here was the man who had taken Cullum in as an orphan babe, had taught him how to fish, how to read, how to pray. He had read Cullum the sermons in the church. He had given absolution. And he always, *always* reminded Cullum that through everything, right or wrong, holy or damned, in his actions, he had a choice.

"Many men pray to be good. Few men act to be good. It is actions that the sun sees," he had told Cullum often.

"Father," Cullum said now as he bowed and kissed the archdeacon's azure ring.

"My son." The archdeacon patted Cullum on the cheek. "Tell me of your mission."

Cullum did just that, his gut churning as he recalled the corpses of all three of the taken farm girls.

"You and Herres did well. The Luminescent is pleased," the archdeacon said, his fingers steepled in front of his belly.

Pleased? All the girls died a most horrific death. Cullum had allowed Herres to be injured nearly unto death.

"What about the girls, your holiness? I failed them," said Cullum. "I was too slow, too dim-witted to follow the signs given us, until it was too late. The Sisters, they had shown me the sewer, the hovel, the cave…all three ritual locations…the faces of the ones taken, but I could not reach them fast enough." Cullum's fists were clenched so tightly that the bones in his fingers and his knuckles began to ache and throb as if his hands might implode. He breathed deeply. He thought of the sun's holy light rising in the east, rising to its zenith and warming his soul, his wayward broken soul. He silently prayed to be punished.

"Those young souls, they are with the Luminescent now." The archdeacon's steepled fingers rose until the tips touched his lips. "They are living and learning new life, afterlife, forever touched by the light. They witnessed you, Cullum; they witness you now. And they know that you avenged them. They know that their oppressors felt the same fear and agony as they before the end. In its small way, celestial order has been restored." The archdeacon raised his palms to hail the Luminescent.

But Cullum could not.

He felt sick. He saw their dead faces, their naked, defiled bodies, split apart, the gore and blood, the devils all about. He heard the screaming, his screaming, his anger. The killing, the torturing, the emptiness in his heart—all was fresh and raw.

Fill me with your light, he silently begged of the sun.

"They are proud of you," Archdeacon Lazarus said. "Those young girls, those Enlightened Luminescent-loving souls, they know how you fought. The Sun has shown them. They know how you suffer. They would tell the two of you, Vicar Cullum and Brother Herres, that they are safe now, in the Luminescent's arms."

How do you know? The question haunted Cullum, but he could never ask it aloud. The sun was setting in the west of his soul, his faith. Its warmth was fading and the questions of the dark were rising. *How do you know, Father? How can you stand there and tell me where those girls are now, and what they are thinking? The pagans believe the girls' souls are bound now to some demon in some beyond where they cannot be reached or saved.*

"They will never know pain again," Lazarus said.

Cullum kept his head bowed, his eyes on the floor. *How can you stand there and spew that shit? I was there. I saw the corpses. I buried the ones that were still intact. I stared into the dead eyes, and more and more of late, inside of those eyes, inside those empty mirrors, I can see your lies.*

The thoughts shamed him. He wanted to believe. He needed it as he needed air. But he couldn't.

Shame for his failures. Shame for his doubt.

"Vicar Cullum Shrike, your shame only strengthens your soul," said Lazarus, appearing to read Cullum's thoughts. Or perhaps Cullum was just that simple. "It is a testament to the incandescence that looks down on you, my son." He extended his arms, and in his embrace, Cullum felt loved and warm, like a happy child, and both his questions and his shame ebbed, at least for the moment. It was a marvel that such a small old man could still seem so large to him, so much grander than anyone else.

Lazarus released him.

His expression became somber, his frown dripping off his jaw.

Cullum's stomach and throat tightened. This was always as it was: a mission was completed, a mission was given, and the journey began again. He relished the next mission. It would take his focus from the doubts that assailed him and the ever-present guilt that was his sole companion in the darkest hours of the night.

"Vicar, the Luminescent has whispered to me," Lazarus said, his posture changing as his shoulders drew back and his chin rose. "We have spoken, and he warns of an ancient power's rising, a power most wicked, one that would see the world of the Enlightened return to the age of the beast… mayhaps an age even before that. I dare not think on it."

Lazarus paced before his towering shelves of books, his steps slow and careful, his hands behind his back. He reached up for a volume he had tucked away behind others, his arm thin and frail, his shoulder creaking.

The tome was large and heavy, and Cullum started forward as the old man's arm dropped with the weight, but the archdeacon waved him back. He struggled with the book as he moved to the parchment-and-scroll-covered table, where he let the book fall with a thud. Its covers and spine were formed of a shimmering black stone, and it opened and closed on gleaming gold hinges.

"It is a tome most ancient, from a land distant and foreign," the Archdeacon began, his voice soft, his eyes staring straight ahead. "It was given to me by a long-haired, bearded man-giant. In a dream, he spoke to me in an angelic tongue I did not know and yet understood. He was tattooed like a pagan raider of the north, wild-eyed and fierce. But I had no doubt, not one, that this man was holy..." The archdeacon's voice trailed away, a small ship on uneasy winds, and when he met Cullum's gaze, there was fear in his eyes. "When I awoke, this book was here on my very table."

Magic. Yet Cullum felt no emanation from the heavy tome.

"He gave me no name... I feared him, not as I fear our Father the Luminescent, but as I may fear a stranger, nay, an outsider...from a place so far off that I questioned if it was not mere distance that separated us but even great leaps of time. In the dream, I knew not if I was his visitor or if he was mine."

It was normal and expected for the archdeacon to speak to God and his emissaries.

It was not normal for books to be passed by man-giants through dreams. This was old magic, from before the forma-tion of the Order, and as Cullum stared at the book, a primordial fear rose inside him. His Order burned books that were dangerous. So what was this abomination doing here? Why had Lazarus kept it?

Lazarus flipped open the book's cover and exposed the first page, and while Cullum's instinct was to step back, step away, he found his feet drawing him closer. Painted in a dark, faded red ink—*blood*—were archaic drawings of spear-wielding stick men in different positions in a sequence across the page, left to right. It was a language, but as to its meaning, he had no insight.

"The giant became a demon before my dreaming eyes," Lazarus whispered, his lip trembling now along with his hands. "His features changed. His skin became scaled and his tongue forked, and it flicked from his mouth as he spoke. His language decayed from its angelic speech to something terrible. Guttural utterances and croaking that I could somehow comprehend. Terrible warnings. Words dripping with doomed prophecies of dread times." The archdeacon stumbled and clutched at the edge of the table. Cullum steadied him, his palms clammy with the rising tide of helplessness. It was a feeling he knew well, one he associated with his many failures, but never with the archdeacon.

"Father?" Cullum asked.

"'Wardbrook,' the man-giant said." Lazarus stared through Cullum into the beyond.

Cullum frowned. Wardbrook. He knew that name, that place, but could not recall why.

"'This book, it is the invitation sent. You have been chosen, you have been summoned; you must answer, or send proxy,' said the man-giant." With a gasp, the archdeacon slumped forward, deathly pale, bearing his weight on his forearms where they pressed against the table.

"Father!" Cullum gave the archdeacon a jolting shake. Icy terror encroached around his heart. "Lazarus!"

After a long moment, Lazarus gasped again, the way a

man does after near drowning.

"I must sit down." He patted the back of Cullum's hand. "I'm getting old. I beg thee, help me to my chair." His voice was frailer than the remains of a dried-out corpse beetle.

Cullum helped Lazarus sit, and saw that the right side of his face was twisted and scrunched into a grimace. The archdeacon's right arm hung at his side.

Cullum turned to the door and yelled, "Medicus, we need—"

Lazarus dug the long, curved nails of his left hand deep into the flesh of Cullum's wrist.

"Bring me the book," Lazarus said.

"You have suffered an apoplexy. A medicus—"

"The book." Cullum hesitated. A strange and unfamiliar fire burned in the archdeacon's eyes. "The book," he said again.

Cullum fetched it and settled the heavy tome in Lazarus's lap. With his left hand, the archdeacon flipped through the pages, the little stick men that served as letters appearing to run and hunt as the pages turned.

Then Cullum's attention veered from the pages. The back of the archdeacon's hand was distorted, not in the way of the *Bloodburn*—this was no *Bloodburn* that Cullum knew, nor should any Seeker experience the burn within these hallowed halls. The veins had swelled so they were nearly as thick as his fingers. They stood out, marble white and hard against the thin skin.

With a feeling of disorientation and wariness, Cullum reached out and rested his fingertips on the back of the old man's hand.

"What is this?" he said.

"Nothing of import. Look at the book, boy."

Cullum looked. Spanning the entirety of the left and right pages was a single image. Cullum had seen it before, many a time, in books and scrolls and even etched in stone. In the ancient texts and cave drawings of cultures spanning from the Northern Isles of Ygdrasst and Blodjord, across Romaria and all the way southeast to Kehldesh, and then northeast to the Dragon Dynasties and the Steppe, the image painted into this mysterious tome had repeated. The medium, the style, and the level of artistry varied, but the subject did not: the father of monstrosity and chaos, the stirrer of fear in the dreams of mortal and mythical beings alike, the grand devil king of a thousand names and a thousand heads.

Leviathan.

Devil god of the first age, the age before the Era of the Beast. Evil men, wise men, those drawn to darkness, men who cried out as they burned at the stake…all spoke in whispers of this time, a time when all things were of the sea, eons ago, and the true ancestors of man swam through the black depths of the abyss.

Archdeacon Lazarus flipped one page, and then another and another. In the second half of the tome, the spear-wielding stick figures crossed the page from right to left, instead of left to right, as they had in the first half. Their shape, too, was altered. As the pages went on, the stick figures hunched lower until they were on all fours and crawling like animals. By the time the final pages were reached, the figures were unrecognizable, with only drawings of waves on the last page.

"What does it mean? What does it have to do with the lands of Wardbrook to the south? Why did the man-giant send you such a summons?" Cullum asked, then shook his head. "Let me summon the medicus, Father, I beg you." The archdeacon was pale as chalk, his eyes red-rimmed, his breath coming in shallow gasps.

"Ah, Wardbrook. This will not be the Order's first visit to those lands," the old man rasped, again catching Cullum's arm and digging his long nails in. "Before you were born, when I was a young archdeacon, there were two investigations launched on Wardbrook. Reports of mass pagan rituals and even human sacrifice had been brought to the attention of the Order. The first investigation ended with floggings of peasants for starting rumors and an apology issued to the knight errant, Lord Robart Everest Howalder, lord of the estate and its lands. The second investigation ended the same way. The only difference was the apology was issued to the new lord and lady of the estate, Alexander and Diana Ward." Lazarus let his head fall back and stared up at the painted ceiling, a red and golden sun looking down on him.

"I will get the medicus now," Cullum said softly, placing his hand on Lazarus's shoulder.

"You will not," Lazarus said, and removed Cullum's hand. "Cullum, did you see any men of our Order on your way to me? In the halls, I mean."

"None," Cullum answered, and then squinted upon the realization that such a thing was strange. There were always at least initiates walking the halls.

"Sit down, Cullum," the archdeacon said, and tugged on his arm with surprising strength.

Cullum sat. Lazarus leaned in. "I have more news, none of it good. Some of it will fill you with great rage, Cullum. Remain calm, and do only as I say." He paused. "Cullum, my boy, my son." Lazarus put his hand to Cullum's cheek. "Your mission took you away from here for many months, and in those months, the Ministry of the House of Deacons was replaced."

"What?"

"A ship came from the holy land. It arrived at the western docks not a fortnight after you left... Deacons of Lordan, sent by the High Patriarch himself. Men with strange titles like Lord Regent and Bishop Witch-Finder. When the

Lordanian deacons arrived, it was with word from the High Patriarch, letters written in his hand and sealed with his sigil. There was naught we could do but obey the orders, strange as they were." Lazarus began to shiver.

Cullum sprang to his feet and took off his coat, then draped it over Lazarus's trembling shoulders, feeling helpless.

"Deacon Mikael, Deacon Berkaltr, Deacon Fenrae… They and all the others, all the deacons are dead but me," Lazarus said, tilting his head to look up at Cullum. "The others were sent on separate missions, missions of such secrecy that they could not relay their tasks even to me, on pain of death by immolation. In the months after, one by one I received news of their deaths from the smiling lips of the Lordanians."

Dead. All dead. Cullum could not imagine it.

Lazarus's head whipped toward the door. "They are coming. Now, right now."

The hairs on the back of Cullum's neck rose, and he looked at the closed door, listening intently for steps coming down the hall. There were none. He tried to feel dark sorcery stirring in the forces, but he sensed nothing.

"Father—"

"By the sun, it is too late for me," said Lazarus, grabbing Cullum by the wrist. "It is too late for me, but not for you."

"Father—" Cullum started, his hand straying to the hilt of his sword. Again, he listened to the hallway, homed in on the forces, and he heard nothing, felt nothing. But his hand stayed on his sword.

"Their magic is old, preceding all that we understand of the arcane. They are *his* seed, *his* children that he raped into this world countless eons ago. They have risen, and the children call the father back! They would see the waves of the sea rise like mountains and eat the clouds and drown the sun." Tears rolled down the archdeacon's face.

Cullum looked over his right shoulder, then his left, into the dark corners of the room. Was Lazarus speaking truth or madness? "Who? Who is the Lordanians' father if not the High Patriarch?"

"Cullum, my son, I am not mad." Lazarus tried and failed to lift his limp right hand. "My body betrays me, but my mind and my faith do not. These are the very children of Zole, penetrated deep into our Order and all the Holy Church of the Luminescent, even to he who sits on the golden Sun throne in Lordan. The Leviathan cometh, the eater of worlds."

Lazarus slammed the book shut and shoved it toward Cullum. Cullum's stomach roiled like a coming storm, cold sweat forming on his brow and trickling down his spine.

Somehow he had not seen it at first, but the book's cover was sculpted in relief with the form of a hydra bursting up from the sea...

*No...t*he book was upside down. The hydra was not bursting up from the sea, but rather ripping through the very fabric of the sky and descending.

He had not missed it before.

It was not there before.

He saw that now as the veins in his left hand pulsed. The *Bloodburn* was upon him. What vile magic was this that he had failed to sense it before?

"Give it to me," Cullum said. "I will burn it. Throw the ashes in the sea."

Tears streaked the archdeacon's cheeks as he only shook his head.

And then Cullum understood, the horror of his realization dripping through him. A thing like that would corrupt the elements of its destruction and bend them to its will. No earth, no sea, no fire could contain that evil book.

*T*here would be no need to force the one known to the villagers only as "the hermit" to kneel before the block. He would do so of his own accord. He was prepared for this; he was waiting for it, patiently and without fear.

He was excited for it, for the hermit had been promised this end.

He had been promised a second life, one of meaning, of service... of revenge upon them all, the whole race of them.

The headsman was a morsel of a man; the axe was not sharp. Still, the hermit smiled.

"Kneel, sorcerer," said the somber lord over the sound of the downpour, his rain-soaked hair hanging around his face in a heavy mop, falling water spraying off his lips as he spoke. The hermit knelt and placed his head on the block, staring out at the small crowd of wet, cold-fleshed, hot-blooded peasants. They cried out for his death.

All but one, a young man, the cleanest of the lot by far. He walked close enough to the hermit to speak.

"You have my sympathy, hermit, for darkness is a disease, and those touched by the devils have no choice in it. May your soul be saved in another life, vile sinner."

The hermit spat in the face of the young man, who reeled back in revulsion and joined the rest of the peasants in screaming for the hermit's death.

"Your last wards, speak them now if you will, or take them with you to hell," the somber lord said.

"I never wanted yar sympathy, I never wanted yar love. I just wanted this...yar drooling hatred and for the sun to turn black above. I will return, you sheep of Brynth. The wrath of the Leviathan cometh. Soon you will sleep, and in this sleep such horrid nightmares you will be forced to imagine. Imagine all the unimagi—"

The headsman swung. He hit skull, not neck. The hermit's teeth burst. Blood ran from his eyes and ears as a massive gash opened on the top of his head.

～

In the woods by the village of Wardbrook, beneath the great black house on the hill, a hunter's moon glows as wolfish, howling winds blow.

A mangled, broken wretch twists and wriggles in the muck. Little bones snap into place; spilled brains move with life, scuttling back into the fiend's skull.

"Hehe." The sound comes from the creature as its human head re-forms, no larger than an egg, and its ratlike body rises anew, orange and red boils glowing as they swell on the thing's belly.

"Hehe."

～

CHAPTER FIVE

OUTSIDER

"Seeker Wardorf," Cullum greeted the twenty-stone holy doorman who guarded the solid black portcullis to the Chamber of Inquisition. If anyone other than a Seeker tried to enter, he would bash their brains out with his iron mallet. He always held the weapon in his hands, moving it from left to right throughout his shift at the door. The holy serums kept him vigilant. Yet he looked beyond exhaustion and defeat now, as if his shift was never-ending.

"Hawthorne?" Cullum asked.

Wardorf shook his head. The other guard of the door was dead or compromised, then. Cullum felt a pang of regret.

"How long have you been at this door?" Cullum asked.

"I have not left it," said Wardorf. "Does Lazarus yet live?"

"Barely." Cullum ground his teeth.

Wardorf's shoulders sagged, then he drew them back and raised his chin. "Since the arrival of the Lordanians, the archdeacon and I have had limited communication. We used letters out of fear of being spotted having lengthy conversations. We used a trustworthy initiate—"

"A trustworthy initiate?" Cullum interjected. "I did not

know there was such a thing. Why did you not use a veteran Seeker?"

"Our personal network of trusted veterans was sent out with our deacons. You and Herres were the first to return," Wardorf said. "I fear the others are dead, compromised, or they have fallen into hiding." He paused. "The initiate wound up dead in a tavern three days ago, his throat slit ear to ear. What's more, two days ago, four of the Lordanian deacons came to me, and they demanded entry to the Chamber of Inquisition. They demanded to speak with the Sisters."

"Demanded?" Cullum asked, his unease overflowing into his tone. Only those of Brynthian blood, summoned by the Sisters, were allowed entry. It had always been this way. But Cullum had been sent, not summoned. Would they see him?

"I told them that even if the High Patriarch himself demanded entry to the chamber, I'd demand he walk away," Wardorf said. "They stood there a long while, staring at me, frowning… Cullum, when you stand next to a mortal man, what do you feel?"

"Feel?" Cullum asked.

"What do you feel, vicar?" asked Wardorf.

"I feel his life energy. I feel his soul. I can see his anguish or his glory hovering in his spirit above him," Cullum answered.

"And when you stand next to a monster?" Wardorf asked.

"You know what I feel. You feel it, too. The *Bloodburn* writes itself into the back of our left hands and we read the signs." He thought of the strange *Bloodburn* on the back of Lazarus's hand…white, hard, swollen…

"Those Lordanians, they give off nothing."

"Even corpses have energies," Cullum said.

"Those nine men and their scribes, the handful of Seekers they came with, not one of them gives off anything."

Seekers relied on their sixth sense to keep them from

the dark.

"I see by your face that you share my concern." Wardorf opened the massive doors.

"I was sent, not summoned," Cullum said.

Wardorf snorted. "You were summoned."

Cullum stepped into the Chamber of Inquisition and all its secrets. He felt the draft of the heavy doors closing shut behind him. The stone-tiled hall had no windows and no torches. It was lit by thousands of small, glowing blue Seeker sigils on the walls. He kept his gaze directed forward as he made his way toward the Pool of Finding, his footsteps light and silent despite his fatigue.

The sight that greeted him when he reached the pool was one he had seen many times before, but it never failed to give him a twist of unease. The Sisters' bodies were completely submerged in the circular pool, making it appear as if their hairless heads hovered above the water.

With glowing, lidless eyes, they stared at him.

Waiting.

"Cullum… Cullum… Cullum," they whispered to each other.

One laughed.

One cried.

The third hushed them both and said, "Cullum." This time she spoke to him instead of her sisters.

Cullum took off his hat, then slipped off his coat and let it fall to the ground behind him. His leather armor and black tunic came next, before he moved on to his trousers and boots.

The liquid that filled the pool was infused with powers of the arcane, causing the vibrant blue essence to forever whirl and stir. Small waves formed and fell, white-blue vapors rising from the crests. The waves lapped at the hand-formed tile edges and spilled across the floor.

Cullum went in, right foot first. The vapors swirled around his body as he submerged, step by step, until he was chest deep.

The Sisters began their whispering, and Cullum watched their frail, smooth bodies swim toward him under the surface. He tensed, as he always did, when the first one's fingers touched his chest, her nails scratching lightly at his skin.

"Vicar," she whispered.

"Vicar… Vicar," the other two echoed.

"Cullum," said the first.

"Shrike!" the one on his left shrieked. It made Cullum's ear ring. She grabbed his hand, her skin smooth and slimy, like an eel's.

They all touched him now.

"Don't resist…don't… Accept it. Accept," they said at once, and he loosened and let them tilt him back so he floated, arms and legs spread wide. He let them submerge him beneath the surface of that holy pool.

They pushed him down and held him there. He let them and did not close his eyes.

The pool changed from blue to black, dark as ink. The sisters' hairless heads grew long white hair; their skin sagged and the blue glow of their eyes turned red.

He was ripped from his body, and he floated up…up…and saw from above. He saw from beyond.

The walls lined with Seeker sigils, and the high ceiling deconstructed, bricks and stone rolling in a slow cyclone, revealing the sky and a village in a valley. Past the village, atop a hill backed by forest, was an ominous estate. It was a great black house, the size of a small castle but without the same degree of fortification. The sky was heavy with roiling charcoal clouds that looked ready to pour lakes. Still, beams of sunlight found their way through and mixed gold into the gloom.

The Sisters and the pool remained far below him.

Their bodies decayed in the ink-black water, their flesh slowly dripping off their bones like honey from its comb.

"Wardbrook," they whispered. "Wardbrook… Wardbrook."

Thunder boomed.

Lightning flashed.

The black ichor in the pool turned to crimson flame, and as Cullum burned with the Sisters, he saw what was coming.

Fragments, viewed only for an instant.

A golden-haired woman screaming in a bath of blood. In ecstasy, in pain, her eyes roll back into her skull, her neck straining.

A brown-haired girl with freckles, her skin darkened honey gold by the sun, weeping and collapsing in an emerald-green dress, red staining her abdomen. She writhes atop a stone altar and then goes still.

A grizzled beast of a man running through dark woods, dead branches cutting at him as tears run down his bloodstained cheeks.

Wardbrook, Wardbrook, Wardbrook. *The whispers echo. A still crimson lake rests beneath a black sky as unseen men and women's screams mingle with the disembodied sound of a babe's laughter. Flames everywhere; licking tongues of red and yellow and orange turn and twist into tendrils. The vibrant colors go white. Tentacles wrap around Cullum. His left hand feels like it is afire, like his bones are fusing one to the next, his veins turning to stone.*

Cold. So cold.

The beautiful golden-haired woman, the brown-haired girl, and the grizzled blond brute are all there with him, tentacles pulling them apart, plunging into their mouths, their eyes, reaching deep between their thighs.

A typhoon, a maelstrom, a behemoth of a storm made of blood, washes over Aldwick under a sky dripping fire.

A church, tall and white, the sun sigil at its zenith, gleaming gold, melting into the rivers of blood that run through the streets. The dripping flames of the sky descend lower and lower, and from the blood, tentacles of white rise up.

They touch the fire.

The Sisters are flayed by pale demons.

Archdeacon Lazarus rising from the grave, things squirming from his eyes.

Cullum is screaming now.

In the dark, he is screaming now.

The darkness fades away, leaving a yellow sky. A forest of massive arms and hands reaching up to the black sun moon.

Cullum gasped as his head broke the surface of the pool. His lungs filled with air and his sight returned. His sight of the mundane world. The Sisters were there around him, staring hard at him, unblinking pale eyes surrounded by paler flesh. They looked dead—in a way, they were, and yet they saw and lived so many lives.

"Cullum?" one asked.

"Did you see?" asked another.

"Did you see her?" they asked all at once, and then they began to giggle like three little girls. Like the girls they had been when the Order had taken them.

He spun and stared at them. He had seen a blond beauty and a brown-haired girl. It was the girl who clung to his thoughts. "Who did you want me to see?"

They laughed again.

He would get no answers here. He slogged through the water, climbed from the pool, and made his way down the steps. The Sisters kept on giggling.

"You look cold, Cullum," one of them said.

"You look scared, Cullum," said the second.

"Are you Enlightened?" the third sister asked.

He did not respond to them; they always did this. They

carried on making their jokes and having their spiteful fun. Who could blame them? Not he. He wasted no time in drying off and getting his clothes back on. He wanted to be away from the Sisters as quickly as possible.

Cullum banged on the inside of the great portcullis to the Chamber of Inquisition. His back was still wet from the pool; he wiped the last beads of enchanted water from his skull then donned his hat.

The door opened.

"Did you see what you needed to see?" Wardorf asked as he held the door for Cullum.

"Always," Cullum said. Had he? "The signs have been given, Wardorf. Now I must only interpret them."

~

Within the first moments of his arrival in the town of Wardbrook, Cullum asked questions, the answers to which were tales of an old witch, her young disciple—a seductress with whom she colluded—a cursed son, and his vengeful father, both dead. He was told of more bodies in the woods found at night in the pursuit of the seductress.

So he went to the witch's hut, set in a field of tall grass, trees to the north, trees to the east. The great black estate, Wardbrook, topped a hill in the distance.

The witch's body lay before the open door to her abode. He looked into her eye, the same color as the parchment of an ancient scroll. The eye looked as if the woman had died four moments ago, not four days. It was all that was left of her face, the rest of which was pulverized into a decaying mush. Cullum could be sure it was the face of a human being only because of the body that was attached to it. The woman had been tall and burly, and in the winter of her life. Beside her outstretched hand was a small brass saucer with a curved handle—a candleholder.

Rot was well at home in the corpse, and the stench was atrocious. The body had marbled green and purple and black; foul blisters filled with fetid liquids covered the dead flesh. Dark red, congealed blood rested at the bottom of the corpse and melted through the skin, leaking from the body in jellylike pools. Cullum waved away flies as he leaned in.

Maggots ate away at the stone-smashed head, and eggs were visible by the wounds surrounding the pitchfork still sticking upright from the woman's belly. Corpse beetles scurried into burrows of flesh.

"How did it happen?" Cullum asked, turning around to the slack-jawed yokel standing several yards from him, the signature distant stare of daytime drunkenness in the man's eyes. Callum had been asking questions of the man all morning and had yet to receive a single usable answer. He had heard various tales in the village, but this man had been here when it happened, and Cullum wanted to know what he had seen.

"I told ya, sir. We all told ya," said the idiot as he shielded his eyes from the sun despite the fact that he was wearing a hat—but not on his head. He had it on a string wrapped around his neck so that it hung down his back.

"And you will tell me again, peasant," Cullum said, and stared into the pit of the jackass's soul. "And I will tell *you* again…I am a vicar among the holy order of the Seekers. I receive my holy missions from the archdeacon, and he receives his orders from the Luminescent. You will answer my questions when I ask them, or you will know my wrath." Cullum walked closer to the yokel as he spoke, and brought himself as near as he could without causing their noses to touch. The man's breath was near as foul as the scent of the corpse.

"U-u-understood, sir," said the yokel. "Jeremiah the elder." He indicated the second corpse, who had suffered a fate far grislier than the stout old witch. His flesh was melted off his bones from the chest up, muscle and sinew turned to crimson tar that trailed down the lower portion of the corpse and made a sticky pool that had burned through the long grass in a perfect circle perhaps ten feet in diameter. The yokel frowned and shook his head. "Something...happened to him..."

"So it would appear," Cullum said.

"Jeremiah's son," the yokel said, "Jeremiah the younger... he had been seein' the young witch who lived here, with that there old one there. She lived here for..." Again, he shook his head. "For... I can't recall..."

Cullum closed his eyes for an instant, then opened them again. He'd heard all this already, more than once. And each time the fool seemed to recall less and less. What Cullum wanted was a description of the actual events, but this man was either unable or unwilling to provide it. "Silence. The words you speak are not worth enduring the pong of your breath, man." Cullum stepped to the mess that was Jeremiah the elder, until the toes of his boots touched the edge of the thick goo. He knelt by the body. It smelled of rot, and something else...a smell Cullum thought of as the scent of the sky burning. It was often residual around magical killing grounds.

The sky burning.

The sisters had said that one by one, and then a final time in unison had whispered, "The sky burning." They had sent him here, not specifically to this scene, but to Wardbrook. And he felt this scene before him was illusion in the face of the greater problem. His problem was that he didn't know what that problem might be.

"I was just doin' as you said, sir," said the yokel, leaning close. The words and the stink of the man's breath pulled Cullum back from his thoughts.

"Did you consume pig shit for your last meal?" Cullum asked.

"My last meal… I don't recall… I don't know what I last ate, but I do know I've not once eaten the shite of swine, your holy sir, and I take offense to such a brandished accusation." The yokel punctuated his sentence with a belch.

"You recall very little," Cullum said, then waved his hand. "You are void of any use. Go back to your home and continue further honing your vocation."

"My vo… What now?" the yokel asked.

"Go home and drink, peasant."

When there was no sound of movement, Cullum rose and turned back to the yokel, his predator's gaze already carved upon his features.

No more words were spoken.

The yokel turned away and took off bumbling down the path that descended the tree-covered hill back to the village.

Cullum removed the glove from his left hand and turned his attention back to the melted man. He squatted and hovered his outstretched fingers above the crimson-black tar. His skin tingled, and the blue veins darkened from a central point on the back of his hand. The color grew darker still as it seeped outward until it was the same hue as the tar. The blood inside of him burned as if corrosive oil was being pumped into him through some unseen insect's sting. The dispersion was slow, and the burning blood felt as thick as turned cream. He pulled his hand away and stepped back from the grisly scene.

The pain faded at once, and he shook his hand out. His blood pumped as it should. He had expected magic, and magic he had found.

Does the blood go black? Black-red? Gold? Yellow-gold? Green…

Is it boiling or is it blazing? Does it thicken or does it thin? And how fast, how soon? Does my vision blur; does my stomach turn; do I see other places? Where and when?

All of these questions and more Cullum asked and answered by studying the *Bloodburn*.

Cullum went back to the corpse of the pulverized witch. Just as he had with the melted man, he hovered his open palm over the body. Again, the back of his hand burned and turned the color of her blood magic. Cullum read the *Bloodburn*, and it was no flexing of skill to determine that the dead witch cast the spell on the dead man, after which the rest of the angry mob murdered the witch. His gaze slid to the candleholder, only metal now, a threat no longer.

Cullum pulled his glove back on and whistled to his grazing horse, who stood close by—as always, unfazed by the heavy reek of death.

His work was far from done. There was still the body of the son to inspect, and two more villagers and their dog were also unaccounted for.

Cullum had paid a visit to the town's coroner and surgeon before coming here, and he intended to pay him another.

The coroner-surgeon was perhaps fifteen years Cullum's elder. His hair, cut in the shape of a bowl, was as deep as jet. He was not tall, but his perfect posture made him appear as though he was. He spoke with a confidence that Cullum had only seen in one other man, and that was the archdeacon. It was for this reason, and the fact that their words were spoken in private, that Cullum did not punish the man for his insolent addresses to a holy vicar.

"Oh my, a Seeker, in the small town of Wardbrook..." the man had said when Cullum first arrived in the wee hours of the morning, the sun not yet risen. "You must me be here about the killings. The yokels here have only brought me one of the bodies. They refuse to go near the others. Superstition and all that…fears, you see?"

"I see all, for the sun is my sight," Cullum had replied.

The coroner-surgeon said, "Ha-ha," in his deep, clear tone and clapped his hands together once.

"Where are you off too so early, sir?" Cullum had asked, for he had come upon the man already fully dressed and ready to leave his domicile.

"I am the coroner-surgeon of Wardbrook. But someone in a nearby town is much in need of a surgery. So, I am off to the tavern to drink, and then I am off to…to…a town—"

"Which town?" Cullum asked.

The coroner-surgeon frowned. "A town. The name matters not. I know it by sight."

Cullum stared at him, wondering if the man did not wish to name the place, or if he truly did not know. "And what do you there?"

"I am off to cut and sew and pry and burn and grind and dig about in human flesh until the patient is saved," the coroner-surgeon said in a voice that overplayed boredom.

"Or dead," Cullum had replied.

"Yes, that is the unspoken alternative. My, my, you were not lying when you said you see all, were you?" The man had stared at Cullum a moment, and then, perhaps sensing Cullum's rapid loss of patience, continued, "I am sorry. Playfulness is my nature. I sometimes ponder if it is more a disease than a trait of nature. Then I suppose a disease *is* a trait of nature, one of countless many." Then, abruptly summoning an impressive cheerfulness, the man finished, "Accompany me to the tavern, if you would. Share a drink. I will tell you all I know from seeing the one corpse, that of the young fool, Jeremiah."

"Show some respect for the dead," Cullum had said.

"Sir, I respect nothing. Especially not the dead," the coroner-surgeon had said, again completely shifting his tone and demeanor as smoothly as any master actor of the stage. There was no cheer, no jokiness, no sympathy, no mercy to be found in his inflection.

Snap.

His sneer and joviality returned. "But when I return late this night from saving a life, we will talk about death. After you have finished your inspection of our happy town and the snug woods around it. Come, let us drink now."

"A strange hour for a drink. Stranger still to have one before carrying out a surgery, no?" Cullum said, pumping all his Enlightened condemnation into his tone.

"Oh, yes, strange indeed, and yet stranger things happen every day. Every night, too." And the man had offered an unsettling wink.

At that, Cullum surrendered and went with the strange and absurdly confident coroner-surgeon to the tavern, for there were many ways to gather information, and he was used to taking advantage of any opportunity.

Now the sun was dropping below the horizon at Cullum's back, and he watched his own shadow as he trotted his horse down the thin dirt path that split the ravine on the hill in half, all the way down to the clearing where the village lay. The tree branches formed a tall and tight arched ceiling over the path. And despite it being deep into spring, one in three trees appeared leafless, yet very much alive, perhaps more so than their green contemporaries, for in the twilight, the barren branches seemed to be caressing one another, their movements suggesting life. And the wind that passed through them sounded much as if they whispered sweet nothings to each other, sweet nothings about the dark.

"Are you plotting?" Cullum asked them.

The wind answered with a howl.

PART II
THINKING OF MEMORIES,
REMEMBERING THOUGHTS

I am not a man for addressing the events of my life to a diary. Although I do keep extensive notes, they are of a scientific nature. I write this now, not as a man of science; I write it as a man in awe of the sheer vastness of it all.

For a hundred nights, I gazed on that single star as I sat in my rocking chair in the university solarium. The moonlight washed in through the domed glass ceiling. Trees and plants from all over the continent and beyond surrounded me.

I have always enjoyed gazing up at that black infinity as a way to end those long days of studying the same infinity. For my learning of the stars was endless. Be that learning from books written by wiser men long dead—those pioneers to first navigate the stars and commit, with the magic runes of written word what they found on those expeditions of the mind—or be it my learning from simply gazing up and navigating the cosmos on my own at night, I was always in the stars.

I know not what pulled my focus to the single particular star that beamed next to the formation of the Goose of Galjernon, but that it glowed more incandescently than those near it. Over time, the glow began to fade. At first I was not sure. I'd focus on the star and sit wondering as to whether or not it had shrunk, and as I did, I would nod off into sleep. Sleep, heavy with the most lucid dreams. I dreamed of other worlds, and in a single night, I'd bear witness to an eon. I'd walk among the races of these distant realms, and I'd walk in their forms. At times, they were near human, and at times, they were things that the mind could neither comprehend nor explain. Regardless, I will attempt it.

The fly people of a world which cannot be pronounced by any tongue of man and has no suitable translation that would not cause great laughter among any human race eludes proper explanation. For they believed their planet was a turd of a god, and the cosmos was a great and endless swamp. Every million years of swimming through it only set the start of the journey for a million more. In their understanding of the universe, god ate god and the fly men fed upon their shit.

They built great cities made of silver ore beneath green skies; they fought no wars and had no crime. They worked together, in perfect, unquestioning, unfaltering unison. They communicated in silence; their antennae did all the speaking, speaking that filled in all the holes that spoken word left open. They did all that they did with the certain, unified knowledge that they were insects feeding on the defecation of something greater. And aren't we all?

What separates the hairless apes in my world from the fly people of the cosmic turd is that human beings will go to war, they will murder and maim, they will oppress and enslave their own, just so that they don't have to be the flies sifting through the shit.

From the fly people, I have come to learn about the hairless ape that, above all else, he fears equality. For death is a kind of equality. As our memories become shadow, as our bodies fade to dust, are we not all the same? Are we not all just the elements that be? And in the same way that death is equality, is equality not a kind of death? For if all is fair, if naught is foul, if all is good and satisfaction and comfort are king, then we may be happy to wake and say unto our world, "Today nothing can go wrong. I have my spot, my safe little spot, where I harvest the ore from the mud and the next fly does the same. Others gather feces from the roach-oxen. I return and I build the nests, and my comrade returns and we feed together—equally—upon what he has gathered. The queen will be inseminated and a new brood will rise, forever in perfect harmony. Hail, hail the cosmic turd and the Great Swamp!"

Yes, this is the hairless ape's fear.

It is a fear shared by the dragon men.

After suppressing all the other races on their jungle world, after wiping multitudes of species from existence on their great spine hunts for the Sky Father Calteca—the dragon of cloud with lightning breath—they battled perpetually amongst themselves. They warred for no greater purposes than to claim the title of the strongest bloodline. And what wars they fought—fortresses fell; mountains of corpses piled. Sword and sorcery were put to the deadliest of tests, and again and again new levels of slaughter were reached. All to be seen as higher than the rest, all to fight off that thing they so feared...equality.

Calteca saw only those who dominated with fists of stone, as do all the pantheons of gods belonging to every race of man I have ever known. I have seen us act as flies, and I have seen us act as dragons. I am still trying to understand what it means to act like a man.

When I'd wake, I'd write as much as I could recall of the dreams before they faded forever in the black holes of my memory.

As I said, each night the star paled, the star under which I had these most absurd, terrible, and magnificent of dreams. On the hundredth night, it was no more, the once gloriously vibrant star that had out-gleamed the Goose of Galjernon. I never dreamed of those worlds again, and I spend my nights now questioning if I am here, or if I am in some far world only dreaming of this one, long after its star has already faded from existence.

~Excerpt from *Dreams in the Solarium* by Hector Pearce Lovell

≈

CHAPTER SIX

MANY MONSTERS

*C*ullum trotted into town, stabled his horse, and promptly came upon the two men he had assigned to assist the town gravedigger in excavating the body of Jeremiah the younger. He had left them to carry out the task while he went to inspect the corpse of the old witch woman and the dead man at the witch's hut.

The men were drunk and were playing some game of flipping coins at the well.

What they were not doing was digging.

"I have only been gone a short while," said Cullum as he walked down the dirt road between the houses. The men turned around and their faces went red, like children caught in the act of pilfering sweets. "Have you finished the task assigned you by the Holy Order?" A glance at their boots revealed no graveyard mud. Were he to guess, he would say that they had not even started.

"As you said, your holiness," stammered one, his face as red as his hair. "Ya were only gone a short bit, and we thought we may just fortify ourselves a wee bit with some brew before we set about the heavy task of digging up a boy we just buried."

Cullum did not respond, just frowned and stared and let the silence linger. The red in the two men's faces receded, and they went pale, their embarrassment replaced by fear.

"Your name?" Cullum asked the one who had spoken.

"Samuel."

Cullum nodded. He'd asked the man's name when he set him to his task, but he wanted to make the point that he'd already forgotten, for they mattered little. Had they done the task he'd asked, he'd have addressed both by name. Samuel and Martin.

"And yours, son?" Cullum asked the other man. He very much enjoyed using the term *son* on men decades older than himself.

"Martin."

"Tell me, Martin, where is the gravedigger? Is he *fortifying* himself as well?" Cullum asked, making a show of looking around as if expecting the gravedigger to crawl out and reveal himself.

"Oh, no. Solomon needs no fortification for a task such as that, for it is his job. I'm but a humble potter," Martin said with a little smile.

"Humble men obey the word of the sun. Now shut your mouths and get your shovels."

Both men turned a whiter shade of white. "The sun's setting. We'll be digging in the dark."

"So you will," Cullum said. "So you will."

∾

The night was alive with the song of crickets and the whispering of hidden creatures close by and the howling of ones far off. By the light of a flickering torch, Cullum watched the gravedigger clear the last of the dirt from atop the coffin.

"Give me some ale, Samuel, you useless bastard," said the gravedigger as he wiped sweat from his brow.

"I have a weak back, Solomon. I have for years, ever since I... That is...when I..." Samuel replied from where he rested beside the grave.

The man had "injured" his back when he first put shovel to dirt, and Cullum had taken his place thereafter. He glanced up now and asked, "Are you so dull-witted that you cannot recall how you injured your own back, man?"

"Hey, now. Even clever men forget," Samuel said as he got the large wineskin of ale and handed it down to the digger. Solomon took a long sip then tossed the skin back up.

Cullum noted the man's assertion and set it aside for later consideration, for it seemed that more than one man in the village of Wardbrook had a faulty memory. Two might be deemed coincidence, but three was quite possibly a sign from the Luminescent.

"Hand me down my pry, if you would."

Martin picked up a three-foot metal bar and squatted as he handed it down to Solomon.

The thin pieces of timber that made the coffin lid creaked as the gravedigger wrenched it off. He lifted the lid and placed it on the wall of the grave. All three men looked uneasy in the flickering light of the torch. Shadows danced on the other graves and the wind whistled between the stones.

"Well, here he is," the gravedigger said through the arm that he used to cover his nose. When a gravedigger cowers from a stench, it is certain to be a stench most foul, but Cullum was not one to break from a reek, no matter how horrid. When the scent hit his nose, his teeth clenched and his blood ran hot. He knew without looking, but he took off his left glove and looked all the same. His veins bulged and glowed blue, then orange, then green, and the burn was strong. There was potent magic still lingering in that corpse, but it was not magic discharged by the dead witch atop the western hill.

"I'll need you to bring the body up here. When I am done examining it, take it some miles from the village and burn it to ash. Even the bones," Cullum said. "Do it in the valley, not the woods."

"The stench, by the fuckin' Luminescent. The stench." Martin moaned through his forearm that he held over his mouth.

"Never blaspheme before me again!" Cullum shouted, and took three long strides toward the man.

Martin stumbled back, eyes wide. He dropped his hand from his mouth and quickly bowed on all fours. "Mercy. I beg you, mercy."

"Get up," Cullum said, heaving Martin up by the back of his shirt. "Get that corpse out of the grave." Cullum then looked to Samuel, who pretended to be rubbing his hurt back. They did not move. "Now!" Cullum roared, and they nearly leapt at the corpse.

Martin got into the grave with the digger, and they hoisted the body of Jeremiah the younger up to Samuel, who squatted at the grave's edge and pulled as the other two lifted from below.

Jeremiah's corpse was halfway out of the grave when it gave a bone-chilling moan.

Crying out, all three men let go of the corpse and attempted to scramble away. Too late.

Jeremiah's corpse grabbed hold of the two men lifting him and, with tremendous strength brought on by hellish magic, flung them down into the grave.

They slipped and slid in the loose earth, their screams

mingling with the monster's moans, and in the dark and the shadows, Cullum could not make out the one from the next. He moved closer, the torch illuminating the scene. Samuel grabbed the pry bar and swung it at the corpse, only to hit Martin's foot instead. Martin howled. The corpse howled. Samuel howled, and then Solomon grabbed the shovel and swung it at the corpse, which fell atop Martin.

"Out of there, quickly!" Cullum ordered them, and he extended his arms down to heave Samuel out of the grave. With a whimper, Martin half leapt into Samuel and Cullum's reaching arms. Solomon remained in the grave, pounding the corpse with the shovel.

Cullum's left hand burned beneath the glove. Living, breathing sorcery was about. With Martin and Samuel safely away now, he leaned back into the grave, reaching for Solomon.

"Smash, smash..." the gravedigger said. "Smash." He swung the shovel.

"Back away!" Cullum roared. The corpse's abdomen had swelled as if it carried a seven-month babe, and it glowed vibrant orange.

The gravedigger spun his head around to an impossible angle. His eyes were black but for emerald-green dots as pupils.

"Outsider, turn back!" the digger said in a bestial growl. The pulverized corpse of Jeremiah the younger swelled, a glowing orange fluid swirling beneath the stretched flesh. "Turn back!"

The corpse's skin burst with a loud pop, and steaming orange ichor covered the gravedigger, who howled and wailed as the ooze seeped into his flesh.

The curse was in Solomon now. With his gore dripping, shovel in hand, he sprang from the grave in a single leap.

The bones in Cullum's left forearm and hand vibrated like wind chimes in a storm.

"May your cursed soul find rest, and may you forgive me," Cullum muttered.

Solomon whirled on Cullum and shrieked from deep in his belly.

Cullum opened his palm to the gravedigger as if he were about to command him to stop. The whole world became darkness. The graveyard was gone. The other men gone. Only the sorcery could be seen: Solomon standing, a hunched figure of orange wrapped in blue. From Cullum's left palm, through the glove, the arcane blue chains poured, leaving no mark on either his flesh or the glove's leather.

Solomon's face was a twisted mask of pain. He tried to thrash, but with each movement, the chains grew tighter. Cursed or not, he screamed from the agony. Cullum yanked him close, pain erupting up his left arm. He ignored it, and he drew and swung his sword with his right hand in one fluid sweep. The gravedigger's head came off, and as it spun, falling through the blackness, Cullum saw the caster of the spell.

A small creature stood at the edge of the darkness, a rat with a grotesque little human head and too many limbs, orange boils glowing on its underbelly. It moved its lips and its evil little hands. Cullum released the chains from the gravedigger's corpse and whipped them out at the little sorcerer, but it was too fast. A symbol shaped like a human skull formed in an emerald-green mist in the air before the creature, and then both symbol and rat were gone.

Cullum pulled back the chains and returned to the earthly realm.

"What th-th-the fuck…was th-th-that?" said Martin. He cowered beside a distant grave.

Cullum walked to the bushes where the rat sorcerer's

magical trace remained. "Burn the gravedigger's body and head," he said. "Burn whatever chunks you can pick up of Jeremiah the younger. Burn them to ash," Cullum added without looking back. He'd told them this once, but they seemed like a people who needed multiple reminders.

The rat sorcerer had not gone far; his presence was still strong. But he was not in the bush. Cullum scanned the tree line, the ancient trees so tall he would struggle to leap and touch one of their lowest branches.

A nameless force pulled his vision toward a wooded ravine close to the great black house on the hill.

Cullum whistled, and his horse came cantering toward him, his shadowy mane swaying as the fine beast tossed his head. Cullum pulled himself onto his steed's back and hooked his small lantern to the saddle and his steel-toed boots into the stirrups. On the nightmare-black mount, Vicar Cullum Shrike entered the woods to hunt a rat.

The sound of flies was strangely loud, and simply strange —for whether or not a corpse lay about, flies were not usually active at night. The mixed scents of fresh spring and rot hung in the air. Moonlit mist walked over the forest floor like a legion of ghosts.

Only when he got close enough to the stinking masses of rot strewn about did Cullum realize he had not chased the rat—the rat had led him here.

With his lantern held close and his *Ordeal*-sharpened vision, Cullum discerned the carnage about him to be the remains to be both human and canine. The two missing villagers and their dog?

"By the sun, what words can describe such a scene?" Cullum whispered. To say they had been *killed* would be an offensively gross understatement, as would the use of *slaughtered* or *butchered*.

The dog's head was twenty or so feet from the body, its

maggot-infested entrails spread across the forest floor and up and over a low branch of a nearby tree. Below the branch, a man's remains were propped up against the trunk. His face was gone; bloody pulp and an eyeless skull remained. His chest was ripped open, his ribs pulled wide apart like open doors, and a piece of wood—half the man's walking stick— was rammed through his heart.

"A storm, hehe, is what it looks like. A storm," came a rasping voice from somewhere above Cullum.

No. Somewhere below?

"It looks like the wrath of nature itself… Look there at the other one. The moon wolf ripped out the vermin's spine." The voice came from the direction of the other dead man. Of course, it had not come from the man himself, for even if he had been reanimated by some spell, he had no lower jaw, no throat, no tongue, and, as the voice said, no spine. He was a scrap of rotten meat. *It* was a scrap of rotten meat, no gender, no identity anymore, just minerals, ores, and enzymes to seep back into the dirt.

But the sun will rise, and from the dirt, life will grow anew. This is why the Seeker fights. Because the sun rises and the light always finds a way.

"Where are you, little sorcerer?" Cullum asked.

"Hehe," answered the voice, and it echoed from all around. "Haha." The voice changed; it was no longer high in pitch but had dropped to a demonic depth, and Cullum recognized it as the voice that the gravedigger had spoken in after he was possessed.

"*Little* sorcerer? I assure you, I am grand."

Cullum urged his horse forward. They had taken only two steps when the leaves, twigs, and dirt on the ground swirled up into a cyclone as wide as the widest tree's trunk, and a massive shadow in the form of a bearded man with four long arms appeared.

Neither Cullum nor his mount were fazed; their arcane eyes saw through the trick.

The shadow form burst, and when the voice came again, it was high-pitched and wretched.

"Hehe, good eyes youhave, Seeker. Special glowing eyes. So open them wide—your ears, too," the sorcerer ordered him. "Turn back, outsider. The coming fight is not your own."

"This is Brynth, rat," Cullum answered, his tone somber. "This is a land of the sun, inhabited by the children of the Luminescent. There is sorcery here. I will kill it, and I will kill you. Then I will kill the thing that did this," Cullum said, referring to the peasants and the dog, his outstretched hand slowly panning over the scene. "For I know it wasn't you, rat. You work your filthy magic at a distance."

"You know not a thing about how I work my filthy magic, Outsider. You know not how far out of your depth youare. You know not how absent, how uncaring your God really is. You know not, you know not… You. Know. Not. But you'll learn, you'll learn, angry, little man. You will learn."

"I'll not turn back, devil. Show yourself, that we may fight." Cullum focused on finding the origin of the spell being cast. In less than a blink, a curtain fell, and he entered the black, ephemeral realm of the forces. Skulls of green smoke hovered around him, speaking the words of the rat sorcerer. They obstructed his vision and hearing as he searched the expanse of infinite darkness for his enemy.

"Hehe, you're right. It be best for you that you not turn back—with what's coming to your beloved Order of the Seekers, it be best that you just turn away. Go hide with the peasants until the sun turns black and you see the truth. The truth that will make you mad…it will set you free."

Cullum's calm wavered at the mention of doom coming to the Order. Not because he had not heard similar squawking from other mages and demons in the past. No, the words assaulted Cullum's calm because, for the first time, he knew a heathen's words to be true. Something terrible was descending upon the Order, and the already long-lingering idea that this whole mission was a trick intensified tenfold.

The rat might know nothing; he could be spewing false prophecies promised him by some troglodyte master. Or the rat could have entered Cullum's thoughts while hiding in the distance in a moment while Cullum's guard was down. It could have sifted through his anxieties and fears the way a thief rifles through dressers and drawers in their victim's home, even as they sleep.

"You know my vocation, sorcerer," said Cullum, his calm returning, and he silently thanked the sun for granting him strength of mind. "You know I shan't turn away. You know that I won't accept any of your lies. You know I am going to keep searching for you until I kill you. I have heard enough excrement spill from your fetid lips, rodent. Show yourself so we may fight."

Cullum clenched his teeth as the chains exited his left palm. His horse trotted in tight, slow circles in the blackness as the green vapor skulls flew around them. He whipped the chains out, and several of the skulls burst and disappeared, while others escaped, laughing as they flew and hovered in the air, speeding up and down and to and fro like flies circling the dead.

"Hehe! Hehe! You idiot! That won't do at all, you fool," said the sorcerer, and each word came from a different skull. "I'll not show myself. I'll not fight you. I'll let you continue down this winding, branching path... I'll even point you in the right direction. But if the wicker man don't kill you, the moon wolf will. And if by some cosmic rule you defeat him too, you'll cross the Goddess herself, you fool. And you shan't kill her, you can't kill her.

"If you escape her, you angry little man... Oh, Black Brenna can promise ya, there won't be any fight left in ya, none left for killing a wretch like me." The skulls converged to a single point; the green smoke turned to emerald fire that blazed in a lantern that swayed in the powerful hands of a mighty four-armed man, hunched and bearded, with a wild mane of black hair, black eyes but for dots of green as pupils. His translucent black belly glowed orange from the inside.

"I will always have enough in me to kill a wretch like you," Cullum said.

"I am one wretch of many. *His* children have risen." Before Cullum could demand an explanation, the sorcerer said, "Follow," in a voice as deep as black oceans. Then he turned and sprinted into the dark, where he and his lantern disappeared, leaving footprints of green fire.

Cullum called back his chains, and the blue tethers whipped back into his palm. He returned his sight to the mundane world.

Where the sorcerer had just been, Cullum could see the footprints. Not of a hulking four-armed hermit, and not of a rat. They were the prints of a slight human. As he looked upon them, in his mind's eye flashed the image from his time in the pool with the Sisters, a weeping brown-haired girl in a green dress, fear in her forest eyes.

The footprints went through the woods toward the great black house on the hill.

Wardbrook.

The house was obscured by the trees and the night, but he could still make out its silhouette. He swore he could hear the girl's cries, and it was his name on her lips.

But no, it was just the sighing of the wind.

He raised his left hand to the structure that seethed with

the very atmosphere of sin, then he took off his glove and closed his eyes.

The *Bloodburn* did not stir. Either he was too far off, or there was no magic in the place. Which he doubted.

He was about to don his glove when he realized that he felt...*truly nothing*. There was no sensation on the back of his hand, for the moist fog and chill wind that touched his face and ears and fingers did not do the same to the center of his hand.

"Cloaking amulets," Cullum said. It was Cullum himself who had first documented this phenomenon in the Seeker Manuals.

He snarled and nudged his horse into a trot toward the house. It was time to make inquiries.

"Be careful in how you ask your questions up there, to those *pagans* in the manor on the hill, young man," the coroner-surgeon had said that morning with an imperiously knowing smirk. Cullum despised that word, *smirk*, and as far as he knew, he despised every man he had ever met who carried out the action of the smirk. The lip up on one side, the exposing of the fang, the slight wink—it was enough to earn any man a beating from Cullum's righteous fists. But there was something about the coroner-surgeon that seemed above such a beating.

The man was smart. And he was hiding something. But in his warnings about Wardbrook, he had been forthcoming.

So Cullum chose a different path than the one that would carry him to the house on the hill. He turned his horse and headed back through the woods to the town. He would wake the coroner-surgeon and he would bring him to the grisly scene. And in the heart of the violence, he would begin asking his questions.

～

Breathe.
Breathe it in. Breathe it deep. Breathe in the fire. Choke it down.
Drown it in the abyss. Suck the blood from death's sweet kiss.
Know that I am true, know that I am real.
Know that I am pain through and through.
Know that you'll always love me.
When you sleep, when you dream,
I am you.

～

CHAPTER SEVEN

OH, SWEET DREAMER

$\mathcal{T}$he sun was setting, and Nyva nibbled away at the last of the picnic that Diana had brought with them—hard cheese and bread and a flagon of wine that they poured into goblets. Odd that no matter how much she ate, she could taste nothing, and her belly never seemed to fill. Odd, too, that the weather was so warm, for spring had only just begun. But it had been a warm day when she had seen the rat outside Nan's hut—

"I feel guilty," Nyva said, and pulled the bread away from her lips without taking a bite. The warmth in her heart disappeared, and she thought of the sounds Nan made before that horrific, echoing crack. Nyva's whole world had cracked with it. Her reality had split like Nan's skull, and everything she had known and understood poured out like blood and brain, all to rot. All to decay. "I miss her."

"Beautiful girl, you need to listen to me," Diana said, and she grasped Nyva's chin and turned her head so that she stared right into Diana's eyes. What wonderful solace Nyva found in those azure depths. "You are not at fault. Those who *are* will be punished."

Heat rose from Nyva's chest to her eyes, and her vision blurred as the tears formed. "My lady, that whole village is at fault. They became more and more fanatical every year after you left. Those backward sheep-fucking inbre—" Nyva stopped speaking, horrified by her own brashness. This was the lady of the land, and what a formidable lady she was.

Diana only smiled down at her, then she caressed Nyva's hair.

Nyva frowned, for while she saw the movement from the corner of her eye, she did not feel the touch.

"I am so sorry, my lady. I meant no insult in that, none at all," Nyva whispered. She reached out to offer a touch to Diana's hand, then, afraid she was overstepping again, she pulled her hand away.

Diana reached out, took Nyva's fingers between hers, and wiped away her tears—again, her touch was one Nyva did not feel. Then, without warning, she pulled Nyva to her breast. In a voice smooth like silk, as she rocked Nyva back and forth, she said, "Oh, beautiful Nyva, I take no insult. Many, many more than those who live in my village are at fault, and they too will be punished."

"They will all be punished," Diana whispered.

Her embrace was strong and protecting.

It was very strong. It was becoming too strong, constricting.

Nyva tried to push away, and when a gentle press of her palm achieved nothing, she pushed harder, then harder still. But Diana was more powerful than any man.

Nyva gasped as her breath was squeezed from her. She heard and felt the small pops as pressure released between the joints of her spine.

"Let me go!" The words were loud in her mind but less than a whimper as they slid past her lips. Sound without form or meaning.

Why are you doing this? Nyva tried to ask, but she had no breath with which to speak. Her head spun and flashes danced before her eyes.

Diana was her safe place. Nan had sent her here. But in this moment, Nyva felt anything but safe. She felt betrayed.

Again, she tried to push free, but Diana's arms were like chains, binding her. She could not move. Could not breathe.

In that instant, she regretted not dying with Nan. She regretted not listening to the rat who had warned her that Diana was no safe place. She regretted ever lying with the farm boys. All Nyva could do as she sank toward oblivion was regret...regret...regret.

Then Diana released her.

So abruptly did Diana let go that Nyva tumbled backward onto the grass. She turned and crawled away coughing and heaving, desperate to get precious air back into her lungs. She pushed to her knees and, with tears in her eyes and questions on her lips, turned her head to look at Diana.

But Diana was there no longer.

The black house of Wardbrook loomed like a dark shadow. It looked exactly as it had moments ago. But everything else was changed, completely and horribly changed. The tall, thick trees of the ravine that bordered the northern side of the house were no longer trees. They were colossal, gray-skinned human arms reaching up from the earth, hands and fingers flexing and stretching in and out to form grasping claws. A yellow-green miasmic fog hung in the sky above.

Stumbling to her feet, Nyva turned back in the direction of the brook, preparing to flee as far as she could from Wardbrook, from Diana, from the forest of hands and the choking fog. The sight that greeted her on the other side was changed now too.

The previously clear blue brook was a putrid orange-brown, and the grass beneath her was not grass at all—every blade of green was now a writhing white worm. The trees of the apple orchard had mutated so that their trunks were like human spines, and the greenery atop had metamorphosed into giant brains. Where the apples had once hung now grew black, bulbous tumors that pulsed like hearts.

"Hehe," came from the direction of the brain orchard.

She knew the voice.

"Hehe," came from the forest of hands.

"No!" she screamed.

"Hehe," echoed all around her, and she shut her eyes tight and screamed over the laughter of Black Brenna. Then, as if it were sliced off, her scream went silent.

The cackling grew louder, and against her skin she could feel the grass of the living white tendrils growing around her. They squirmed over her ankles and around her wrists. The ground beneath her began to quake, and just behind her, from the black house of Wardbrook, she heard a sound that thrummed through her bones and belly as much as through her ears.

It was the sound of the world screaming, the earth splitting.

Don't look, don't look, don't look...

She threw back her head and opened her eyes against her will, like phantoms had yanked her by her hair and with cold, dead fingers peeled back her lids.

The yellowed sky was now below. A black sun-moon dwelled in the center of it all, like a black hole torn into some mad artist's design in a fit of rage-filled indecision as to whether the plot was night or day. From the earth—from the below which was now the above—the shadow home ascended even as it descended. Emerging from the earth, from above it, *from beneath it* was a pyramid of black stone.

Hehe... As above is below...the endless beyond lies within.

Hehe...wake. Wake. Wake! And let the nightmare begin. Before ya, behind ya, inside ya. In the earth and in the air. The labyrinth will bind ya...hehe.

Nyva opened her eyes. Her heart pounded. The silver moon was above; the high trees of the ravine surrounded and sheltered her. She got to her feet and looked up from the foot of the hill to the great black house of Wardbrook.

She had been here before.

She was here again, but she could not remember how she got here. She had run from…

Why had she run?

What happened last?

Nan had sent her here…

The memory of Nan's murder flooded back, and Nyva felt as if she would be sick. She remembered running. Fleeing through the woods. She remembered the cry of a man when he spotted her. She remembered the barking of a dog and the sound of…

Something had howled at her back, something like a wolf. But bigger. So much bigger. And then men had been screaming and a dog had been yelping and Nyva had been —*was*—running again.

She ran to the beat of her pounding heart, and she ran up the hill toward Wardbrook.

She had been here before…

She was here again…

Strange memories of a forest of hands and an orchard of brains that she did not understand started to take the place of the thoughts of Nan as the howling at her back grew louder.

And louder.

And louder.

Nyva blinked.

She was inside Wardbrook. How had she come to be

here? Her thoughts spun. Her pulse raced. She was upstairs, in the guest wing—

How did she know it was the guest wing? Paintings of warlords, kings, queens, philosophers and so many beasts hung on the walls. Small candlelit lanterns were spaced through the hall. Closed black curtains over glass windows suffocated the light of the brilliant moon that managed to penetrate the house with its glow despite the fabric pulled to block it out.

Nyva's heart still pounded like it had as she fled the beast, but she felt no fear.

Why do I feel no fear?

Without thought or will, she strode with silent steps to the door at the end of the hall and swung it open. Someone slept in a huddled ball beneath fur blankets on a finely carved bed. A hearth fire glowed in the room's corner, and it took the lump in the bed and grew its shadow on the wall. The shadow looked like a hill, and something monstrous in Nyva wanted to climb it.

Something good in her died, and, with a sick premonition, she somehow knew what awaited her under the covers.

She knew what made the shadow hill on the wall, and she wanted to run.

She needed to stay.

Or did she *need* to run, and only *want* to stay?

She could not know; she could not be certain until she saw what lay beneath. Slowly, she advanced on the form in the bed. It did not stir; it did not wake.

Nyva lifted her left hand. There was a black glove upon it. She stripped her fingers naked and saw the hand of a man. She placed her palm against the form of the lump under the fur, and a vibrant green glow surged in the veins in the back of the hand that was hers yet not hers. She ripped the blanket away and saw herself.

She wore a green dress, the same color as her eyes. She was not sleeping, she was just waiting, and she said, "Open me up and come rest between my thighs." She stared down at herself and wrapped her hands around her neck.

She turned to dust in her own hands, and blackness engulfed all again.

She saw rings of blazing blue, like two glowing irises in an otherwise opaque darkness. They looked into her until she burned, burned all over. Burned like the very heat that was infection.

I am plagued; I am cursed; I am corrosive...and the loneliness never stops.

I dream.

~

Nyva awoke alone to a humming sound and soreness all over. Five nights she had been here. Five nights she had dreamed. She had been dreaming again, but she could remember nothing. No, not true. She remembered how she had come to be here, running up the hill into Diana's embrace.

She remembered a picnic with Lady Ward—but that had been only a dream...hadn't it?

She shifted on the bed. The soreness was sharper in her heart than it was in her feet and legs. Still, her rapid flight through the woods had left her with more than a few bruises and sprains. The way the big toe on her left foot ached, she questioned if it was broken.

Diana had said it was not. Diana had said there were no breaks. "Nor any loss of digits or limbs," she had added with her warming, motherly smile. Nyva remembered that now.

She had nursed Nyva, the lady herself, not just the many servants. Diana had taken Nyva into her arms and her house, and she was doing all she could—for what reason, Nyva could not say—to make Nyva feel at home. It was working, and the sense of comfort Nyva was beginning to feel was giving her a strange sense of guilt.

Nan had been good to her, treating Nyva like she was her own daughter.

Diana was treating her like a treasure.

Yet Nyva could not keep the words of the devil rodent from surfacing: *The Lady of Wardbrook, what do you know of Lady Diana Ward? Eh? Hehe.*

She stood from her bed.

Your bed? Getting quite comfortable, aren't we? She winced at the sound of the rodent's voice in her thoughts. He was not here. His words were mere phantoms.

She walked toward the table across the large chamber, where a tray had been left bearing food and wine. "You will need much spirits to help you through this, my child," Diana had said. "My husband and I…we have tried many a time to have a child, and every time, the child is stillborn." Nyva was sad for her. "We drink many spirits afterward; there is no shame in it."

And so Nyva felt no shame when she poured from the jug to the cup and the cup to her belly. She stood there for a time wavering like a reed in a light breeze, and then she drank a little more. Leaving the jug and the cup on the table, she walked to the open window that looked down the hill to the village, where lights in a few houses and the tavern were still lit. On the town's southern fringe, where the farmland began —at night it was as dark as the sea—Nyva could see the house of the coroner-surgeon. It was the largest house in the village.

The coroner-surgeon and Nan had been on better terms than Nan and anyone else from the village. Nyva did not like him.

He was still awake now. Light glowed in his windows, like small orange stars in a sea of black. Nyva wondered how he had responded to the death of Nan. Had he berated those who killed her, or had he clapped them on the back?

Then she saw another, smaller orange star approaching the house from the north—a lantern bobbing and swaying. A rider was on their way to the coroner-surgeon's house.

He was so far away he was little more than a black smudge against black sky. But she saw his face, a once-handsome, now-scarred face. Still handsome to her. Blue eyes, so very blue.

She remembered him, remembered the sound of his voice and the tilt of his chin and the line of his jaw.

But how could she remember a man she had never met?

～

Where this war begins, no trumpets blow and no drums beat,
No, not where this war begins.
When this war begins, there is only passion, only heat,
That is when this war begins.
That is why this war begins,
In love, not sin, is how this war begins.

Where this war begins, you need sail no ship, ride no horse,
No, not where this war begins.
When this war begins, they are sightless and know not remorse,
That is when this war begins.
That is why this war begins,
In welcomed threat is how this war begins.

Where this war begins, the child's eyes in the mirror,
Looking back at the man, at the woman it has become,
Yes, that is where this war begins.
When this war begins, hear all the voices screaming,
"Let me tell you what you should have done."
War in the village, war in the home is how this war begins.

Where this war begins, inside your love, sitting atop your liar's
throne.
That is where this war begins.

~"Where This War Begins" by Lionhard Conahan

～

CHAPTER EIGHT

❦

A HEALER, A TEACHER, A GUIDE

*I*t required none of Cullum's talents, none of his gifts from the *Ordeal* or otherwise, to know for certain he was being watched. Cullum bobbed in the saddle as he rode his horse down a narrow mud road that went from the ravine southward to the largest house in Wardbrook's village. Since coming to this place, he had felt uneasy. More than that, he had felt impotent. He had felt shame. He had failed those three girls in the hall, sewer, and cave. He had failed his Order. And his thoughts followed that path until he could think of nothing but his failures and his shame.

Which made him think of a time he had not thought on for a long while, a time he locked away in a dark coffin buried six feet under the dirt of his shame. He thought of a time when he had broken his vows of chastity as a young man, before the *Ordeal*.

He'd had a woman in a brothel down in the wharf. Afterward, driven by regret, he had run naked through the briars in woods south of the city. He had prayed that the thorns would take hold of his cursed cock and rip it from his body, thus forever saving him from sin. It did get caught and it did get cut, gashed wide from shaft to head, and the pain was horrible. The agony was every bit the opposite of when he had released all his pent-up youth into the whore by the fish seller down in the wharf. And so, the agony was every bit the same as the pleasure, for a thing's opposite is only as far as the other side of the coin.

When his prick had caught and split, he had kept marching. As the thorns plunged into his thighs and his shoulders and his chest and belly, he had kept marching, kept begging the Luminescent above to make it stop. Not the pain of the thorns but the temptation, for temptation was pain. It was the worst of them, the pain of seeing the thing you want most on the other side of the bars. The agony of not knowing which version of yourself is in the cage and which is looking at a pathetic beast from the outside. The lust for a woman was naught but the peak of an iceberg, the lust for the magic inside himself, the lust for the violence he always wished to carry out, the lust for the dreams to stop.

If only the dreams could stop.

When Cullum had finally made his way out of the briars, his bloody cock was still attached, as were his balls. And he had been left alone in the moonlight with nothing but his naked pain and his returning sanity. The sanity that must deal with all the shadow has done in its absence.

It took long, long months for the wounds to fully heal from that night in the briars, and every time an impure thought entered his mind and his loins tried to stir, Cullum would vomit from the sheer torture of it. After he had finally healed, he had become still below the belt.

Cullum got off his horse two score strides away from the house and began his approach with quiet footsteps. The wind whispered along the back of his neck, a caress, then stroked his cheek. He froze and looked around. Someone watched him, but not in malice. Female fingers stroked his lips. Emerald eyes flashed in the night. And then she was gone.

To his horror, he realized his cock had stirred, even as the *Bloodburn* flared. The situation was both alien and confusing. Accompanying the unexpected and unwanted stiffness in his loins, fear worked its way up his spine, a thousand little spider legs creeping and crawling up his vertebrae like a bone ladder.

Cullum. She whispered his name.

He shook his head. There was no whisper. There was no carress. It was the wind, just the wind in this place riddled with magic. The *Bloodburn* subsided.

He adjusted his trousers and walked on.

Light came from several of the coroner-surgeon's windows, despite the late hour.

The man had been awake when Cullum first arrived that morning—*the previous morning. It is well past midnight now*—and he was awake now.

Cullum stared up at the moon, then looked back to his destination.

A silhouette passed by the windows, a pacing shadow in a house that stood with a black sea of farmland at its back.

When Cullum had first arrived in the village with the sun yet to rise, the coroner-surgeon had been awake and dressed to start his day. Now Cullum saw that the man was again dressed for the day, though the moon was full in the sky, the sun far from its time to rise. Had the man already dressed for the next day? Or had he simply not disrobed from the prior?

Everything is foul in the lands of Wardbrook. The thought came to him, a parody of words he had read in a play.

A lit lamp sat on the ground to one side of the door, giving off a pinkish glow. Thin, translucent sides boxed in the lantern flame. Cullum had never seen such a lamp. He squatted, licked his forefinger, touched the lamp, and brought his finger to his tongue. Salt. An interesting choice. A way to ward off evil spirits—pagan and Enlightened folk alike put salt at the doors of their homes to keep wicked entities from entering.

Cullum rose, snuffed his own lantern, and placed it up against the wall. He knocked twice, and his fist was about to deliver a third rap when the door swung wide. Standing before him was the familiar form of the coroner-surgeon, and yet he looked different than he had when Cullum had first encountered him the previous morning.

The man in the doorway looked decidedly...*younger* than the man Cullum had met. The bags beneath his eyes—bags attesting to years of no sleep, not simply the slight darkening above the cheekbones of a night's poor rest—were gone. His perfectly cut bowl of dark hair seemed fuller and shinier, and the curls of his mustache and his chops were pristine. His posture was more erect.

The coroner-surgeon smirked at Cullum, exposing his right canine. Everything in Cullum rebelled at the man's expression, his condescension, the secrets Cullum had no doubt he was keeping, and the brazen way he wore a chain with a large golden sun sigil hanging from it around his neck.

"I've been waiting for you," the coroner-surgeon said.

Camaraderie had achieved no results. Cullum would try the blunt approach. "By the order of the Church, by the order of the king, what the fuck is going on here?"

"You don't give the king's order, young man. Or have you forgotten the rules to the game?" the coroner-surgeon said, the slightest distortion in his words caused by his perpetual smirk.

"There is no game here," Cullum said, forcing his tone to

stay low and calm. "Sorcery is at work and people have died, people you call neighbor have died—"

"Do not presume to tell me whom I call neighbor, *friend.*" The coroner-surgeon spat the last word with the seething animosity with which a man may call another a filthy rodent or a no-good dog's cunt.

The corner of Cullum's eye twitched. Who was this man? Never had he suffered so much disrespect from a simple civilian, wealthy and educated or no, *a man wearing a sun sigil, no less.* It was clear the amulet meant nothing to him, for only a despicable pagan would speak to a vicar so heinously.

Before Cullum could decide whether to speak or draw his sword—he was not sure which he wanted to do more—the coroner-surgeon laughed and said, "You are too easy to bait. Please, your holiness, do come in. There is much we must discuss, much I must tell you if you wish to win this game." At this point, the coroner-surgeon's tiny smirk turned to a full-toothed smile, and he stood aside in the doorway, extending his arm to the interior of his vast home, bidding Cullum welcome.

Scowling at his host, Cullum took off his gloves and put them in his pocket. He took off his hat and held it in his hand. Then he entered the home.

"It would seem you do not sleep," Cullum said as they walked down the stone-walled hallway to the coroner-surgeon's great room. Firelight from the hearth danced along the walls.

"It would seem neither do you, your holiness." The coroner-surgeon indicated a low, comfortable-looking chair covered in pelts. "Please."

Cullum sat.

"A drink, a glass of wine? A bottle, perhaps?" asked Cullum's host.

"Men of the Order do not drink spirits. I told you that at the tavern—"

"Did you? I don't recall. Besides, I've met plenty from the Order who do." Again, the coroner-surgeon offered that obscene wink. "I won't tell the arch—"

"I do not trust you. To drink spirits with a man, I must trust them—"

"So you *do* drink spirits," the coroner-surgeon said, and Cullum heard the word *hypocrite*, though it was not voiced aloud.

Cullum held his temper by a thread. "You wear a holy sun sigil around your neck." Cullum waved a hand at the necklace then reached across the space between the two of them, pointing his finger at the coroner-surgeon's nose. "But you do not act like you believe. I suspect you to be a pagan, as most men of *science* are. You *oh-so-wise* skeptics, calling better men *young man*, only to conceal the constant dread in your soul that has been summoned by your lack of belief.

"Yes, you lack belief in all the things that can't be explained, and there is far, far more of that than there ever will be of the explainable." In his thoughts came the whispers of guilt for his own lack of belief. But Cullum's finger did not waver. His stare did not waver. Only his lips moved. "That's right, I know you. I know the lot of you, so drop your false airs and understand this for what it is."

The coroner-surgeon's smirk finally melted away. "And what exactly is *it* that is happening here, in the great room of *my* home where I so humbly bid you welcome?" he asked, his eyes partially crossed as he stared at the tip of Cullum's pointing finger.

"Your welcome was anything but humble, and this is a Seeker's interrogation, *civilian*. You went somewhere today. You did not carry out a surgery. The closest township is still nearly a day's ride from here. There is no way you could have gone there and back for the conversation we are now having. And you carried no surgeon's bag with you."

The coroner-surgeon's brows lifted. "My name is Damos Castaros, not *civilian*."

"I don't give a shit about your name. You just homed in on the wrong part of what I said. Why did you lie about the surgery? And why did you come back from wherever you went looking a decade younger than when you left?"

"Why, thank you for noticing. My work keeps me youthful." Damos' stare shifted from Cullum's finger to his eyes. "I've never known an interrogator who offers compliments." His tone stayed flat, and his irritating smirk re-formed at the right corner of his mouth.

"Worst of all," Cullum went on, ignoring Damos' words, "is the feeling I am now acutely aware of in my left hand as sit I here with you." It was not the *Bloodburn* but something else.

"What feeling would that be?" Damos asked, shifting in his chair, his muscles tensing. Cullum's did the same just in case he had to spring.

Cullum did not intend to answer, yet the words came. "It is a sensation like a wide, circular hole has been cut in the center of the back of my hand, but it is done without pain, and no pain comes." He did not think Damos used sorcery to pry the words from him. It was something else, something inside Cullum urging him to speak. "The circle flexes and swells, then shrinks and warps only to flex and swell again—"

"Ah, like time," Damos said, looking up at his ceiling. Cullum stared at him, stunned that Damos had interrupted him yet again. "A circle of nothingness that grows and shrinks, that warps and writhes, that changes and changes, yet is always the same." He looked down, back at Cullum. "This is the sensation to which you refer?"

Damos' words were the ones Cullum had meant to speak next.

He surged to his feet.

Damos was faster, and he launched a kick into Cullum's chest so hard and quick that Cullum flipped over the back of the chair at his rear.

"Draw your sword if you want to fight. The chains will not work on me." Damos was no longer calm, roaring his words as Cullum lay on his back looking up. "They did not work when your order of hypocrites first found out what I had become while serving the Bastard King Athelram in Leavon. That was my payment for saving and healing so many hundreds of his mortally wounded men! Being hunted. Being chased by your kind."

Cullum rolled backward and got to his feet, drawing his sword. Damos paced and bayed. His eyes were black. Pupils, irises, the whites of his eyes—all were a shimmering black.

"What are you on about?" Cullum said, circling, sword held at the ready. The nothingness in his left hand continued to swell and contract, but there was no burning, no reading of magic that he could understand. "The Bastard King Athelram fought his crusade in Leavon more than five hundred years ago!"

"That is why I call you *young man*," Damos said, circling as well, his eyes on Cullum.

Five hundred years old… Damos was undoubtedly a man of magic. Yet the *Bloodburn* failed Cullum, offering him no reading. "The sun sigil around your neck is a cloaking amulet, isn't it? You are hiding the nature of your true magic under its illusory shield."

"Impressive guess, but the answer is stranger still," Damos said with a laugh. "I have changed my mind. You should put your sword away and we will talk like gentlemen. We can forgo the titles and speak each other's names, and I will answer for you any question you ask. And some you won't think to ask."

Cullum was tempted. So very tempted. "If I recall, you were the one who struck first," he said sullenly. "And quite violently, I may add. I fear you cracked a rib."

"You leapt up not to ask another question but to stick me with your sword and only then ask another question. Do not deny it," Damos said like a father catching his son in a lie.

"You were faster," Cullum admitted. "I give you that."

"We are on the same side," Damos said.

"Which side is that? I am on the side of the Church. I am on the side of the Enlightened."

That Luminescent-damned smirk. I will flay his lips.

"I pity you for the day you must suffer the truth about your order," said Damos. "The day when you are forced to suffer the sins of all the Order's fathers and vicars and Seekers who came before you, and all the deals they made with the devil underneath the robes of men sworn to God... And it *is* coming, this day of reckoning, a day that will overflow at the brim with blood, and the fabrics of reality will warp from the roaring thunder."

"Shut your fucking mouth, you mad dog," Cullum said. He hated the words, not only for the threat of them but for his own suspicions that they might be true. He trusted his Order, the order of his father, but he did not trust those twice-damned Lordanians. "When we first crossed paths, I thought you had a brain in your head. Now it is clear that you do not. What do you know of God? What do you know of the Luminescent?" Cullum demanded, and to his horror, he realized his voice was shaking.

Damos lifted his sun sigil from his chest. He raised it to Cullum the way a superstitious man may raise his sigil at some ghost or unseen phantom. His smirk was all snarling lips now. "This is no amulet of cloaking, young fool. And if you saw as much as you thought you did, you'd have seen that too. This is but an amulet of belief and love, in the sun and the woman who showed me the light so long ago. I know much of God. I have been speaking with him since before your archdeacon crawled from his mother into a brave new world. I have watched your church warp and bend like the circle of nothingness in your left hand. I have seen it rise and fall and become again and again what it was and what it will be, and I always see the heartache... Your church does not know the one they name the Luminescent!" Damos walked forward and placed his throat against the tip of Cullum's sword.

Cullum tightened his grip on the handle.

"Look around you, at least with your periphery if you fear taking your eyes from the *beast, the heretic, the demon*...the honest coroner-surgeon in front of you. Tell me what you see on my high bookshelves."

Cullum did as he was told.

"There are no books. There are no rugs on my floor. No paintings on my walls. I have been meaning to leave this place for a long, long time. The recent deaths, your arrival...I am sick of it. I have watched this play out too many times before. I dug through the corpses. I found the answers that only the dead can provide. And with those answers, I could do nothing but know the guilty and the wicked in silence, for I am a man sworn against violence, and even if I were a violent man, the evil here is violence beyond man."

Damos turned away from Cullum and sat back in his chair. He sighed and went on, "My house is empty because all is packed away in the cellar below. My healthy horses have long been ready. I raised them myself. I raised their parents, and their parents' parents, too. The cart is well built, and I built it a decade ago. I always meant to leave. I just never did, and every day I wondered what was keeping me.

"Beatrice told me that one day I'd do something that mattered, mattered even to me. I used to sneer at her the way I sneer at you and all the world. But maybe she was right, for right now I am realizing the thing that I must do, the thing that matters, has finally come and it has come with you... your *holiness*."

Cullum could not help but hear the ring of truth in it all. He did not understand. But he did believe. He lowered his sword and, after a lingering moment, sheathed it.

"Call me Cullum, Damos... I will have a drink with you. I need a drink, badly. And I need to eat." Cullum's stomach growled, and he slumped back into the chair. Even with the gifted fortitude granted him from the *Ordeal*, he had gone too long without the essentials of the living.

"I will fetch you something to eat, as well." Damos stood.

"You don't have servants to wake, in a house this large?" Cullum asked.

"I do not believe in servants," said Damos, and before Cullum's very eyes, the man morphed and melted into a pitch-black mist and gusted from the room in a blink. Cullum's heart pounded, and he surged to his feet, drawing his sword, though it would be no use against black mist. He spun around, waving the blade, reaching up with his left hand to try and sense something.

Nothing.

"Damos!" Cullum turned another full circle. "Where have you gone? What trickery is this?"

"It is trickery most convenient," Damos said from behind him.

Cullum spun, ready to cut his host to ribbons if need be.

Need would not be. Damos had returned to his physical form, wine in one hand, bread in the other. His eyes were still orbs of jet, and from his back grew eight spider limbs longer than his human arms. They held instruments: a lute, a flute, a skin drum, a rattle.

"I thought you had put your sword away, Cullum," said Damos. "May I still call you Cullum?"

Cullum sighed. This was sorcery. This was magic. This was all he was sworn to oppose. Yet he sheathed his sword, for this was also an opportunity for knowledge. "You may still call me Cullum," he said as he flopped, for the third time, into the chair. "What the hell are you, anyway?"

"The ones who killed me, the ones who brought me back...they call me *Dahkah.*" Damos' obsidian eyes went wide, and his thick brows rose as he said the ancient word.

Cullum got gooseflesh at the sound. The Order of the Dahkah, the shadow blades of the *Shahidi...* Archdeacon Lazarus had spoken of orders older than the Seekers, older than the Church of the Luminescent, as old as when man still ruled the below and beasts the above. An age before the light.

"Eat." Damos handed Cullum the bread.

Cullum accepted it. The bread was still warm, and the smell... His stomach growled and his mouth watered.

"Drink." Damos handed Cullum the wine.

Cullum accepted it. He sipped it, and the wine tasted of ambrosia. He bit the bread.

Bliss.

"Rest, and listen as I play a tune. I will show you what so many decades of honing my dark gift has wrought." Damos laughed as he plucked the lute with his shadowy spider limbs. It vibrated in the vast, near-empty room, and it vibrated in Cullum's near-empty soul. "In the morning, we will carry out your mission. In the morning, I will do something that matters." Damos closed his eyes and opened his mouth, and just when Cullum thought the demon was going to sing, a black snake with red eyes slithered out, a spider limb brought the flute to the black snake's lips, and the serpent began to play. Damos' arachnid claws strummed that lute, and thrummed on that skin drum.

Cullum closed his eyes, and in the dark abyss, he felt the sun's light.

The demon played.

The holy man prayed.

*A*lexander Ward stared at his wife.

  She was a perfect picture, the woman to make any man's heart ache, to make him fall to his hands and knees like a dog just to be close to her feet. He stared at her pale, naked splendor, painted with the moonlight that cascaded through their open window. She did not tell him where she had been for three years. She did not tell him what had happened to her. Instead, as they had made love, she showed him. Through the use of her magic, her thoughts and memories became his own. His empathy, his sympathy was hers, entirely hers.

  She showed him how she was betrayed by Elyra yet again, that emerald-eyed bitch, how the rogue sorceress had betrayed them all. She showed him how she had been overcome by too many foes and how she had been taken to the city of black stone ziggurats in a world foreign and strange.

  He wept as she made him see and feel what she had felt as the Murlur tortured her, seeking the whereabouts and the workings of her allies and kin. She had told them nothing, only endured.

  She had survived until Therick and Stiggis had come for her, and together, before they escaped a dying world, they had killed hundreds of their foes.

  As she shared the vision of her triumph, they shared their climax.

  Alexander stared at his wife now, that perfect picture, and he felt the closing of a circle. She had shown him so much; she had shared so much. She had made him feel everything, made him feel like they were one. She had done this so many times, so very many times before.

  He was always the hopeful fool that thought each time would be the special time when she revealed all, when she finally treated him as her equal. But this time, like every other time, she hid parts of her experience. And he knew she would leave him again. She would leave him with hate and revulsion and lust. And love, a love so strong that nothing could tear it asunder.

"I learned something there, in that other existence, that world like a distorted mirror image of our own. I learned a way that we may have a child...children, even." Diana did not look at Alexander as she spoke. She kept her focus on some unknown point in the sky through the open window.

Her words ought to bring him joy, but they did not.

Alexander's stomach rose in his throat, and he swallowed it back down. The shadow hands of anxiety closed in. He would have loved to have children, but it was not supposed to be. There was a natural rhythm to birth and death, a time in a life span during which there was but a brief opportunity to have a child.

But his wife was a sorceress. Her life span had far surpassed the norm. Still, her opportunity had passed long, long ago.

The memories she had shared were truth, but what she had kept hidden made them false. The price of a child would be too high.

"I don't want to become the wolf again," Alexander said.

"Alex, my dear, you haven't even heard what I have to say," Diana said.

"Diana, please..."

"Oh, it will just be a short while, I do promise." She turned her face from the window and looked into his eyes, and Alexander knew there was no escape. His soul was already howling.

~

CHAPTER NINE

❧

BLIND THE DAY, WAKE THE DREAM

*D*iana had brought her to the stable, and as far as
Nyva was concerned, all five of the horses here
vied for the title of *most magnificent beast to ever roam the flat
earth*. Two grays, a red-spotted white, and a white-spotted
red. They were sixteen hands tall, and their short, shining
coats gleamed overtop of defined, sleek muscle. The fifth
horse—this one golden beige with a mane as blond as the
tumbling waves of its beautiful mistress—was now Nyva's
focus. She decided this one was the most beautiful of the
horses. At first, she thought it was the mare's coloring that
drew her. But then she realized the coloring could not be
enough to explain the most immediate and intense growing
attachment to the animal.

Was it the eyes, perhaps?

They were just as black as the eyes of the other four. And
yet there was something about them...something melancholic, yet proud. Such an absurdly poetic thought. Nan had
often said, "There's no bigger fool than a poet, those filthy
word wizards." Even though she kept many books of the
Northmen's sagas, which she loved and read nightly, Nan

had something against poets. Nyva closed her eyes for an instant, her chest tight, tears pricking the backs of her lids.

It is *the eyes. These proud, melancholic, and so human black eyes.*

Nyva reached her hand to the horse. It dipped its head, and its wet nose touched her skin. Nyva laughed. She'd not had much exposure to horses in her life, not since she'd been a small child, but she had always admired them from afar and always wanted to ride.

"Ah, you have your eye on Ishtarra. She is magnificent, isn't she?" Diana asked. The smell of her perfumes and the pong of the stable commingled into something both sickening and seductive.

"I was just thinking how magnificent they all are, my lady…but yes, this one is the most beautiful, I think," said Nyva, then she whispered, "Ishtarra," and the horse nickered in recognition as Nyva lightly caressed her velvety nose.

"Nyva, how many times must I say this. You are to call me Diana. Think of yourself as my friend. A friend of my family's, and friends use names when conversing, not titles." Diana waved her finger as she spoke in a mock-chastising voice.

"Diana," Nyva said. "Diana, you must have the most wonderful horses in the whole world, I think."

Diana threw back her head and laughed. "Oh, my dear, how you know just the way to make me blush. There are many horses like these specimens, but to find them you must go very far from here. Far off to the southeast. Past Romaria. In the lands of Kehldesh, there is a vast and wondrous city-state called Kallibar. And in that place are bred the finest horses the world will ever know. Some of the most beautiful men and women, as well."

"What is it like there?" Nyva asked.

"Perhaps one day you will visit and see for yourself."

Diana opened the gate to Ishtarra's stall. "Right now, we must discuss the day's affairs. Because today we are going to be as busy as bees, my sweet."

"Busy?" Nyva asked, her interest piqued.

"Yes, tonight is the party." Diana snapped her fingers at the stable hand, and he hurried over and began saddling Ishtarra.

"The party?" Nyva felt like an idiot after asking. She felt as if all she had done since her arrival was ask questions. But she recalled no mention of a party.

"Yes, the party. I must have mentioned it to you. No?" Diana shook her head, brow furrowed.

This woman cannot be confused, Nyva thought. Then she shivered as she realized it was not her own voice that whispered in her mind, but Black Brenna's.

She wanted to dismiss his words, but she couldn't. Diana had been nothing but kind to her. Too kind. She understood that some debt to Nan saw Diana take her in, but that did not require the lady of the manor to entertain and coddle her. Nyva hated that she was so ungrateful, yet she couldn't quite trust such kindness and couldn't explain why.

"Perhaps you did mention the party," said Nyva. "I just—"

"Don't you even stress, my sweet child," Diana said, and she reached out ran a hand through Nyva's hair.

I had bad dreams last night. Dreams I can't recall but that saw me wake with my nightclothes sweat-dampened and stuck to my skin.

"You have had so much happen to you," Diana said. "You cannot be expected to remember every little thing I say." Nyva nodded, but Diana's observation only increased her unease, because, yes, Nyva did remember every word the lady had said. And there had been no word about a party. But was that a reason to feel wary?

"We have much to do, but I promise today we are going to have some fun." Diana lifted her brows.

"I'm not one to turn down fun," Nyva said, surprising herself, because she meant it.

A smile formed on Diana's lips, and she placed her hands at her hips.

"A young lady after my own heart," said Diana. "Have you ever ridden before?"

"In a manner of speaking. Nan had a horse once. Well, I think he may have been a mule. But he was a tall mule and he…cantered," Nyva said, and shrugged.

Diana offered a strange smile, one that made the hairs on Nyva's nape rise. Then the lady clapped and tossed back her head, her light golden curls stroking the air like a painter's brush on the canvas. Her deep laugh filled the rafters.

"You are the most precious," Diana said, and grabbed Nyva and pulled her into her breasts, burying her there. Smothering her there. "I know all about Nan's mule. Did you ever wonder how she managed to buy such a creature? How she managed to feed it?" Diana's tone was dark and forbidding.

I had bad dreams last night. A forest of hands, an orchard of brains, a river of old blood and rotten meat.

Diana let Nyva go and stared at her a moment.

"I'm sorry," said Diana, and in her eyes, there could be no mistaking the sheen of tears.

"Diana?" Nyva whispered, her voice caught in her throat.

"I'm sorry for what happened to Nan," Diana said, blinking away her tears. "Nan had a special magic."

Nyva nodded. "Sometimes she would try to show me, but I am no witch."

"No magic in you at all?" Diana asked with a tight smile.

For an instant, Nyva felt uncertain of her answer, as if Diana knew something about her body and soul of which

Nyva was ignorant. Then Diana turned to the stable hand, who had finished equipping Ishtarra and one of the grays, and said, "Help the young lady up. Today we shall call each other huntress," and Nyva's uncertainty flowed away.

Nyva set her foot to the stirrup as the stable hand helped her up, then gratefully accepted a quick lesson from Diana, who adjusted her posture in the saddle and her grip on the reins. Then Diana mounted the gray.

Outside, the smells of spring carried to Nyva and filled her nose with life as they paused in the yard. The breeze felt like kind fingers combing her hair, and the warmth of the sun made her empathize with the Enlightened in believing the sun to be the one God, even though she knew it wasn't. Nan had told her of so many gods.

She stared at the horizon, enjoying the sun and the breeze and the view of the trees. And then she saw him, Alexander Ward, his moon-bright hair falling to his shoulders. He walked at the edge of the forest, and after a moment, he paused and turned, and she knew he'd seen her. She felt his gaze, though he was too far away to make out his features.

He half raised his hand, as though about to wave a greeting, a welcome, to *her*. Then he went stiff and turned away, and Nyva glanced back to see Diana staring after her husband, a forbidding cast to her beautiful features.

"Have you ever gone hunting, Nyva?" Diana asked, and on the heels of her question came the nearing sound of baying hounds from the direction of the great black house of Wardbrook.

Nyva's stomach knotted. She did not like hounds. She did not like the stories Nan had told her about hounds. And she did not like the memories so recent of running from one through the woods.

"Worse than wolves, they are," Nan would say. *"A wolf stops hunting when its hunger is satiated. A hound does not stop hunting.*

It cannot stop hunting. Thousands of years of killing for man have seen to that. So, that killing lives in their blood now, just as it does in their race of masters who, too, are just a kind of hound."

"Ah, speak of the devil, as *they* say," said Diana. "There is the hunt-master now."

The joy of the day evaporated. Nyva wanted to ride. She did not want to hunt. Nan had been hunted by the villagers. Nyva had been hunted in the woods. She most definitely did not want to hunt. But where was her voice? Where was her protest? She felt powerless in the face of the lady's confidence and wealth and bearing.

"Well, Nyva? I hope you are not a squeamish sort. I doubt you are, having lived with old Nan. So, have you ever gone hunting?" Diana asked again.

"For hares. Nan taught me to be a good trapper. And I bagged a single buck in my life two years past with a bow. I will admit, it did make me feel quite sick. There was a lot of blood when I slit its throat." Nan had been next to her, urging, "Do it, wimp. Don't keep the creature waiting for its endless pasture. Set it free." Nyva thought of that buck. She remembered its eyes and the surrender in them, the calm surrender of a thing that was at terms with its own death the moment it breathed into life.

"I knew that day why we pagans worship the stag as a god," said Nyva. "Because it is life. It is death. Its blood is like water, because it changes into the form of all it enters. Its death becomes life. Dammar the Antlered God looked at me through that stag's dying eyes and said, 'We are one, you and I. Oh, child of mine.'"

Nyva shuddered. Thoughts of memories, memories of thoughts. *How oft is the past the present now? How oft now is the present the past?*

"Nyva, you have a wisdom that astonishes me," said Diana.

"Nan taught me well." Tears filled Nyva's eyes. *Tears of a melancholic pride.*

"Nan was a good woman, and a good teacher. May she be feasting and fighting now in the axe-hall with the warriors and pantheon of gods she loved so dear," Diana said, looking off, back toward the house and the man in the distant foreground, a half-score hounds with him. He was riding a small nag and had what looked like a bow over each shoulder. From this distance, Nyva could see no quivers.

"Nyva," Diana said.

Nyva turned back to Diana. The lady was staring at her, a wet glaze of emotion over her eyes again, her head ever so slightly tilted to one side, the loving, knowing smile of a mother illuminated under the light of the late morning sun.

"My compliment to you just now was to you and you alone," said Diana. "The wisdom that you carry is not one that is taught. Rather, it is wisdom one owns. A primitive thing that follows a river of blood that has cascaded since the start of your line and runs now through you."

Diana was very serious now, her expression so intense that it made Nyva's heart flutter with fearful anticipation. She felt something coming up from her gut and didn't realize it was a question until it left her lips. A question that was hot and bitter.

"My line?" asked Nyva. "My blood? The only family I have ever known was Nan. And I heard her skull burst not a week past. I had no family but her, and now not even her." Tears made warm paths down her cheeks, and she thrust aside the memory of Black Brenna's false whispers about a mother she had never known.

"You are much like Nan," Diana said softly. "And she will always be watching you, and loving you, as you will always know she is watching, and you will return her love. But you are so much more than that love, too. There is magic in you that Nan could never dream of conjuring. That magic is your line, it is your blood and it cannot be taught. Only awakened."

"I-I-I am not…" Nyva said, "not a sorceress… I can't be."

"You can't be?" Diana asked.

"I have never felt it."

"Are you sure? Because I have felt it, and others have felt it, too." Diana said this in a matter-of-fact way that made Nyva feel like a character in a narrative not her own. "That is why that filthy rodent Brenna has come."

Nyva gasped. "How do you know—"

"He has come even though he was not invited," Diana continued as if Nyva had not spoken. "I took him off the guest list right after I escaped that *world*—" Diana cut herself off and looked around, squinting, as if trying to see the rat-mage, like he was skulking somewhere in the shadows.

Diana's words and their implications made Nyva wish that Ishtarra would all of a sudden tear off running. Then keep running, away from the house, away from the town of Wardbrook and all its happenings that grew stranger and stranger still. She wanted to ride like hell with her eyes closed through the many miles of death fog that smothered the Marsh Betwixt, a terrifying expanse that connected Brynth to Romaria. She wanted to go to Fracia and make a new life, maybe go further still. She did not want to be here.

Yet what exactly had Diana done or said to make her feel this way? Why was Nyva so afraid?

A hand touched her shoulder, a warm, nurturing hand. Nyva felt calm again. She glanced down at Diana's fingers where they curled over her shoulder.

A touch. A delicate clutch.

And Nyva fully understood: she was under Diana's spell. She no longer wanted to run. She was still afraid, scared of the things the lady had just said, about Brenna, about her blood, her magic. But she wanted to stay close to Diana Ward.

She didn't understand why that wanting made her wary.

"My fair ladies!" shouted a man, accompanied by the barking of dogs.

The man with the bows slung over his shoulders galloped toward them on his small horse, and Nyva was surprised how fast the steed moved despite its size.

"Welfric!" Diana called, and waved her hand with such a wide, bright smile that the man must have seen it from as far off as he was. "Hurry along. We are nearly dying, you've kept us waiting so long!" Diana winked at Nyva. They had not been waiting very long at all.

"Hyah, hyah!" Welfric cried at his horse, and dug his heels. The tall, rough-coated wolfhounds were in full sprint across the field, their tongues hanging out the sides of their mouths.

Nyva's heart pounded. She swallowed.

"It's all right," Diana said.

Nyva did not turn away from the dogs; she could not. Her gaze was transfixed on them. On their fangs. She could feel their eyes on her, closing in. Angry, ravenous eyes, eyes like ale-drunk men looking to get drunk on blood. *Eyes like their race of masters.*

"The beasts here obey me, Nyva. Every last one of the stinking, lusting, hungry things. They obey me above all. These lands are my lands, and so you need not fear the dogs here." Diana's tone was firm and commanding as any man's had ever been.

Her words did not quell the fear; they heightened it. If she spoke falsely, if she spoke out of a heightened ego, then Nyva should still fear the dogs, the men, and any other beast in the lands of Wardbrook. The alternative was worse, for if Lady Diana truly did have complete control here, then she had allowed the horrific events that had brought Nyva here to transpire.

She had allowed a ravening mob to kill Nan.

When the hounds and the lone rider drew close, still charging, Nyva was certain they would not be able to stop before making impact.

"Woah!" the horseman roared, and pulled hard on the reins. His small, long-coated horse pulled up onto his hind legs and whinnied at the sky. The hounds lowered their haunches and dropping to sit while still running, and slid across the grass, stopping just at the feet of the horses. They wagged their tails uncontrollably, thudding each other in the ribs as they all huddled in and lifted their heads to sniff and lick at Diana's boots where they were set in the stirrups.

Nyva could not help but laugh at the unexpected sight, quickly finding reason to ignore the dark suspicions and premonitions of moments ago regarding her gracious and loving host.

"Sorry to keep you waiting, Lady Diana," Welfric said in a lowborn smuggler's accent. He was likely from Baytown—at least, he sounded like a man who had stopped by Nan's once from Baytown.

"Welfric, this is Nyva, the young lady who is now living at Wardbrook," Diana said.

"A pleasure to make your acquaintance, Lady Nyva," Welfric said, and bowed his head so Nyva could see his balding pate.

Nyva nodded to him, both stunned and pleased at his form of address. She almost corrected him, then pressed her lips together and said nothing.

He was by no means a pleasant-looking man. Perhaps only in his twenties and already balding. The bags under his eyes were so dark they were nearly black, and they sagged to his cheekbones. His eyes were bloodshot and he reeked of spirits. He had a patchy beard and rotten teeth, and enough muscle to strangle a boar.

"Nyva, this is Welfric, a longtime friend of my husband's and mine, a fine hunter and master reveler."

"Oh aye, that I am, that I am." Welfric contained a burp and winced like someone was screaming in his ears.

Diana studied him a moment. "I told you and Alex not to open the aged stuff until the party. And with one day left, you went and did exactly what I explicitly asked you not to do." Her voice was still pleasant, but there was something underneath it. Something dark.

"Oh, not to worry, Lady Diana. We did not open the aged stuff, just far too many rounds of ale last night, is all," Welfric said, then closed his mouth and struggled to contain another belch that filled his cheeks.

"Welfric, my dear...I can smell it in your filthy sweat," said Diana, her teeth gritted into a smile as she spoke, her lips hardly moving.

"We just wanted to have a wee sample of it, was all." Welfric turned red and scratched the bald spot on the top of his head.

"Oh, yes, you look like you had a *wee* sample," Diana said.

Welfric was about to speak, perhaps apologize. Diana cut him off.

"Shh... That's enough from you. Now lead us to a boar, fine sir."

"It would be—*belch*—an honor to escort two fine huntresses such as yourselves." Welfric trotted his shaggy little horse past Diana and Nyva, and when he whistled to the dogs, they barked and went after him. Diana followed, and though Nyva gave her mount no command, it did the same.

The group went south to a small stone bridge that

crossed the brook, and then they made their way back north, and then east through the apple orchard.

An orchard of brains: black tumors grow like fruit; yellow miasma fills the air; tentacles of white play the part of living grass. The brook is old blood and rotten meat. The earth is splitting. The labyrinth is rising. The black house of Wardbrook makes a mountainous shadow cast by the dark light of a black sun-moon.

Anxiety washed through Nyva, and she didn't know why. Memories that were not memories, things murky and unclear, tugged at her thoughts. But all she could truly remember was that she had woken in drenched nightclothes, terror in her throat.

The orchard this morning was beautiful. The sun touched the apples, painting them a majestic red-rose gold. They were plentiful, and the sweet smell of their blossoms was enough to make Nyva's mouth water.

So what is this revulsion that I feel lingering deep inside of me?

"You may pick some, Nyva." Diana waved a hand at the trees. "The baking is already underway. But fresh fruit at a feast is always enjoyed, and the apples of this orchard grow to sweetness so very quickly. I see many that are just begging to be plucked and consumed." Diana lifted her right hand and plucked a fruit from the closest tree. She bit the fruit, closed her eyes, puckered her lips, then moaned. She chewed, swallowed, and opened her eyes. "Oh my," she whispered. "They are perfect."

Welfric let out a low groan from Nyva's left, and she turned to see him eating one of the apples. "They are magical." The way he said the word "magical," it did not sound at all like hyperbole.

Some of the hounds wagged at the feet of Diana's horse, some at the feet of Welfric's. Diana plucked another apple and then another from the tree and tossed them to the hounds. Laughing, Welfric plucked fruits from his tree and fed them to his group of four-legged followers.

"Won't the seeds upset the hounds' bellies?" Nyva asked, genuinely concerned. She was afraid of them, mightily so, but she knew the seeds could cause them considerable harm, and she did not want that.

"Oh, to be sure," said Diana. Her eyes widened and she erupted into a fit of laughter that had her bobbing and swaying in her saddle. Soon, Welfric was doing the same. The hounds started wagging and yapping and running about, puppylike excitement overwhelming them. They nipped and pawed each other. Their tails swayed back and forth with such force that their bodies rocked and twisted.

For a moment, Diana brought her fit of hysterics to heel. She pointed to the tree next to Nyva. "Will you have a bite?"

Nyva looked to the apples on the trees, then to the hounds, then to Diana, then back to the apples. And Nyva thought of Nan's Golden Goat and the way she had felt when she smoked it.

The last time she had taken something that altered the way she thought and acted, something very, very bad happened. An image of Black Brenna biting Jeremiah in the hand flashed. The sound of the rock thudding against Nan's skull rang through the orchard. Nyva closed her eyes, and when she opened them again, Diana was smiling at her.

Here was the lady of the land—the most magnificent lady of any land, for that matter. She was Nyva's savior and she was bidding Nyva to be happy.

Why would I say no? Why would I be afraid? Even the dogs were laughing.

Nyva heard Nan. *Do you know what happiness is, Nyva? Happiness is a liar; it is a handsome man that promises you comfort and bliss, safety and joy. He tells you that you deserve him and that he will never leave. He swears that this is how things should be. He fills you with his seed of hope. But, child, the babe is never born. And he leaves you with a last letter and it says he was never really there.*

Nyva did not want to listen. She wanted to be happy, even just for a moment.

She held the apple. It was heavy, smooth, and cool, and it glimmered in the sunlight. Her mouth watered. She took a bite.

Shockingly bitter juice filled her mouth.

She opened her mouth to spit it out, then froze.

Euphoria. It washed down her spine, and she arched her back.

Happiness is a liar.

She took another bite.

Quieter now: *Happiness is a liar.*

Another bite.

She would not hear Nan. She could not listen anymore. She would not listen anymore.

I am the snake. I am the megalithic serpent that slithers in your mind. My black scales slide in circles around the borders of your understanding. I may sleep for eons, I may sleep for seconds, but my eyes are always open.

You feel their red glow upon you even when they are unseen, and you know I will find you because all hands are born unclean. When I wake, my tongue will dart and taste the air that is befouled with the corruption of your human kind. As I slither, as I follow, always know: there is no escaping the ties that bind.

The Python.

The Anaconda.

The Viper.

The Rattler.

The Cobra.

Revere their holy names. Know they are my brothers, the brothers of the fang. When you see them, if you survive them, prayers in silence should be sang.

To the dark I am married. It is fear I have taken as mistress, and suffering as my guide.

~Onyx Viper, the first Chieftain of the Dahkah

CHAPTER TEN

∞

TOP OF THE MOURNING

*C*ullum sat alone in the morning light, sprawled out in a chair. He had sipped the wine and eaten the bread. And he heard Damos' song even now.

The song had started soft, and as Damos—*the Dahkah*—had tapped the skin drum with the tips of his arachnid shadow limbs, Cullum had thought of a gently beating heart.

Has my heart ever beaten gently?

The strumming of the lute had been faint. The shaking of the rattle had been like soft rain. And when Damos had called the flute-playing black snake back inside himself, he had sung as he pounded the drum with the flute.

"I can feel the poison rising.
I can see the temples burning.
The only sound is children screaming.
Rivers growing from mothers weeping.
And I am running, ever fleeing,
Never smiling, always hiding."

As he sang and played, Cullum had not been able to stave off the coming sleep. He had not—and still did not—fully trusted Damos, but the music, the bread, the wine made

Cullum unable to cling to his mistrust. His eyes had closed and he had fallen into slumber. And in his dreams, the song remained, playing again and again on a loop. A loop like dancing children, skeletons in day clothes singing, "Hale, hale, come morning, the sun rises. Hale, hale, come morning, the king rises."

Damos had repeated the verses. His voice had deepened and cracked, and the instruments had stirred louder with agitation.

The loop, the song, the nightmares, the burning dreams.

The memories.

All remained now, the morning after.

The wheel was spinning; the loop was unwinding.

"*I can feel the poison rising.*" Cullum's thoughts and memories merged. He saw his left hand beneath the water of the pool, the Sisters around him. He saw glowing, multicolored lights patterning his veins. Burning in his veins. Then all the color faded to white, thick like cream. He watched it spread into smaller veins like fire eating a tree as it crawled along the trunk then greedily reached out to devour the branches.

"Am I going mad?"

"*The only sound is children screaming. Rivers flowing from mothers weeping,*" Damos sang in his head.

Too many faces of too many dead boys and girls—chosen sacrifices—eyes on Cullum as they did not cease their screaming. His belly was eternally cold from the sound of those mothers weeping.

Damos' voice had grown angrier and angrier still, as did his playing as he delivered his chorus twice over.

"*And I am running, ever fleeing! Never smiling, always hiding! And I am running, ever fleeing! Never smiling, always hiding!*"

Cullum frowned and stood up now as he pulled the rim of his hat low, trying to get the Luminescent-damned lyrics out of his head. But he could not chase away the final lines, sung by Damos like a sigh as the instruments thrashed then died.

"And I close my eyes,
just to see,
That all I am,
is misery."

Cullum closed his eyes. He saw the Order dying. He saw the church falling into the clutches of those infiltrating enemies who had come from Lordan. He saw his world burning.

He thought of a woman, the whore from the wharf. She was silently crying as men in blue hats walked away with a screaming babe.

Was that him? Had he been that babe? Had his mother been a whore? Was that why there was no father to take him after she died in childbirth? But the woman in his mind had been crying...so, if that was him—had they lied to him?—then how could she have died in childbirth? And if that was him, then how could he remember this?

All I am is misery.

He thought of the briars that had torn his flesh as he ran through them. *All I am is misery.*

He longed for their bite in his flesh now. *All I am is misery.*

The briars would kill all the thoughts and all the memories. At least for a time.

"Am I going mad?" Cullum asked to the empty room.

"You can't go to where you already are," Damos said, entering. "You can't go to where you have always been." His voice was deep and brooding. His stare unforgiving. Then, *smirking*, he said, "How did you sleep, your holiness?"

"Cut the shit. Call me Cullum, and none of the sarcasm this morning. Or I'll stomp you out like I would any other spider. And I slept like a calamitous storm, thanks to your lullaby."

"You have previously demanded I refer to you as your holiness. Has something changed? Are we now friends? Partners even?" Damos asked, the smirk remaining.

Cullum only glared.

"Understood, partner," Damos said, and Cullum could tell the man was putting considerable effort into controlling his irritating smile from growing any further. "I have readied some fine morsels to take with us as we head to the site of the bodies you wish me to examine. We will walk instead of ride, and eat on the way. I will share with you the history of this land and the great black house that rules over it."

"Thank you for your assistance in this task, Damos," Cullum said. Then, after a pause, he mumbled, "I'm sorry."

Damos' brows rose. He lifted his hands to his face to twirl the curled ends of his mustache. "What are you sorry for?"

"For being difficult," Cullum said, and he was aware as he said it that his tone was still one of imposing condemnation. He was apologizing in a tone that demanded an apology. So why had he apologized at all if it was only to get one back as reward? *That is a very un-Enlightened thing to do, vicar. Worthy of a time spent in the briars, that is to be sure.* "Well, let's be off, then," Cullum said. "But I need to take a shit first."

"Right," Damos said, laughing. "You are a very gritty holy man, aren't you, Cullum?"

"I'm a Seeker. We are not some choirboys turned priests. We are wrathful men sculpted from the forms of beasts."

Damos made a grand gesture. "The shitter is yonder."

∾

For hours, they walked and talked at a leisurely pace, and when Cullum and Damos arrived at the place in the woods where Cullum had seen the mutilated bodies of men and dog, the scene had changed. The bodies were gone.

The reek of death and decay was no more. Now that the sun was up, he could see the surrounding forest clearly, and he could no longer feel the rat sorcerer's eyes on him from 'neath the shadow of night. In fact, at first glance, the place was but the same as any tall-treed woodland in spring.

Cullum turned a full circle, suspects running through his thoughts. Was it one of the yokels who had moved them? No reason for that. Was it Brenna? Perhaps... But some instinct made Cullum turn his face to the hill and the great black manse that sat atop.

"Are you sure this is the place?" asked Damos.

"Of course I'm sure." Cullum gritted his teeth. "Do you think me some kind of amateur?" he asked, unable to stop himself. He always had to fight back. He always had to take everything as an affront, even if it were just a question. He knew this trait of his to be unacceptable, and he kept on doing it anyway.

He sighed, trying not to wonder too long about free will.

"This is the place. It was night. Magic was being cast, and I had not slept and hardly eaten for too long. I have wounds from a recent fight not yet fully healed. And I felt them burning, as they burn now. But I assure you, my mind was and is entirely sound." *Is it?* "This is the place, Damos," Cullum said with steely conviction as he scanned the scene for anything, anything at all that would prove his assertion. He could feel the seeds of doubt sprouting in his belly, their beanstalks growing.

Then he saw it. *Evidence.*

"Look there...proof." Cullum pointed to the ground where mud was uplifted and twigs lay broken; leaves were scattered and tufts of grass were partially flattened. In places, the mud was darker than others—in smears and sprays, the dark color speckled the leaves and grass as well. Lines of near-black dried blood connected the scene from last night.

Trails went to the tree where half the dog had been strewn in the branches, and the impaled man with his chest ripped open had been propped up against the trunk.

Damos walked to where Cullum pointed and squatted for a closer inspection. He ripped out a blade of grass and held it near.

"Good eye, Cullum." His compliment sounded genuine enough for Cullum to not assume it to be an insult wearing sarcasm's cloak.

"A Seeker's vision is enhanced by the *Ordeal*. My good eyes are but the Church's good eyes," Cullum said, then gave the humblest bowing of his head he could manage.

Damos laughed as he walked, following the dried blood smears and splotches to the tree.

"If ten thousand ordinary men were gifted an eagle's eyes," said Damos. "If they could look as an eagle looks, ten thousand ordinary men would still not see what the eagle sees." Damos stood still and looked up into the treetops. "The Shahidi told me that."

"What does it mean?" Cullum asked.

"That is what I asked. I said, 'What does that mean, you many-eyed-mutant? I've heard enough of your fucking riddles. Say something that makes sense.'"

Cullum laughed.

"It means that just because you put a man on the finest, fastest horse, does not mean he can win a race. Indeed, it does not mean he will even be able to ride at all. Riding is a skill. Seeing is a skill, a skill that belongs to you. Forgive me for using a metaphor to explain a metaphor, but I am unaware of any alternative methods of effective explanation."

Cullum frowned.

"Indeed, in my era of undeath, that is what I have come to know," Damos went on. "We humans are always trying to explain things, trying to make sense of them, so we say what this and this is like. We try to make a circle of what we know."

Cullum knew much of circles.

"It starts with our first memories, our first thoughts. This differs for everyone, but what does not differ is the burgeoning, blooming desire to make sense of it all. We see in seasons, life and death, then life again. We see in nature as the wolves hunt the slowest in the herd of elk that only the strongest survive. We say a new love is budding, because we have seen a flower do the same. When we light a candle in a cellar so that we may find the stairs and make our way out, we understand a little more about our souls. On the inside, we must always keep a fire lit, lest we wish to become forever lost in the cellars of our fears and sorrows." Damos sighed. "You see? I am plagued by it, always trying to reduce everything to the only thing."

"How did they kill you?" Cullum asked. "The Shahidi, how did they do it?" Before Damos could answer, Cullum said, "My apologies." This time, his voice was sincere. He had surprised himself with the question. "That was a perilously invasive question, and as you are no longer under a Seeker's investigation, I had no right to ask it." Cullum tilted his hat enough to have the brim cover his eyes.

"On the contrary—you have every right to ask any question you'd like. And I have every right not to answer it. But I will," Damos said, squatting at the base of a tree and poking the grass before he rose again and faced Cullum. "I have never shared the events of my death with another soul. Your arrival is significant, though. Your arrival is the variable, the change that I have not yet seen. So, with you, Cullum, I will share the events of my death."

"And I am most interested in those events…" said Cullum, his voice trailing away as he recalled their surroundings and his investigation. "However, we have a pressing matter to attend to first."

Damos indicated the clearing. "The investigation will wait for a short time. The bodies are gone for the moment. The bloodstains are not going anywhere."

Seeing no argument, and being curious, Cullum said, "Very well."

Damos laughed. An empty, heartless laugh. The laugh of a man dead and brought back to walk the world absent a soul.

"I was in a foreign land stitching and burning and fixing good and bad men alike. Just so they could all be certain to die bad men. For that is what the crusades were, what they still are. The war that makes bad men of us all. I vowed never to kill a sentient being, and I suppose that is *admirable*." Damos laughed again, hollow, dead laughter. Cullum's skin crawled. "In that place where all one is expected to do is kill, and all I did was pointlessly snatch them from the edges of death, just to keep young men in hell a little longer so that some far-off king's ambition could be filled as he sat on his liar's throne…I couldn't do it anymore. I could not see a purpose in it, not at all."

"What about the woman? The one who gave you the necklace…the sun sigil?" Cullum interrupted. "Beatrice."

"She came after. She made me believe after. And that is a story I cannot bear to tell. Not now. Not yet. Perhaps never."

Cullum thought now not of the ones he had failed to save but of the faces of those that he *had* saved. The men and women he had brought back from the certain death at the hands of the demons, pagans, and heretics. Mostly he thought of the children, those little faces with ancient eyes that had seen too much.

He had killed those children's oppressors; he had cut off their heads and opened their guts, sawed their throats and flayed and burned their flesh. He had seen them drawn and quartered, had watched the hounds and the rats eat them alive. And none of it, not one of the punishments, would ever get rid of the sight in the knowing children's eyes.

"I'm sorry I interrupted. I should behave less like a child," Cullum said.

"Do not be sorry. Your interjection only betrays the goodness of your heart." Cullum thought there might be sarcasm in the words, until Damos continued, "And no, your church didn't give you that. You had it already."

Cullum did not respond. He felt an imposter, to trick a man, *a Dahkah*, of Damos' age and intelligence into thinking he was an inherently good man. Because every time he punished the wicked with hammer and nail, with stake and torch, with tooth and claw, he did not feel good. But he kept on punishing, because wrath was intoxicating.

"I had a wife and four children," Damos said. "All grown up, they were. Even when I was still in Brynth, my wife had not kissed me in years. I was detached, empty, hollow even before I went to the sands.

"In that place, I came to understand what sand really is. It is everything. It is all of us, and it is nothing, just the grains of the meaningless. I was watching a fourteen-year-old murderer and rapist die in my arms, on my operating table. He wept and apologized for all he had done, begged me for forgiveness, as if it were my place to give him absolution. So many young sinners...orphans, farm boys, quarry workers, slaves, all brought over to fight for the king and those wealthy lords, died on my table as that boy did. And there was nothing special about him or his death. Nothing stands out from the rest. It was simply the thing that broke my fucking heart. I could not take it anymore. I was past sick of it. I was dead inside, truly dead. I saw the hands of endless night rip the sun from its invisible mantel in the sky, and I was finished with this life."

Cullum's faith had wavered often. He *wanted* to believe, but he didn't, not always. But this...this image of the sun ripped from the sky by darkness was an articulation he had never made, yet now that he heard it, he could see it, and he knew that he had long felt it.

"We were in a city we had taken called Leavon. I had my quarters in a room in a vast palace. My window was twelve feet or so above the stable roof. That night, I leapt out and climbed down into the stables, avoiding the guard out in front of them. The horses knew me well, for I visited them often with apples or carrots, and they did not stir when I entered.

"I took a pair of reins and climbed up a stall to hang them from the rafters, and then I saw the spider. It was right there, inches from where I placed my hand to climb up. The *Death's Kiss* with the pink lips on its thorax. When it bites you, there is no pain. Instead, a warm sensation of euphoria starts at the lips, down the chin and up the nose, over the eyes and over the neck, then washes over the whole body. Bliss, ecstasy, and joy. The victim laughs and weeps, and then they die. Some people even reach orgasm in their death throes."

"Did you?" Cullum asked, and he could feel his face turning red. *For your depraved curiosity, there will be a long walk in the briars when this is all over.*

Damos laughed so loudly his voice echoed in the woods, and black birds took flight from nearby trees, cawing into the sky.

Maybe laughing with the demon as they fly.

"No, no..." Damos laughed again, then his laughter ceased and his stare hardened. "I did not reach orgasm in death. I was not so lucky as that. Though at the time, I thought the spider's bite was my final gift, my only real gift, a way out and in pure bliss, no less. I did not even take a moment. I did not even hesitate. I felt too lucky, too blessed."

Cullum swallowed a rising dread that he was perhaps going to regret this conversation. Sometimes conversation was all it took to bring one to the blackest pits of themselves, each word a key to a door that opened further and further to where the mirror forever waited.

It waits to show me what I am.

"There is another spider in Kehldesh," Damos continued. "The *Liar*. It is the same size and color as the *Death's Kiss*, black, with two curved pink stripes that look much like lips on the thorax. Where ecstasy is the bite of the *Death's Kiss*, the *Liar* fills its victim with agony so severe it alone is what kills them. Pain, sheer pain, so much pain the heart stops."

He looked at Cullum and lifted his brows. "Do you know, even as a Dahkah, I still feel pain, but nothing has ever since compared to the agony of the *Liar's* bite. I will not bore you with the minutiae of it all, but I managed to snap my own spine during the convulsions. I tore out my own eyes."

Cullum looked away from the Dahkah's black eyes.

"At some point, it ended. At some point, I woke up. Leavon had been retaken by the Kehldeshi forces. I was sitting in a temple before the statue of Hor-Na-Thoth, and the many-eyed Shahidi were whispering and smiling around me. They punished me for taking my own life by making me live eternally. They gave me new eyes, ones that saw more."

What was the more that Damos saw? Cullum thought of the Sisters and the pool and could not help but wonder if the Dahkah saw as they saw.

"Was it always inside you, the need to end yourself?" Cullum whispered.

"Need?" Damos shook his head. "I would call it a drive, a want, a possibility, a choice."

Choice. Yes, it is that. Isn't it?

Had Cullum trusted this man, this monster, before this moment? He thought that after such a reveal, he might.

He was as stunned as he would have been after any good punch to the head. For a long, awkward moment, he had no idea what to say. Then, in a flood of words, he told Damos about the briars, and why he went there. He told of all his battles with temptation, and how they never stopped. He told the demon about the deep desire he fought at all times, the desire to vacate from this life, to shed his mortal chains and succumb to oblivion.

"That is what makes a good man, Cullum," Damos said. "A man who constantly wants to do the wrong thing, but he does the good thing instead. Even though so often he seems to be punished for it." Damos paused. "Are we friends, then, Vicar Cullum Shrike?"

"We are." And this was a first for Cullum, for friendship was not a requisite of the Order. And it was not a thing he had allowed himself. *Why do I allow it now?*

Damos clapped him on the shoulder and said, "What luck. A clue." He strode to the tree he had been examining prior to their conversation and plucked something from the bark, then turned and drew near.

The back of Cullum's left hand tingled beneath his black glove.

Luck? He thought not.

He pulled off the glove and extended his hand to Damos, who dropped a single strand of fur onto his palm. Cullum clutched it in his fist. His hand ignited with sensation; a pulse at the center, an intensifying, radiating heat emanated like the waves of river rapids flowing through his veins. He looked to the back of his hand and read the *Bloodburn.*

He had expected the color to be silver, a pale silver like the moon, for the sensation was akin to the sensation he knew from touching the fur, or flesh, or blood of a lycan. His blood glowed like the moon now, but not a silver moon, a different moon, a yellow gold nearly as incandescent as the sun itself. *Nearly.*

"A lycan," Cullum said.

"Alex…Alex…Alex," Damos said, shaking his head with a look of disappointment.

Evidence too easily found. A name that came too quick on Damo's lips. "Who is Alex?" Cullum asked, and barely restrained himself from warning his new *friend* not to lie.

"Alex was—and it would *appear* still *is*—the moon wolf. Diana's designated dog for all her dark deeds. He said he had found someone, someone who could remove the curse while she was gone. It's too late now. She is back. Why didn't he follow through?" Damos asked, looking up at the sun, the canopy of tree branches dampening its light.

Diana. Alex. The Lady and Lord of Wardbrook. Cullum looked past the trees up the hill to the house that looked dark and forbidding even on this sunny morning.

"I have to go to the house," said Cullum. "You said it. You said that Alex is the lycanthrope we seek—"

"No, he is worse than just a lycanthrope. He is the moon wolf. He could shred a pack of the wolfmen you're used to."

"You have no idea what I'm used to," said Cullum.

"Oh, drop the bravado, man. Caution is the only thing that is going to see you through this," Damos said, then rubbed his jaw. "But it is unlike Alex, even in his moon wolf form, to attack those from his lands. There must have been a reason, a specific reason…"

"You had better start talking a whole lot more about what you have so conveniently holding been back until now."

"I hold back because I cannot remember. I cannot—" Damos put his hands to his head and gasped. "My time in this place, in the lands of Wardbrook, has been naught but a hazed dream. I cannot recall."

"What the hell is the matter with you?" Cullum asked. "Your madness is unsettling me."

Damos pressed the heels of his hands against his closed eyelids. "By the sun," he whispered. "By the sun. I am remembering, and I am shamed by my memories."

Cullum stared at him, recalling the yokel and the gravedigger who were also stricken by a strange forgetfulness.

"That house," Damos muttered. "What have I done in that house?"

Wardbrook. A chill crawled up Cullum's spine.

"I keep a journal… We must go back to my home. We must verify these memories whirling now in my mind." Damos spun his fingers in circles around his head as he went on. "So dark, so strange and alien are these thoughts. I can only hope my mind is deceiving me. That I am mistaking a nightmare for a reality."

"You know what truths you will find written on those pages," Cullum said.

Damos raised his eyes to Cullum's. "Do I? Things I remember. Things I forget. They blend into one, and I trust neither."

"Then we will go together and read your scribblings to ascertain the truth."

"And then we will go together to the great black house of Wardbrook and we will both ask our questions, about the nature of this place, and what dark deeds are now transpiring as they have so many times before on these cursed grounds." Damos' pupils filled his eyes to complete blackness, as they had the night before. His usual smirk was absent, and instead he wore a grimace of anger.

"Lead the way, Damos," said Cullum. And the two very angry, confused men returned from whence they had come.

∾

I was born alone 'n' I was made to pay.
With all my rage, ran away. Ran away.
Holdin' my hate, I walked astray.
So damn far, miles out the way.

Went through every lonely city, every empty town.
Thought I was a man, was a jester, just a clown.
Then I crossed that border 'n' I met the Soul Hoarder.
Waist deep in the water,
Blood boiled hotter.

That demon rose on up, thick like a house, tall like a tree.
He said, "Mortal man, bleeding man, bow down to me.
I come from the deep down, up from the bottom of the bog.
I been sleepin' with the fishes, been singin' with the frogs.
I'm the dirty devil, 'n' I'm moanin' with the banshees in the fog.

I see them soldiers comin', I hear the barkin' of them dogs.
Come on in, my door is always open, eat your soul, kill your God.

~The Soul Hoarder

∾

CHAPTER ELEVEN

PRESSURE

*N*yva didn't know when she started laughing, and she could not recall when the horses started running. But she was laughing now, and the horse was running now, and the three riders charged through the orchard like demons, the yapping hounds at their heels.

She was having trouble recalling where she was. She knew she was hunting, hunting with strangers... *No, no, no.* She was hunting with friends, dear friends.

"Do you feel it? Do you feel the thrill?" Diana called, looking back at Nyva as she charged ahead.

Did she? Did she love hunting? She was nearly sure she loved hunting. Didn't she?

Open field and open air. The smell and sights of the orchard were left behind. She glided over pasture now, toward trees and hills in the distance. The wind felt like a lover's touch, and that lover was earth and sky. She only now realized what they were chasing. There was an agile hog squealing and darting in zigzags through the fields, attempting to reach the hilly tree line. Froth streamed from the side of its mouth.

In the hills and trees, the pursuers would have to dismount. Nyva did not wonder if the hog knew this. She *knew* the hog knew this. She felt her heart beating with the beast's, the same beat as Ishtarra charging beneath her thighs. The dogs, Welfric, his shaggy little horse, and Diana on her spotted gray…all were in syncronization.

The horses and the hounds were faster than the boar, but every time they drew near, ready to end the chase, the hog would cut a jagged hard right or left on its short, stocky legs, and the dogs would tumble and the horses would need to make wide circles to not do the same. When they were ready to pursue again, the hog was that much closer to the tree line.

The game continued as the hog reached the bushes and brambles at the base of the new terrain and charged its way onward. Ishtarra slowed instinctively and then stood on her hind legs, forcing Nyva to lock her legs tight and grip the reins firmly.

The dogs leapt and sprinted into the brambles and went after the boar.

"Dismount!" Diana ordered Nyva as she ran past her after the dogs and the hog, a bow over her shoulder. Nyva started to get off the horse, and Welfric appeared at her side. He helped her down and handed her the other bow. Nyva took it, uncaring that she had a bow but no arrows.

She laughed as she and Welfric ran through the dense bush after Diana. Branches and pines poked and cut, but she did not feel the pain. She just felt the euphoria in her pumping chest and thighs as she sprinted up the first hill, leaping from root to root, the ancient trees a forest of ash and pine towers watching over the chase. How many thousands of hunts had they witnessed, those ancient trees?

The hounds were ahead. So why did she hear their barking at her back, their growling in her ear? Why did she feel their teeth nipping at her heels, the trees all around her as she ran and ran?

Unsettled, Nyva stopped and turned a slow circle, staring up at the branches where they grasped at the sky.

"Run," Welfric called from up ahead, and she ran.

A hundred strides more, over root and stone and hill, a leap over a bush, a step and jump off a large, ramp-shaped stone. And then a thousand more such actions and the hog—exhausted from the pursuit on horseback and running through the harsh terrain away from hound and master—was cornered.

Its back was tucked into a tight crevice between a tree trunk and a small natural rock wall that was part of the rocky-hilled terrain. The only opportunity for attack was for the hounds to be head-on to its tusks.

It no longer looked afraid to Nyva, only furious. Truly furious. Nyva and Welfric jogged up to Diana, who stood at ease ten strides behind the wall of barking, snarling hounds.

"Nyva, draw your bowstring—fell the boar before it makes a final charge through the dogs and straight at us." Diana's voice was stern, her eyes on the boar. The big black boar, spit foaming at the bases of its twelve-inch tusks.

One of the dogs got too close and took a swinging tusk to its face for its efforts. It yelped and rolled to the ground, whimpering before it stepped behind the line of other dogs and pawed helplessly at its broken jaw.

"I have no arrows," Nyva said.

"You do," Diana snapped. "Lift the bow."

Nyva did as she was told.

"Set eyes on the boar. Aim well."

Again, Nyva obeyed. Her focus now was only on the tragic beast; everything else was becoming a blur.

"Now draw the string."

Nyva hesitated.

The boar seemed to understand—it squealed and made a feint charge forward. All the dogs leapt back, still barking. Some went to circle to the flanks. The boar again retreated to his crevice between rock and tree.

"The next time it will charge," said Welfric, his words sizzling with excitement, and Nyva could hear his long sword leaving its scabbard. He walked between Diana and the dogs, five strides to either. The boar's squeals grew louder with every step he took toward it.

"Kill the boar, Nyva," Diana said. "If you do not, the boar will charge and gore Welfric."

"I have no arrows, *my lady*!" Nyva's heart beat too hard; her arm holding the bow was shaking. This was lunacy.

"Draw the string. Use the catalyst!" Diana shouted.

"My lady!" In that second, Nyva recalled that she hated hunting.

The euphoria was no longer wondrous. It was mutating into rage and fear and something else…something foreign and strange. She felt tricked. Trapped. A marionette forced to perform for the lady.

The boar charged, and in one swing of its giant head, two hounds went airborne, blood streaming from one that took a tusk.

"Let loose, you witch!" Diana yelled, a command that Nyva had no wish to obey.

I am no witch.

She drew the string. *I have no arrow. I have no wish to shoot.*

The string cut her fingertips. Blood on her hands. A drop falling to the ground.

Crack. Nan's skull burst.

Crack. Lightning in memory's sky.

A nightmare, a forest of hands, an orchard of brains.

A little rat man, with wicked words and wicked spells.

Lies of the other and ties of blood to a lost and dangerous mother.

She let loose the arrow that was not there.

From her eyes, her nose, her mouth, and the tiny cuts on her fingertips, blood warped out of her and crystalized into a long, thin arrow of emerald green.

A voice cackled in her ear. Black Brenna whispering of the Emerald Queen.

The arrow struck the boar as it charged, high in the ridge of its muscled back.

From the point of impact, the beast's flesh and fur immediately began to corrode. Yellow miasma rose from the wound and spread like fire, engulfing its body. The creature walked a full final step before it collapsed and slid to Welfric's feet, half of its skeleton visible and the rest of its flesh quickly burning away into a cloud of yellow mist.

Nyva dropped the bow and fell to her knees.

Diana knelt beside her. She went to rub Nyva's back, but Nyva did not want to be touched. She did not want to be touched by *her*. The marionette didn't want to play anymore.

She started to crawl away from the lady, and without thinking, she moved toward the corpse of the animal she had just killed.

The hog's eyes bubbled like tar inside the corroded skull.

Nyva closed her eyes and pulled her knees to her chest. She began to weep.

Diana was there again, holding her, rocking her.

"Hush now, child. Hush now. It is all done. It is all over. It has all just begun. Nothing is new here. It has always been part of you, always been there, hiding, just hiding."

Nyva glanced at the hog. *I have done this? I cannot have.*

She wept. "I want to wake up." She remembered a dream of Diana's embrace, too tight. A choking embrace. "I want to wake up."

"I don't think we will be able to eat that," Welfric said.

The yellow mist carried on the breeze. She smelled sulfur and lilies.

"I had anticipated her magic may have been of this nature and that the boar would make a fine meal for no one," Diana said to Welfric as she rocked Nyva. "I sent Alex with some others north to go hunting for the party."

"Always thinking ahead," Welfric said.

"Always," said Diana as she stroked Nyva's hair with fingers that felt like snakes.

An Emerald Queen. Her mother? An emerald arrow. Her own. And something unfurling inside her, sleeping until now, until this moment, this dark moment where she had become a vessel for Diana's will. Nyva knew now she should have listened to the rat; she knew now it was too late.

Silent sobs shook her, and she struggled to free herself from the cage of Diana's arms. To no avail. She was well and truly caught. She closed her eyes tight, and in the darkness, she saw two burning blue rings...two burning blue eyes watching her. Black-gloved hands reached for her and she struggled to free her arms so she might reach for them.

And a man whispered, *You may still be saved.*

PART III
THE DEADMEN'S PARTY

～

I have no illusions about the fact that I will forever rue the day I welcomed the Deadmen into my home. But what choice did I have? What choice do any of us have when the summons is sent and the wax seal of the Red Right Hand upon it is split and the words of terror and doom are read?

"The time has come. You have been chosen. Prepare thy home, for the Deadmen's party is about to begin. The bells will chime, and so you must let them all in."

There was but one thing to do: obey.

I see now that every step I took, every move I made, every quest for the king I completed, and every gift given and title granted led me to that end. I say that end for it has already come and gone. My life has passed me. I am dead, and all the hopes and dreams that used to revive me are dead now too. A phantom has written this, an ectoplasmic emptiness, transient and fading, always fading away into nothingness.

They began to arrive the hour before midnight, and the guests strolled in until the witching hour itself was upon us. First to arrive were the Shahidi, two of the mutated, many-eyed monks from across this world, and with them a sorceress—an ebon masterwork of human art made flesh was she. Nephite was her name. I bowed low and bade them enter. On their heels came the giant from the north, the druid who needed to tilt his head to enter even through the great door at the front of the home. Hardly standing taller than his waist was a dryad-nymph clutching to each arm. They tapped their goat hoofs in a little jig and kissed me on the cheeks with the fullest and most luscious of human lips as they passed by. "Where is the mead?" one of them asked. "Where is the ale?" questioned the other.

In his great voice with his northern accent, the man-giant asked, "Where are the mushrooms and the herbs?" He laughed, then, as fast as any snake, he bent down and leaned in so his nose was nearly touching mine. "Hmm? Where are the treats?"

"Right this way, oh mighty Stiggis...just march that way and find our Kehldeshi comrades already enjoying them," said I.

Then the bell chimed below, and I knew more of the guests were arriving up from underneath the basement. The members of the Deadmen who voyaged from places further than across the world had arrived.

"Pardon me, if you will," I begged of Stiggis and his dryads, and I hurried through the corridors and down the stairs, past the baths, to the hidden room. I pulled the secret lever, shown me by the man who last owned this dreadful shadow home, and hurried down the stairs. Ancient books and scrolls filled the shelves. Cobwebs looked like ghosts spawning from every one of the room's corners. I found the second switch behind the obsidian-bound book, and a stone tile in the floor slid open. And from the hole, the chiming bell echoed into the subterranean study.

"I was starting to think I had the wrong address," said a tall, gaunt man as he stepped up the stairs from the catacombs below. His accent was not of any country I had been to in this world, and I have been to so very many. He wore a long coat of black leather that hung down past his knees. The shoulders were knobbed with rows of iron studs, and he wore a hat similar to those the Seekers wear, but this man's was black instead of blue, and the wide rim curled up on either side to make me think of a bull's horns. His face was as tan as cow hide, and in the place of his eyes were two silver coins. In sheaths looped through the snakeskin belt around his narrow hips, he had strange weapons. Armaments not of this time, mechanical contraptions that the man swore were not magic. At all of the Deadmen's parties, he twirled them on his fingers and blasted fire and iron from their tips to shatter bottles and any manner of thing that the other guests tossed up into the air. Not to mention those who got in his way during "the games."

"Ah, Lawdog," I said, forcing a smile. "So good of you to come. It

has been far too long."

Before answering me, the otherworldly stranger turned around and snapped his fingers at some large, heavy-breathing thing with claws making its way up the steps.

"C'mon, old partner, don't wanna linger down there too long," said Lawdog. Then he spun around and stared me down with brows lifted high above his two coins-for-eyes, a wild smile below. "The wicker man will get'chya," he said, and burst into deep laughter.

My stomach sank then lifted as if I might need to spit it out. My heart and lungs felt like they were being compressed together just at the mention of that thing, that demon, that devil I had made, the deal I had made to make it. I deserve no forgiveness; I deserve every mile of hell that I walk. I knew this then; I know this now. I have always known this.

"Cheer up. It's a party." It was not Lawdog who spoke but the massive bloodhound—as tall as a horse—that came up the stairs. I directed the two entities to the others, and for the rest of the hour I ran up and down, to the above, to the below, each and every time the bell chimed. Visitors from so many beyonds gathered in the great hall, bound by the fact that we were all Deadmen. Skin or scale, fur or hair, from now, from before, from after. We were all Deadmen.

I was exhausted, barely able to stay on my feet, when the honored guests arrived. When I set eyes upon them and all the joyous things they had brought, I knew I would not be able to fight it. I knew that before the sun rose, I would revel, for the lady and lord had arrived.

~The Deadmen's Party
by Robart Everest Howalder,
Lord of Wardbrook

≈

175

CHAPTER TWELVE

WAX SMILES

*T*hree silhouettes stood outside the door of the coroner-surgeon's abode.

Cullum and Damos slowed as they walked on the road, still far enough away that the house was a small lump and the men mere specks, Cullum knew what they were. Seekers. One of whom Cullum knew immediately, for there was only one man that tall, that broad. Seeker Wardorf—the guardian of the door. A door he should not—would not—have left. Not while he yet had breath in his lungs.

"You know them? Are they friends?" Damos asked.

"If that man you can clearly see towering over the other two is here, then something horrific has happened at the House of Deacons." Cullum's gut felt like it was splitting in two, half of it scurrying up and the other burying itself down. He spat on the ground. "That fucking rat was right."

"What rat?" Damos asked, stopping dead.

"Does the name Black Brenna mean anything to you?" Cullum asked, focusing on Damos' response like a bird of prey.

"Perhaps," Damos said. "I might know the name. I might

not. I don't recall. But I do recall a rat, a vile creature. A dangerous creature."

"What the hell does that mean?" Cullum asked with a glance at the distant Seekers. "And why does no one in this forsaken place recall anything I need to know?"

"I believe they have been wiping my memory," Damos said, and rushed to add, "The memories of everyone in the whole village." He paused. "The memories of those investigators from your order who came years ago and who left satisfied with answers though none were truly provided." Again, he paused. "There were deaths…sacrifices…"

"Who has been wiping your memory? Who has been holding sacrificial rites?" Cullum asked, glancing again at the Seekers, who, oddly had not moved at all.

"The lord and the lady here, but not just them. A whole organization…they have a name, a name that I cannot recall." Damos tucked his shaking hands into his pockets. "I think it may be part of the reason I don't leave this place, though I want to I want to so badly I can feel my feet fleeing down the road. But every morning when I awaken, I am still here. It is a dark and powerful spell on me and all the others here."

Cullum swallowed.

Damos glanced toward the house. "They come."

"Vicar!" It was the booming voice of Wardorf. Cullum turned to find the Seekers walking toward him. Though the sun hung low in the late afternoon sky, there were no shadows, for the coroner-surgeon's house stood a lonely sentinel at the far edge of the village.

"Hail the Luminescent, we have found you," Wardorf called. "The sun is good; the sun is kind."

Cullum tipped his head and studied Wardorf and the others. They walked side by side in a perfect line. Right foot. Left foot. Perfectly synchronized. And the way Wardorf had greeted him…

That was not the way he spoke.

"Cullum, when you stand next to a mortal man, what do you feel?"

"Feel?"

"What do you feel, vicar?"

"I feel his life energy. I feel his soul. I can see his anguish or his glory hovering in his spirit above him."

"And when you stand next to a monster?"

"You know what I feel. You feel it, too. The Bloodburn *writes itself into the back of our left hands, and we read the signs."*

"Those Lordanians, they give off nothing."

"Even corpses have energies."

"Those nine men and their scribes, the handful of Seekers they came with, not one of them gives off anything."

Cullum looked down at his left hand. He felt nothing. Not the nothing he had felt when first conversing with Damos. That had felt like an imposed absence. This was a complete absence of sensation. Truly nothing.

His skin crawled. His gut churned. And the three Seekers walked ever closer.

He had been told that the purpose of the *Ordeal*, that in becoming a Seeker, he would be able to sense and hunt down magic in all its forms, in every dark corner. So what was this unfolding before him if not magic? And why could he not sense it?

"These men are imposters," Cullum said quietly, then yelled, "Wardorf! Glory be, it is good to see your face!"

"Imposters? How do you know?" Damos asked under his breath.

"That big man," Cullum said, smiling and nodding at Wardorf. "He has a vocation in our order, and that vocation swears him to guard a door in our glorious House of Deacons. There is no word, no threat, no danger, no saint...not even the Luminescent himself that could move that man from that door until the time his task is up."

"I feel I know the answer, but may I ask, when is the man's task supposed to be up?" Damos asked, smiling and nodding as well.

"When he's dead," Cullum said. "Whatever they are, they are not Seekers. I suspect they are not men. They are here to kill me, so you had better make a choice right now."

"What choice?" Damos asked.

"You were a medic and a deserter from your army and from life. A suicide. Are you going to use your demon gifts to prevent them from seeing their task done, or are you going to use the same gifts to slither away?"

The thing playing Wardorf held his hammer over his shoulder. The other two put their hands to their belts.

Cullum put his hands at his sword belt as he continued forward, smiling and nodding.

"I'm with you, Cullum Shrike. You have my fealty," Damos said, his voice steady and stoic.

"Do you need a weapon?" Cullum asked, refusing to acknowledge the relief he felt at Damos' words.

"I am a weapon," Damos said. "I was a tool of healing the living, a tool of understanding the dead, and now I am a weapon. And now I will make the dead." Damos' voice was distant; he said the words like some kind of mantra. "And now I am the tool that makes the dead."

"And we shall make the dead together. The demon and the holy man," Cullum agreed.

"The demon and the holy man." Damos growled.

"Stand where you are!" Cullum ordered the three nearing imposters. He thought of the archdeacon's fear. He thought of the corrupted white *Bloodburn* on the back of that old man's hand. He knew Lazarus was dead now. He knew he had died alone and in fear at the hands of these things. And it was Cullum's fear that not even the Luminescent had been there for his father at the end.

And what of the Sisters?

"Vicar?" Wardorf called back. He and the other two continued walking.

Cullum picked up his pace. He felt something stirring in the back of his left hand and thought of the vision in the pool with the Sisters. In his mind's eye, he saw his blood turning white.

"I said stand where you are. Stop walking!"

The man on the left lifted his head. Cullum froze. It was Herres beneath the rim of the hat. He was smiling. Wardorf was smiling. The third man, a tanned Lordanian, was smiling. Their smiles looked like wax carved into half-moon shapes.

"Now, now, Cullum!" The words came out, but Wardorf's mouth did not move, not at all. The wax smile remained. As he spoke, he picked up his pace to a jog, his strides so large that the other two sprinted to keep up. "It's only me. It's only us. Just your..."

"Friends!" all three of them said at once.

They tossed their arms back in unison. Their hands exploded into mists of blood and chips of bone.

"Monsters!" Damos cried.

Writhing white coils oozed from the severed wrists, and then Cullum saw they were tentacles that grew and undulated. If the things felt pain, the wax smiles did not show it. Wardorf dragged his hammer across the dirt road, three six-foot-long tendrils holding on to the handle.

"Luminescent," Damos said, "what the fuck are they?"

"I know not," said Cullum. "We'll examine the corpses to find out."

He welcomed the dark curtain that rose from the arcane

and blanketed the mundane, allowing him to see only the monstrous, the demonic, the hellish, a gift of the *Ordeal*.

The three fiends floated in darkness, running across a black ice lake. But Damos was gone. Cullum could sense him by his side, but could not see him with his enhanced Seeker's vision. Damos was a demon, was he not? He should be clearly visible.

The *Ordeal* clearly did *not* allow Cullum to see all magics. An unpleasant discovery to make at this moment.

Pain pulsed with its own heartbeat up Cullum's arm in fiery waves. Agony swelled in his heart, surging through his shoulder and down his arm to meet the fire that blazed. The arcane chains whipped from his palm.

Wardorf's imposter twisted at the waist and threw his shoulder in a wide swing. Tight in the fiend's tentacle grip, the hammer soared for Cullum's head.

Cullum whipped his left arm, and the chains lengthened. Glowing blue links smacked into the tendrils that held the hammer. They tangled, the chains burning the milky-white flesh. It sizzled and popped, yellow blood boiling out. The hammer went spinning and disappeared into the dark.

Cullum heard a whistle of air. A grunt. A gasp. Next to Wardorf, the false Seeker in Harris' skin also disappeared into the blackness. *Damos. Good man.*

The third enemy—the Lordanian—charged.

Pain from the heart through the lungs, into the right shoulder now, agony bending and rippling down the arm, exploding from the palm.

The blue tethers blasted into the Lordanian and wrapped it up like a python does a rat.

The thing wearing Wardorf pulled his tendrils free of the chains, shrank them to the length of a human arm, and drew a sword.

Cullum recalled the chains as both his burned and

wounded foes continued their advance. His full senses flooded back. Sights and sounds and smells. Damos was roaring like a beast, the beast that he was.

The sun gleamed.

The smell of burning sky.

The smell of sorcery.

Damos was on top of the creature that was Herres. Black spider limbs spawned from Damos' back, stabbing and pounding into the shrieking thing beneath him as he wrestled it down with his human arms. Fountains of yellow blood sprayed into the air.

But with each mauling strike, Damos' attacks slowed.

"Pace yourself, Damos. They don't die easy," Cullum called, stepping back as fast as he could to keep the space between him and his foes, avoiding their lashing tentacles.

He had set out on his last mission with three specially formulated flasks. He'd used his hellfire and his frost during his encounter with the bat demon and the heretics that had summoned it. He reached to his belt and unhitched the last flask.

The Lordanian surged to its feet and charged, tentacles outstretched. Flesh and yellow blood dripped from charred muscle still smoldering from the magic burn of the chains.

Cullum hurled the flask and nailed the creature square in the forehead. The flask burst. Fluorescent green liquid spilled out and dripped down the human face. Skin melted away like wax, exposing a bulbous white head. Tentacles took the place of a mouth and eyes. They twisted and undulated, swelled and burst, then shrank and shriveled from the acid in the flask.

Wardorf was nearly in striking distance. Cullum drew his sword and changed his movement from backward to left then forward with a slash. The creature blocked it with a clang. Swords pressed, Cullum stepped in, muscles tightened and locked in effort as he looked up at the big man's waxen smile.

"You'll suffer for what you did to him, what you did to all of them," Cullum said.

Underneath Wardorf's hat were pale, dead eyes. "Join us." The words emanated from the tips of the tentacles squirming out of the husk's mouth.

"Like hell," Cullum said, and kicked the brute in his torso, forcing him back.

"Your order has been taken." The tentacles from Wardorf's mouth had grown a foot long, flopping around in front of his chest.

"By who? Who are you devils?" Cullum asked, holding his ground, heart slamming against his ribs.

"We are no devils." The thing lunged and whipped out its sword arm, tentacles lengthening so that the blade they held went around Cullum and stabbed toward his back. He spun and deflected the attack, then pirouetted as he moved toward his foe and stabbed for the creature's chest.

Wardorf was too fast, stepping aside then winding back for another attack.

"We are your saints!" it said, and slashed again.

Again, Cullum deflected. "Not my saints," he roared. From the corner of his eye, he caught sight of tentacles and shadow limbs intertwined as Damos battled the creature that had inhabited Herres.

The creature stabbed at his throat, and Cullum felt the sharp steel sing against his skin as he deflected.

The tentacles yanked. Cullum stumbled again. One foot left the ground. He rammed it back down and rooted in place as he braced for the next attack. Swords clashed again. Cullum summoned the chains to his ensnared hand. The chains wrapped around the creature's tentacles, and they began a tug of war, yanking and pulling one another. The chains burned into the thing's flesh, sending it sizzling up and over Cullum, burning him with small dots of molten monster, like the spatter of fat in a hot pan.

Still the creature clutched and bellowed, its mouth tentacles elongating and shooting for Cullum's face like spears. The moment slowed, and Cullum saw both terrible possibilities. The tentacles would rip right through him. If he used his sword to swipe at them, the creature's sword would find an opening and run him through.

He called back the chains.

He ducked.

He evaded the spearing tendrils, but his foe's sword still stabbed toward him.

Cullum's swing started low, the tip of his blade skimming the ground as he brought his sword arm up and around in an arcing backhand. He slashed through the tentacles that tethered his hand, and the blade kept soaring until he pulled it straight down to parry the sword attack. Steel cracked on steel. Cullum let out a roar accompanied by three rapid stabs and two short slashes.

They circled again. The thing was slower now. At least it was tiring. Behind Cullum's foe, the bleeding, mangled thing that wore Herres' skin was now on top of Damos, tentacles from its mouth reaching down as its other limbs spread and tangled with Damos' arachnoid appendages.

The coroner-surgeon yelled, more in frustration than fear, and then turned into a black vapor whilst in his foe's very clutches. He reappeared next to Cullum,

"Come with us. Come back to Aldwick. Come speak with your *new* father," said Herres.

"Go to hell," Cullum said between labored breaths.

"Join us," said the Lordanian, getting back to its feet, the words emanating from the half-destroyed skull, a bulbous white swell bulging from the open chasm of the wound like a fungal tumor.

In places, its flesh had burned away to expose pulsing organ and ivory bone dripping with yellow blood. Still, it stood and spoke. "Join us."

"We only wish to be your friends!" they called out in unison, and advanced.

Cullum and Damos stepped forward together. From some point behind Cullum soared an orange orb that hit Herres in its deformed head. The head exploded and splashed Wardorf with hot orange goop, chunks of white, corroding flesh, and fragments of skull.

The creatures turned to the new threat. Two more balls of orange acid flew overhead and struck the fiends, Wardorf in the chest and the Lordanian in the leg. In less than a second, there was a melon-sized cavity through Wardorf that allowed clear sight of Damos' house down the road. The Lordanian's leg folded, the still-human limb dripping skin and muscle off below the hip.

Cullum did not need to turn around to see who their unexpected savior was. He could feel him in his left hand.

Black Brenna.

Still, he turned. The sorcerer was in his larger form, that of a black-bearded grizzled and muscled hermit with four arms, glowing orange boils on his chest and belly.

In his left hand, he held a book.

"That is my journal," Damos said angrily.

Black Brenna gestured toward the house. "Are you going to invite me in, hehe?"

"*A*t that very moment when the demon-doctor held open the door to his home for the hermit sorcerer and the holy man, dark clouds manifested from the depths of nowhere and engulfed the sun like a curtain closing over a stage," the father said to his son, and pulled the boy's blanket over his head.

The boy giggled and pushed the blanket away from his face. His father laughed and continued.

"In the house, a growing gale could be heard, and through the windows, the holy man watched an eastward wind blow the trees so that they looked to him like they were pointing with their branches to the place whose name the whirling squall even now whispered..."

"What name?" the boy asked, eyes wide.

"Wardbrook." The father's voice was hushed, and he drew the word out with an eerie exhalation.

Outside the boy's room, the wind howled. His father told him a new story every night, and the boy liked them all, even if they did scare him a little.

"'A demon, a holy man, and a sorcerer walk into a house, hehe... How does the rest of the joke go?' asked the four-armed hermit, looking back and forth with his sneaky eyes at the demon doctor and the holy man, wondering who would speak first.

"'It goes with you telling me exactly why the fuck you helped us, and—'"

"Darcy!" came the voice of the boy's mother from outside of the room. His father laughed and called out, "He does not understand, my dear. He's just a babe." And then he looked at his son and gave him a wink.

"Now, where was I, Aldous?"

CHAPTER THIRTEEN

PROCESSION

*D*amos laid a hand on Cullum's shoulder. "I am sorry you had to kill your friends."

"Those were not my friends," said Cullum, the words tight. Friendship was not something he had allowed. "Those were the creatures who murdered men of my Order then wore their skin and faces like clothing."

"Will you go back?" Damos asked with a glance at Black Brenna, who stood watching them in silence.

"To Aldwick?" Cullum asked, thinking of all he had left behind. Nothing. He had left nothing in Aldwick. They were dead, all dead, the church destroyed. Even the Sisters' chamber had likely been infiltrated and desecrated. The man he had called Father was dead, and his last act before his death had been to show Cullum the book that had led him here. So here he would stay. "No, I will not go back."

"The church has been dead for hundreds of years," said Brenna. "This is just decay, hehe."

Cullum glowered at the hermit. His stomach turned with disgust just looking at the brute. Here was dark magic. Here was the sorcerer who had infected and killed young Jeremiah and, in turn, the gravedigger, the one whose actions had caused a deadly confrontation between a mob and a witch. Everything in Cullum wanted to purge the creature from this house, this town, this land.

"Why did you kill those townsfolk?" Cullum asked, his tone conveying the venom in his heart. He stepped forward, but Damos moved to block his way.

Brenna's filthy black beard swayed back and forth as he opened his small eyes wide and shook his head.

"You can't be serious, mate?" Brenna said. "I just saved your life. Hehe."

"I'm not your mate, rodent—" Cullum said, but before he could continue, Brenna cut him off in a twisted voice.

"You will be." The sorcerer's words bent and warped in octaves as his body did the same in form. Brenna shrank down, turning into his rat body with deep and shrill pops and cracks as his bones bent, shortened, and thinned. His head and neck swung to and fro and up and down, fast and violent, his face becoming a blur as it grew smaller and smaller. Dark blood spattered out of the blur, perhaps from a bleeding nose, or his ears. Cullum could not tell.

He looked on at the thing with his teeth gritted and his eyes squinted in disgust, the *Bloodburn* tearing at his left hand. A glance at Damos revealed the coroner-surgeon's expression twisted with the same revulsion.

From a puddle of his own blood, the shrunken Brenna snickered before retreating across the floor, looking like a hairy insect as he scurried on his six limbs toward a thin crack in the wall. Much thinner was the crack than the rat, but that did nothing to thwart his speedy entry.

"Sneaky little fucker!" Damos shouted, looking at the crack in the wall as if he had never seen it before. "How many times have you been in here? How long have you been watching me?"

"What is life like for you, Seeker?" Brenna asked, ignoring Damos' ire. The whole house echoed the words, as if it was the home itself that was doing the speaking.

"I didn't give you permission to do *that* to my house!" Damos said. He looked to and fro, trying to pinpoint Brenna's position. It was hopeless. Each word had come from down a different hall, out of a different room.

"Eh, Seeker? How lonely...and miserable...and pointless is your life up there on your moral high ground? So much closer to the sun, and yet so much farther from all the rest of the world, so much farther from what you really are. You lowly scum. You, the child of squirming primordial filth, came crawling from the sea and into the sand like all the rest of us."

"Make your point," Cullum said, clutching his sword hilt, preparing himself to call upon the chains to tear Damos' possessed house apart stone by stone, board by board until he found the rat. And through the agony of the *Bloodburn*, Cullum would shackle Brenna and send him back to whatever dark void he had crawled from. Whatever had motivated the sorcerer to save their lives, he did not trust him.

"I was making my point, and then you asked me a fool's question. You were not hearing what I was saying, and I saw that idiot rage in your idiot eyes that has led to the burning of so many of my kind," Brenna said, his voice coming from the ceiling, the floor, the hallway to Cullum's right.

Again, Cullum was receiving insufferable ridicule to his character in this house; this time his judge was a shape-shifting sorcerer and not a shape-shifting demon. "The burning of black magic, heretic monsters?" Cullum yelled at the house. "Yes, I've killed many of you."

"Yes. Bravo. A man who takes responsibility," Brenna said, his many voices mocking. "So take responsibility for all the rest too, you steaming pile of human shit. Eh? How many have you killed, you and your mates? How many walked in that procession of judges and executioners, the song of the screaming mob that snakes through the streets as the doom march is made to the pyres? All this at your behest. Their crime? They did not do what you did with their magic blood."

What you did.

Cullum had chosen to wield the magic he had been born with in defense of the sun. He thought of the *Ordeal*, of the whip, the serums, the terrors in the night, the visions and the desires. He thought of all the things he did not choose; he thought of all the things the Order had forced him to do. And then he thought of what he did choose, what he still could choose.

"They simply did not want to kneel and beg and lick the feet of the Church like you do," Brenna went on, speaking through the halls and the rooms as the *Bloodburn* grew stronger still. "You're their dog. They have a collar around your neck, and when they say bite, you bite. You run the fox to ground like a hound."

Cullum remembered a time, a chase on horseback...two wizards and a witch fleeing for their lives. What they had done, Cullum had not been told, had not asked. But he had had a warrant for their execution, so he had a right. Although he did not remember their names, he recalled now how the witch screamed as the Seeker hounds sank their iron-tipped fangs into her legs and dragged her down before Cullum speared her with his lance like she was naught but a wild boar. He had whistled, and the hounds left the dying witch, now nailed by the lance to the ground, and they'd gone after the two wizards. One of them had been weeping as he fled. He'd been hardly more than a boy.

Cullum glanced at Damos. Why has he killed them, yet chosen not to kill the Dahkah?

"They just wanted to live on their own." Brenna's voice echoed through the house. "They just wanted to be hermits, and you routed them out. Like hares and foxes, you chased them down. You're an animal too, but you're *their* animal. And I'd rather be a rat than a dog."

The voice stopped a moment. A moment long enough for Cullum to speak, but he did not. He remained silent, waiting for the possessed house to continue. For how many more times would he be given this opportunity to listen to his enemy without having the chance to cut the talk short just as he cut out their tongue?

Cullum stared at Damos, making the connection of the events of right now to the events in the woods with the demon just a short while ago. *A demon who I gave the chance to speak, and am willing to call friend...*

"Know this," Brenna began again. "There are innocent and guilty alike in every single religion, creed, and cult, but the innocent are few and the guilty are many. You and I, Cullum Shrike the holy man, Black Brenna the sorcerer, and Damos the Dahkah...we are cut from the same maggot-infested cloth. We are all very wicked men, we have served wicked masters and wicked causes, for all of our lives. Yes, Seeker, your order and your deacons and archdeacons are wicked. And you served them."

"Speak for yourself, Brenna!" Cullum shouted at the house, fury erupting in him at the mention of his father. Brenna could say what he wanted of Cullum, not of his father.

Idiot.

Not my father. *Lazarus, my shaper, my master...my dead master. I do not know my father. I do not know my mother.*

Cullum again fell silent. He felt like a child. How could a man of the Order, a wearer of the blue hat and a holder of the chains, so frequently find himself feeling like a damn child?

"I will speak for myself—I always do, hehe. I will admit that I fear no man, nor do I fear any beast… I fear mirrors. I fear that I was a man so long ago and now there is just a monster. So I carry a mirror with me. I carry it in my soul, and it is the mirror of empathy and honesty, so I look at you and I see me, and I know that is why you hate me. You hate yourself."

Cullum drew his sword. It only made him feel more like an idiot. Was he going to start stabbing the walls until the house stopped making him feel like the dim son?

"Put your sword away, Cullum. He is not our foe," Damos said. "He is here to help us."

"Help us what?" Cullum asked through gritted teeth. "Help me lose contact with my sanity? Help me rip down my confidence and beliefs?"

"Yes, hehe," answered the house.

The back of Cullum's left hand blazed with the worst agony he had ever felt from the *Bloodburn* He truly thought his arm was aflame. If it *were* aflame, if might be less painful than what he now felt.

In spite of this, he put away his sword.

"We are going to help each other. You're here to help me as much as I am here to help you, hehe," Brenna said. "We are going to save the life of one still innocent. One of the few who remain so in this forsaken world of the mundane." Brenna's last words were localized directly behind the spot where Cullum and Damos stood in the center of the library of empty shelves. They exchanged a glance, then turned together to see the sorcerer again in the form of a four-armed hermit, sitting in the chair Cullum had fallen asleep in the previous night.

"I don't trust you, Brenna. But I'm listening," Cullum said.

"Very adult of you, keeping an open mind," Brenna said with a hideous and rotten smile. "She is magic-born like you and I, Cullum."

At that mention alone, Cullum wanted to stop listening. He wished to hear no more. Why would he help a witch? But he kept his mouth shut and his ears open.

"Damos was magic-made—against his own will, but he was magic-made—and for the sin of suicide, no less, hehe, and he is your friend. You said so in the woods. I was listening. I was hiding, hehe. If you have accepted this demon as your friend, then your moral code obligates you to help in saving an innocent girl even if she is of magic blood, am I correct?"

Cullum did not answer; he did not know the answer. He thought of the dead eyes of those he had failed, of the dead eyes of those he had saved. He imagined them as if they were magic-blooded, as if they had the capacity to one day open portals to the abyss and the beyond to call down rains of hellfire from cosmic black clouds. In his mind, he walked back through the entrance of the cave with the girl who had given birth to the bat—he imagined her as a witch—and as he did so, he did not hesitate a moment in trying to save her; he did not hesitate a moment in trying to avenge her. In his mind, he charged forward for the justice of a witch.

Cullum had his answer. Because her being a witch did not necessarily make her guilty of anything. Cullum was willing to accept that now because Damos had chosen to aid him rather than fight him. Because the rat sorcer, however vile, had chosen to do the same. Cullum was magic-born and he had chosen a righteous path. So perhaps not all those with magic blood were to be hunted and killed... He could at least think it, even if he would not say it.

Outside of Damos' house came the droning of far-off music. Bells and drums, flutes and lutes...other instruments that were older and ones too that made sounds that stirred thoughts of far-off stars and worlds.

"What is that?" Damos asked. He walked to the window and looked outside. It was day, but the clouds above made it dark as night, and the lack of wind and dry air was strange in the presence of these heavy clouds.

"It is the procession," Brenna said. "You know what it is, Damos. Dig into that smart brain of yours and remember. It is the same procession as last time, and the time before, and the other processions from other beyonds are on their way, too."

Damos frowned and opened his mouth as if to interject, but then remained silent as Brenna continued.

"Now I am going to need Cullum to make his catharsis and make it quick. The knock at the door will be here any minute. The invitation will be presented and the option to decline will not be given. Your only option is this: to either help me, or get in my way when I try to save the life of an innocent child. She is my responsibility. I have been sent by her mother. Her survival is both my obligation and my purpose, hehe."

"Someone is approaching the house," Damos said. "They are on horseback, riding from the direction of Wardbrook."

Cullum went to the window. "The lights in the town are all out." He saw the approaching rider. Far to the west in the direction of the tree-covered hill that led to the house of the dead witch, he saw torches. And it was from there that the music came.

He turned back to Brenna, his heart pounding now, and the pain in his arm crawled into his chest, tingling with a strange euphoria down his spine. It was this unexpected feeling of pleasure that stirred a greater fear in Cullum than the *Bloodburn's* pain ever could.

"I'll join you, but I need to know more about your

mission than what you just told me, sorcerer." Cullum was part of it now. He'd made his decision. Perhaps there had never been a decision to make. Regardless, the more he knew, the better.

"There is no good. There is no bad. Cullum, there is just the gray storm where the two mingle and twist and become forever lost. There are only the choices that we make trying to get to the eye of it all. The choices that we must live and die with, again and again. We can only try to make the choice that will ease the war inside ourselves. Don't you agree, hehe?" Brenna smiled his rotten smile.

"Do all of your kind speak in rhetoric and riddles?" Cullum asked, looking at his two ominous companions.

"Just as your kind does," said Damos.

Cullum turned back to the window. The rider from Wardbrook drew closer, cloaked and robed all in black, so that there looked to be a splotch of ink riding a tall white horse.

"Who is he?" Cullum asked.

"The harbinger," said Damos, his tone low with dread that reached over and crawled over Cullum's skin like a leech.

Soon the form was close enough for Cullum to appreciate the vast height of the horse and the rider atop it. And then he saw that the massive horse had no flesh. It was all bleached bone, and a deep crimson fire flickered in the black sockets where eyes should be. The giant astride the black, jewel-encrusted saddle was some ten feet tall when he dismounted and stood on the ground. He approached the house, his gait tentative, his black robes flowing over sharply defined bone, giving the harbinger an aura of frailty.

The pinkish glow from the salt lamp at Damos' door painted the ashen-white hair that fell down the figure's chest beneath a huge black hood. But Cullum could not make out any other features. The hands were a pale gray, the white bones of the knuckles protruding from the thin flesh. At the ends of the long, bulbous fingers were nails like claws.

"Who's this now?" Cullum demanded, turning to look at Brenna, then Damos, then back at Brenna, assuming at least one of them could answer. "Is this another devil you'd have join our league of the damned?"

He was sweating and dizzy, the pain in his left arm becoming too much. And then there was that strange, growing euphoria tingling in his spine juxtaposing with the pain. He took off his hat and wiped his brow, then drew off his glove and looked at the back of his left hand. The web of veins was so swollen it was visible down to his fingernails. Indeed, his hand throbbed with so much blood that he thought his fingernails might pop off. A multitude of colors flashed and glowed beneath his skin. He tried to pull his glove on. He struggled for a moment to get his swelling fingers into the proper holes, but there was no use.

"Luminescent damn it all!" Cullum hurled the glove to the ground. He had seen much, and he had come to recognize so many shades of evil, so many hues of strange, but the events that were now playing out were of a league far different. He had never before allied himself with the monsters he was sworn to hunt. Yet here he stood, a demon at one flank, a sorcerer at the other. Everything that had been taught to him his whole life was screaming inside to keep fighting the sorcerer, to make no deal with yet another demon. But his instinct said otherwise; something that had existed inside him before the Order, before he was even born, said, *Me and this rat, me and this Dahkah, we're not so different.*

Memories of the Sisters and the pool and a black sun-moon filled Cullum with a dread that this plot would become more perilous before its end.

"Are you quite done, hehe?" Brenna asked.

"I'm done," Cullum said, and closed his eyes as he sighed.

The single loud thump upon the front doors to the house of Damos echoed through the halls and the rooms like Brenna's voice had done minutes ago.

"Oh, just a minute, please!" Damos called out.

"What is your choice?" Brenna asked, his gaze fixed on Cullum. "Will you help me save a life? Or would you like to deal with what comes next on your own instead? Hehe."

"I will help you, sorcerer. Although your words nearly enraged me into killing you…I will not deny the truth to them. I will not deny the light that you have just prompted me to see," said Cullum, and although he would have rather looked at the floor, he made himself stare into Brenna's eyes.

"What do you see, hehe?"

"I see through the dark, and it is setting me free."

Brenna's hideous smile went away, and, with a somber expression, he nodded his acceptance. Damos did the same, like two wicked bobbing heads welcoming Cullum to a cult.

The faraway music, the sounds of bells and drums, flutes and lutes, the other instruments too, the ones that were older and the ones that made sounds that stirred thoughts of far-off stars and worlds, was not so far away anymore.

As the sounds of the coming procession grew louder, again the door thumped, followed by the ominous echo through the house, and now a voice as deep and dead as the thumping on the doors: "Open and accept the invitation."

"Hurry, go to the door. Play dumb. Play the games. I will get to you," Brenna said, and again transformed into his rat shape and scurried away down a hall toward an open window.

"Brenna, wait. Where will we find you?" Damos asked.

"Look for the girl in the emerald-green dress," came Brenna's fading voice, and then the sorcerer disappeared from the stage.

An image flashed in Cullum's mind, a memory of the

prophecy he had seen in the pool with the sisters: a brown-haired girl holding a bloody hand to her wounded belly, red bleeding into the fabric of the emerald-green dress. Had Brenna clarified that it was she Cullum was meant to save, there would have been no need for discussion or argument. He felt certain now that she was the reason he was here. He would save her. He would redeem himself. He would not fail again. He felt a renewed flicker of faith. The path the Luminescent wove had led him here.

Damos put his arm around Cullum's shoulder.

"Are you ready?" he asked as he started guiding Cullum to the door.

Ready? How could he know when he was ignorant of that which he must be ready for?

The mad music grew louder and louder still. A beast howled. Another beast roared. A she-devil bawled, and some great behemoth trumpeted to the sky. All this as the other instruments went on with their wild circus of song.

Cullum smiled to the music, and he could not say why, nor could he stop smiling, and nor could he slow his footsteps toward the doors that thudded with a steady pounding now, like drums beating in the nearing procession, Damos rushing along by his side. They exchanged glances, only to see the other wearing the same mad smile. Terror rose in Cullum's belly, but it was smothered by the growing, unnatural excitement.

There was a part of him that wanted to run, a part of him that *knew* to run, because there would be no walking back from the place he now went. The chains wrapped around the runner's neck in the blackness of his soul, and Cullum dragged the cowardly son of bitch right to the door with him. No burn in the back of his left hand. Just euphoria down his spine, euphoria all over that made him want to dance and sing.

Terrifying euphoria.

The doors stood before Damos and Cullum now, and in unison they each grabbed hold of a handle and opened the gateway.

The dead-fleshed, frail giant of a man pulled back his black hood.

Cullum stared at the face of weathered, ancient gray. White bone poked through at the cheeks, nose, and chin. Long white hair ran down his shoulders and chest beneath a black turban fastened in the front with an obsidian brooch. A white mustache fell down in braids on either side of his gaping mouth, for his lower jaw was entirely dislocated, a rotten black tongue dangling from the left side. The hollow sockets of his eyes had dots of crimson flame at their centers, like far-off, aging suns.

"The Deadmen beckon," said the towering corpse. Each time he uttered a word, his crimson eyes glowed brighter so that they flashed with a dizzying, blinking radiance. "The processions are on their way, from north, east, south, and west."

Cullum realized he was tapping his foot uncontrollably to the sound of the mad music.

Get a bloody hold of yourself. But it was no use.

That music...it is just...it is just too damn good.

"From now, from then, and from the hereafter come the guests, come all the guests to the Deadmen's party," the dead man with the turban of black went on, his eyes flashing crimson as he spoke, and with the pink glow of the salt lamp beneath the dark clouds and the closing-in music, it was a surreal feast of sight and sound.

Why am I feeling this way? Damos, what is happening? Cullum tried to ask the Dahkah, but he failed. No words spilled from his mouth, only laughter. Damos turned to him, and Cullum saw that beneath the absurd joy and excitement in the Dahkah's eyes, there was fathomless terror. Damos too tried to speak, but no words left his lips. He only laughed and laughed until Cullum worried his jaw might unhinge.

The devil sage garbed in black produced a golden cup from his robes and raised it slowly until it was directly beneath his chin. A dog's head was sculpted in relief onto the goblet. It bared its fangs and wrinkled its brow atop the two azure gems that were set in the sockets of its eyes.

The glow from the salt lamp beside Damos' doors made the blue stones flicker with life, and Cullum held their gaze.

"I present to thee the invitation," said the skeleton in his ominous drone, and then he let out a sigh like death, and from his crimson eyes, dark blood now flowed. It poured down his hollow cheeks, and the streams met on the bone-white tip of his chin as blood the color of wine cascaded into the cup. When sweet-spiced fumes rose rom the cup, he said, "You must drink of it so that we may begin."

The mixture of horror and euphoria had Cullum momentarily paralyzed. The trumpeting of the nearing behemoth and the music of the procession were ripping his sanity in half. He felt like a living puppet in some mad theatre, and in this moment, he was not merely being made to stand and watch—he was being made to embrace the insanity of a reality melting around him.

Damos moved first, seizing on Cullum's stillness. He closed both hands around the goblet and sipped from it. Cullum was both revolted and intrigued. As the Dahkah's eyes flashed crimson and he extended the cup to Cullum, the skeletal sage threw back his head, and his laughter ascended to the misanthropic clouds above.

Cullum found his arm pulled into motion by some unseen string, and he reached up and took the cup. The music that had been far off was far off no longer. Cullum heard the chanting of savage throat singers, and from the town of Wardbrook, above the roofs of the houses as tall as the town's weathered white church, Cullum beheld the behemoth that was making the trumpeting sound. The silhouettes of six tusks and the long-bristled fur of something larger than he had ever seen swayed a massive head and a long, thick, trunk-like snout.

Cullum looked again to the eyes of the golden hound on the cup, and smells of sweet spices washed through him as he raised the drink to his lips. It tasted like blood, old blood. Half was left, and he drank it all down.

The golden goblet fell to the ground, and the puppeteer set to work, that invisible master of fates pulling all the strings. From the house, with the skeletal sage, went Cullum and Damos to join in the procession through the town and up the hill to the great black house of Wardbrook, where the Deadmen's party was about to begin.

～

I am the dark master, watching, flying in your dreams,
'Neath the shadow, 'neath the blanket of wide black wings,
Only bow as you tremble before the King of Abyssal Kings
I dig up, I unbury each and all of your haunting themes.

Beyond the roiling blackness, in all your torment, in all your terror,
I am right here beside you, inside you, only look now to the mirror.

~Under the Wings of Madness

～

CHAPTER FOURTEEN

THE TRUTH WEAVER

In a time yet to come...

*D*arcy *Weaver took another drink to steel his nerves before resetting his quill to parchment. Upstairs, young Aldous argued with Darcy's wife about making his way to bed. Darcy's wife was making feeble progress in winning the debate.*

"I want to look for the dogs!" Aldous shouted.

Darcy took another drink and tried to focus on the page in front of him. He had not slept in nights, not in nights or days. No, he had not slept. He had not slept.

"You will not find them in the dark, and besides, they have run off like this before. They will return in the morning," Darcy's wife said.

Aldous said something Darcy could not hear.

"Aldous, you have no say in the matter. To bed with you, boy!" screamed Darcy's wife.

"Coward!" Aldous shouted.

Darcy's stomach sank at the sound of his son's remark. But Darcy did not move from his table, he did not stand from his chair, and he did not avert his eyes from the page before him.

"I do not need to sleep," continued Aldous upstairs. "The dogs do! It is our duty to protect them, and we have failed, for they are lost. They are lost and alone in the woods! So damn you, Mother, damn you for forsaking them!"

Darcy's wife screamed at the top of her lungs.

Darcy winced.

There was stomping, then the cellar door flew violently open and his wife's voice soon followed. "Darcy! Darcy, you get the hell up here and discipline this child. He is a devil, Darcy. He is a devil!"

Without turning from his desk, or even taking his eyes from the page in front of him, he slammed a tight fist on the table before him for dramatic effect. "Gods damn you, woman! I am at work here. I am at work!" His voice went hoarse before he screamed the final word, and so he wetted his throat with more drink. All it did was burn.

The cellar door slammed shut.

Stomping.

"Luminescent help me, boy, I will beat you black and blue if you don't get yourself to bed at once. I'll drag you out into the woods and leave you there, forsaken with the dogs. Eh? You want that, Aldous, you little imp?"

"You can try."

Darcy did not hear Aldous say the words, but he knew that was exactly what the boy said. It was what the boy always said when his mother threatened him. He would grin like a little devil and look her in the eyes and say, "Oh yeah? Just you bloody well try, Mother."

Above, Darcy's wife let out a battle cry. Aldous was laughing and running, his little footsteps far faster than his mother's.

"I should not be writing this," Darcy said to himself, eyes still trained on his prose, his mind leaving any thoughts of his family far, far behind. A necessary sacrifice, for he had work to do, he had truths to expose, and that was what a hero did: they exposed truths no matter the cost.

Another drink.

"It is not my place to write this." His voice was timid, and he stamped his foot on the stone cellar floor with such force that he felt the thudding impact up into his knee.

"Coward," he said of himself. "Coward, coward, coward." Darcy went to take another drink.

The cup was empty.

"Fuck!" he growled.

His hand shook. He put the quill down. His cup was empty. He poured another drink, one hand on the cup, one hand on the pitcher. Both eyes still on the page.

The pitcher thudded on the table as he set it back down.

"Aldous!" his wife yelled above.

His son's mad laughter followed.

The cup touched Darcy's lips. He tilted his head and drank all within. Then abruptly he stood and pitched the cup against the wall, where the silver smacked on stone with a clang.

"It is *your* place to write this, you coward," Darcy growled at himself as he sat back down. If anyone else was listening, they'd have thought some mad dog was waiting in the cellar for its owner to come down and axe it. But it was just Darcy, drunk and growling things only he understood.

"It is your duty to write this." He made a fist and slammed it into his forehead. He did not close his eyes at the impact, just kept looking past his arm at the page.

"An honest writer is the most virtuous of heroes. One who lies is the most deplorable of all villains."

He pulled his fist away from his head, and he did not need to look to where his hand moved to find the small, red, gold-edged box that contained the fae dust. A gift from Diana Ward herself, the very woman that the writing of this story would so enrage. Perhaps it *would enrage her even more than his other works enraged the Church of the Luminescent. He opened the box, and even as he looked at the contents, his heart began to pound and his spine tingled with euphoric anticipation. He dipped the long fingernail of the small finger of his left hand—grown just for this purpose—into the glowing pink powder inside the trinket box, brought it to his nose, and inhaled.*

Stars explode inside the writer's mind. Worlds are made and worlds die. Black stone orbs in a blacker cosmic sky burn with veins of life, set aflame by the molten cinders of time.

"It is my duty to write this." Darcy again picked up the quill. His blood drummed in his veins. His sight was as keen as it would be in the light of day there in that dark cellar with naught but a single candle. He dipped the quill to his pot of ink, and he damn well set it to the page.

∾

Black Brenna listened to the nearing processions of man and beast, Deadmen playing their ensorcelled songs. They paraded toward the hallowed point of the great black house of Wardbrook, the entrance to another side, to another place, another world, the world of the black sun-moon. From north, east, south, and west, the processions snaked their way closer. The boreal glowing of the closing portals that had brought them here faded on the four horizons. Sorcery was not merely in the air; the air was buzzing with it, like an unseen swarm of locusts pulsed over the land. The idiot songs of the Deadmen's instruments blared through the sky. In the west, where the village of Wardbrook stood, there was screaming as the fiends played their tricks and terrors on the wholesome Enlightened folk, and some nameless trumpeting behemoth trampled down the street. With each step, Brenna could make out more of its features—*scores of tusks, a trunk nose, long fur*—but it was still far off.

"Hehe, filthy yokels," Brenna said to himself as he watched the shadow of the beast loom over the town, the banners of tribes and sects of the Deadmen flying high as their bearers swayed them to and fro.

Brenna recalled many times when he had terrorized those same locals, and their predecessors and ancestors too. How many times had he been in the western procession? How many times had he wreaked havoc and hell on those victims of his spite? He could not remember. And neither could the victims. "Hehe."

Even with all the distractions of the new night, Brenna remained vigilant. Diana knew Brenna, she knew him well, and if he was too bold, if he did not calculate every choice, she would know he was there. He would be captured and Nyva would die. And whatever would then happen to the hermit sorcerer would be far, far worse than death.

He turned away from the western procession and the silhouette of the hulking, many-tusked behemoth that called to the sky with a trumpeting decree, the deep sound booming upward from its snaking trunk.

"Never seen that fella. Hehe," Brenna said to himself, certain now that the behemoth was a new member of the party. Whether it was a sentient being brought in as new member of the Deadmen or a form of entertainment and then dinner remained to be seen.

Brenna wondered how much blood the thing had. He wondered what the smell would be like if he had to unleash his corrosion upon it.

Then he stopped wondering and got back to his task.

In his rat form, Brenna scurried as fast as any sprinting hound through the long grass then up the tree-covered ravine to the hulking manse that rested above the valley at the top of the hill.

The music of the processions grew louder, and the behemoth continued to boom. They were drunk and mad on the drafts and herbs of dark gods long dead—now resurrected. The procession members that were most near to men and women chanted and sang, and the ones more monster howled at the clouds that had so abruptly—against the known laws of time—eaten the day. And although no moon was visible, the lunacy it wrought was palpable.

The knowledge of a potential eternity in black-magic shackles as a warlock torturer's toy stirred no fear in Brenna, only spite, for he was a thing fueled by spite. He had been rejected as a man, and although he'd never admit it to Damos or Cullum or anyone else, he had been rejected by the magic cast as well. He loved this; he loved being rejected. He thrived on the loathing bestowed on him by others. It fueled his dark soul like love fuels the weak. Demons called him sorcerer. Sorcerers called him demon. Monsters and mutants called him a wicked warlock, and wicked warlocks called him a rat.

Yes, all despised him. He was Black Brenna the despised.

Now atop the hill and beneath the shadow of Wardbrook, Brenna took a last look back at the house of the coroner-surgeon. The turbaned, skeletal sage he recognized as Bulgare walked away from the house, accompanied by both Dahkah and Seeker.

Cullum danced as he walked. The sight gave Brenna a sick chill that squirmed down his crooked spine. He had seen the night clouds eat the day so many times. He had been in the processions. He had melted man and monster with magic. He had mutated into many forms, had died and lived to die and live again... How many times? But never once had

Black Brenna or the hermit he had been before seen a dancing vicar. Dancing in the very face of doom.

"Keep him together, Damos," he muttered. "I know you have it in you, hehe."

Brenna turned back to Wardbrook and scanned from a distance, looking for a crack or a crevice, some black hole, some open window to play as portal. His mind traveled between future and present and past, memories and worries nipping at him.

He had been the one to cause the falling out between Diana and his ladyship the Emerald Witch, Elyra. He had been sneaking and spying, and he had seen a thing he was not supposed to see, a thing being done between a wolf and a witch.

"She had a wolf, why not a rat? Hehe," Brenna asked himself as he reminisced. But he already knew the answer. He could love the Emerald Witch in the secret corners of his shriveled heart, but he was her servant, her property. She would never see him any other way.

After seeing Elyra entwined with the moon wolf, head thrown back, face a mask of ecstasy, he had been filled with jealousy and heartache. He was no moon wolf. He was nothing for adoration. He was just a rat.

So, he went and did what rats do: he spread a disease, a plague of mistrust and innuendo, and this plague was deceit and ripped alliances apart. It tore lovers asunder and it spawned a cloak-and-dagger civil war between Diana's Deadmen and those who sided with Elyra. With the Deadmen fighting their own—now their enemy—the Cults of Leviathan were given time to rise, given time to infiltrate the Brynthian Church and its holy orders.

As he scurried on, Brenna knew he could not make right the wrong he had done. Too many were already dead, or worse.

And those who hated him to their rotten cores far outweighed those that would tolerate his existence, so he would find few allies. But he knew that Nyva, the child who was born of the act he had unrightfully witnessed between Elyra and the wolf, and then unrightfully confessed to Diana, the child who was the heart of this terrible feud, did not deserve such a fate.

Brenna reached the house and kept moving, eyes focused on the dark shadow of the clouds as he looked for little cracks, holes in the walls, or open windows for him to crawl his way in. He saw it: a crack so small a roach would struggle through it. The ordinary eye could not see how deep this crack went, or if it would even provide entry to the house, but Brenna did not have ordinary eyes. He had an infiltrator's eyes, and those eyes knew all there was to know about cracks in the wall. That little black hole was all he needed to rat his way in.

"Hehe."

Brenna was careful to use only the most modest of spells as he infiltrated the great black house. The place was seething with sorcery, white magic, black magic, blood magic, earth magic, more and more and more magic. And still the vast majority of the guests were yet to arrive. He whispered words in tongues and made sounds that could not be called words as he traced signs into the air with his twenty fingers, streams of green smoke coming from the tips, leaving emerald miasma hovering in the air in the shapes of ancient runes.

When he was done, the signs converged upon him and he opened his jaw, his black tongue extending with a flick, his rat claws pulling the miasma to him. He swallowed up the symbols and the transformation began. His little bones snapped and popped and twisted and torqued. He stretched and lengthened and he became a thing as much a snake as a rat. A hairy, six-legged snake-rat. "Hehe."

He slithered his way into the black hole in the wall, and in the oblivion of dark, he felt his way. He dematerialized to shadow-blink only when it was absolutely necessary to move further, for shadow blinking was a costlier spell than a transformation. If he did it too often, Diana would sense the pull from the forces and, like the bitch she was, would sniff him out. He was careful enough, and soon he saw in the light and not the dark, and he was staring into the kitchens of Wardbrook. A place he had never before visited in the house, but he knew it to be one of the subterranean chambers…

Glass exploded on the cellar floor. Small shards flecked against Darcy's nightclothes and into his hair. "Are you some kind of idiot, Darcy?" someone screamed.

…subterranean chambers…

"Darcy! Why won't you just damn well listen to me, you stupid fucking animal." It was his wife doing the screaming; he was sure of that now. He looked away from the page. He looked into the kitchen, and at Diana, no…at his wife. He was looking at his wife in the kitchen…in the cellar of his house in Wardbrook… No, his house was in the lands of Aldwick. Diana was at Wardbrook.

…subterranean chambers…

"I am in my house, in Aldwick," he said to his wife.

Her eyes grew wider, and the vein in her thin, beautiful neck bulged like she was about to breathe fire. Then she just sighed. There wasn't even smoke.

She started to cry.

"I'm going to look for the dogs!" Aldous called down into the cellar.

"Dress warmly, please, and be back before dark," Darcy said.

"It is already dark," his young wife whispered, and collapsed to her knees, weeping all the louder.

"Why are you never here?" she wailed.

Darcy stared at her. "I am here right now."

"You're not. You're not here!" she yelled, and pulled on her hair.

"Why? Why? Why?" She scratched at the stone floor as she cater-wauled. Like she was trying to escape this cellar by digging her way to hell.

Darcy stared at her a moment and tried to recall what it was that he was doing. Oh, yes...he was writing. He was writing, and he was not supposed to be disturbed.

"Why?" His wife truly looked like she might become a lycan at any moment, so animalistic was her posture and fury.

Then they could both be beasts together.

"Because I have a gift," Darcy answered calmly. "Because all I see is death, all I see is darkness, all I understand is the suffering and the abyss, and, ultimately, the true beauty of it all. It is my oath to share that truth. I told you this at the start. You agreed to the terms. That is why. Now please, my dear, I have work to do."

Darcy smiled and indicated the rickety wooden steps going up from the cellar.

She did not move.

He didn't care. No, it wasn't that he didn't care. It just didn't matter. He turned around and poured another drink before sitting back down and taking up his quill again.

...subterranean chambers...

Tiny claws scratched against wood and stone as Brenna scurried on.

~

"She who makes a monster of herself kills all the pain and misery of being a woman, and in doing so is reborn a goddess."

~Mother Roots,
Chieftain of the Bloody Root Tribe

~

CHAPTER FIFTEEN

∞

HELLO, DARKNESS

*T*wo emeralds set in the golden goblet stared at Nyva like two faceless eyes; she stared back at them. Vapors swirled in the air above it like translucent ruby tongues.

A hundred voices whispered like the ghosts of murdered children, a single word: *"Drink...drink...drink."*

And this word, although whispered, somehow drowned out the sound of the furious music that blew through the cracks in the walls and the locked window and under the closed door of the chamber. The music rode to the house on the four winds, and the resonances met and created a cyclone of spine-chilling clamor. The cacophony was equal parts method and madness...method to what end, Nyva did not know. She did not want to know.

"Drink...drink...drink."

The whispering helped her to not know.

"No!" Nyva screamed at the voices and the cup. She pulled her knees to her chest and hugged them tight as she rocked back and forth on the bed of the chamber where she had believed herself to be a guest. Nay, she was a prisoner.

The door was locked, and beyond it Welfric—the hideous man who had accompanied them on the hunt—stood sentry.

"What did they do to me?" Nyva muttered to herself. "What did the apple do to me? I am not a witch." She thought of the emerald arrow, formed of her blood and dark magic, and she rocked as she spoke, her words in rhythm with her rocking. "There was something in the wine all along. Yes, they enchanted the wine...ensorcelled it to make me magical. I am not magical...I have no magic."

She wanted to stand and walk to the cup, wanted to lift it and throw it at the wall, but she knew if she got that far, she would drink it. She would have no other choice. Its pull would be too strong. The whispers would be too loud.

"Who are you talking to in there, my lady?" asked Welfric through the door.

"I am not your lady!" Nyva screamed so loudly it hurt. "Your lady is a devil's whore!"

There was no sound from the other side.

Nyva's sanity twisted even further in the presence of the man's silence. Had she just gone too far?

Too far for what? How could this get worse?

Don't be an idiot. This can get much worse.

Nyva heard the crack of Nan's skull. It cracked with the sounds of the drums of the oncoming parades as they converged on the house from all directions. It cracked with Nyva's pounding heart. It cracked as she realized that Welfric was not silent on the other side of the door—rather, he was laughing.

"I can call you sir, if you'd like," he said cheerfully. "I can call you queen, or Your Highness, perhaps...I can call you goddess if you'll just drink the wine."

"Fuck you!" Nyva could not say it as loudly as she wanted to with her knees hugged to her chest. She could hardly hear her own voice or Welfric's over the sound of the music, and the sound of the whispers obliging her to drink.

How could they be so loud? How could whispers scream over a scream?

"Drink...drink." Defying reason, the words came again and again like the endless tide battering down stone, battering it to dust to blow away on the wind of the word, *"Drink."*

Welfric punched the door.

Nyva pushed her back against the headboard as her heart punched her ribs.

"Eh! I can call you cunt, too!" Welfric shouted. "I can open this fucking door and say, 'Drink, cunt,' as I force the wine down your throat. I don't give a shit either way. Mother Roots is out here with me, and neither of us can go down to the fucking party until you drink. That was Lady Diana's explicit order." There came the sound of a fist slamming on the door again, and in his most animalistic tone yet, Welfric cried, "By the gods, I do not want to miss the opening ceremonies."

"I don't care what you want," Nyva said, surprising herself by the ferocity of her assertion, and surprising herself more still when she sprang up from the bed and marched right up to the door. "Do you hear me, you idiot? The marionette is done dancing. Do you hear? Done. Fucking. Dancing. So bang your drum and pull your strings elsewhere!"

"You little c—"

"Come in here if you want to call me that word again," Nyva said. "I'll burn you alive like I did that boar." There came no response. "I'll boil your fucking eyes out. You want some of that, eh, you balding shit?"

Welfric pounded so hard on the heavy, lacquered oak door that she could not be sure if it was his fist or a hammer that delivered the strike.

"I've chopped up witches and wizards meaner than you

while drunk before breakfast! They won't let me kill you, but I'll break your knees, bitch. I'll make you kneel."

Someone, a woman, murmured something to Welfric on the other side of the door.

"All right…" said Welfric. "Yes…all right…I understand… I said I understand. It won't happen again… I know I said the last time… Yes… No… I said I understand, Mother Roots."

Silence.

The music still streamed through the locked window, and Nyva saw the whispering ghosts. Little naked children, ephemeral and translucent, glowed a haunting white-green. They reached out, each with one hand, and pointed to the cup with the other. More and more of them pulled themselves out of the cracks in the walls and the cracks in the floor.

"Drink…drink…you must drink…" They spoke each word like quick, shrill birds.

"Mother, you must drink, drink…Mother."

Nyva wrapped her arms around herself. *Mother?* What did that mean? Why would they say that? Why would they call her that? Doom and dread manifested in her like some rapid cancer eating her alive from the inside out. She did not know how much longer she could suffer this tumor of fear.

Mother? she tried to ask, but she just screamed as the little dead children advanced and commanded her to drink. *Mother?* she tried to ask again, and again she could only scream.

"Nyva." It was voice that she did not know, a woman's voice from just on the other side of the door. Warm and soothing, strong and comforting, a voice like Diana's but not Diana's. This voice was foreign, accented in a manner Nyva did not recognize.

"Stay away from me!" Nyva shouted, both at the woman on the other side of the door and at the nearing children.

The children laughed.

"Nyva, drink the wine. Drink the wine and the children will sleep," said the woman.

The ghostly hands of the nearest child were upon her now. She could feel them, cool and moist, like snails sliding over dew in early spring. *They are not real.* And yet she *could* feel them. She tried to pull her arm away, but she had no more "away" to pull to. She was huddled right up against the door, and no matter how hard she commanded her mind to realize that *this* was not real, that it was just some terrible aftereffect from the apple she had eaten in the orchard, it all felt too real.

The hunt...it did not happen, she tried to tell herself as she closed her eyes and sank down to the floor, her back to the door. The hands touched her all over now; they clung to her.

Snails and slugs and toads.

I used no magic... I ate the apple. I fell ill. I am sleeping. I am sleeping and I dream and I will wake. But what if I am dying? What if I am already dead and this is the dream of death, the dream that never ends?

"*Drink, Mother, driiiiiink!*" The child ghosts' whispers turned to screams. "*Drink! Drink! Drink, you bitch! Drink!*" They started punching her and kicking her with little fists and feet.

"*We fucking said drink!*" commanded a little girl.

And then a ghostly fist hit Nyva, but it felt more like someone had just splashed her in the face with a cup full of some cold, thick fluid, and it was seeping into her through her pores and into her blood. It felt like it was making her like the ones who whispered, "*Drink,*" so that soon she, too, would be one of these dead children that surrounded her.

Her hands were beginning to glow the ghostly white-green. She knew she had to stand now. She knew she had to drink.

As she stood, one of the children leapt upon her. She tried to push it off, but her hands melted through it. *How can such a thing be? How can it both be clinging to me and be untouchable at once?* On trembling legs, she went toward the cup, and with every step she became heavier and terror and dread commanded her forward. More and more of the children leapt upon her even as they beckoned her onward.

She reached the table; she reached for the cup, and the moment her white-green, paling finger touched the lustered gold of the goblet, the unnatural glow to her flesh faded. All at once, the whispers died and the ghosts fled back like pallid beetles, back into the cracks in the walls and the floor.

The ruby fumes of the wine rushed up into Nyva's nose, and tears of relief welled in her eyes and ran down her cheeks. She did not sip; she drank. It was sweet, like honey, cloaking the salty, metallic taste of blood; it was sickening.

She drank it all.

Nyva gasped.

The joyousness, the bliss, the presence that the draft summoned was...was...indescribable. This journey had started with the low of the Golden Goat, like she had just been stoned in the head without any of the pain and only the disorientation and dreamy madness. There was the wild peak her sensations climbed to when she consumed the apple...and then there was whatever she was feeling now. She was not flying high; she was not slithering low; she was drifting in stillness. She was splitting in two, or she already had split in two. Or had she always been divided and only now, after drinking this evil wine, did she understand the truth?

Nyva watched herself from outside. That brown-haired, emerald-eyed girl was a marionette. Nyva had rejected that fate after she had killed the boar. She had affirmed that she was no one's puppet.

Yet here she was, a puppet again. She felt naïve to have made herself such a powerful promise, one that others refused to let her keep.

"Did you drink?"

Nyva the girl pressed her lips shut. Nyva the marionette called out, "I have drunk your potion," her voice steady and clear. The music from outside did not seem as loud anymore. Her heart no longer raced; it pounded out a heavy, slow thud, like a bass drum in her ears. Even her heartbeat felt warm and somehow soothing to her now.

The door was locked. Nyva had turned the key. Yet the door opened.

The marionette did not perform; she stood stock-still, though Nyva screamed and raged inside. A woman stepped through the door and onto the stage.

She wore a headdress of long black and red feathers, which made her appear at first to be well over six feet tall. She had almond skin and almond-shaped eyes with purple irises. Over her sleek figure she wore a gown of golden mail, the interlinking rings so small that there must have been millions of them to form the garment. In one hand, she held a water pipe of black volcanic glass. Over her other forearm —which was bent at the elbow and held across her abdomen —was draped a garment of emerald silk.

"I am Mother Roots," she said, the words spoken like a devil's kiss, the S on the end of "Roots" soft and sinful. A snake's hiss.

Nyva's marionette smiled and curtsied.

"I'm so, so sorry about the way Welfric speaks." Mother Roots' eyes rolled back into her skull as she spoke so Nyva could only see the whites through her hardly open lids. Her head swayed back and forth, chin tilting side to side, like a pendulum being slowed by the fog of a dream. The big black and red feathers of her headdress danced as she moved her head, and Nyva could see traces of the red tips lingering in her vision. And then the blur of the red tips became the blur of the full headdress, which morphed into the blur of the whole tanned face until Nyva was seeing many Mother Roots in front of her.

"It's…all right," Nyva said. It was not all right. It was anything but all right. But Nyva did not want to rouse this woman's rage; she was finally feeling easy, no longer afraid.

I am still afraid! something in the Nyva that was the watcher tried to shout, but the marionette and the one holding the strings had no use for what the audience had to say, or think, or feel. This play was for the players and the plotters, not the watchers.

Mother Roots—with both hands occupied—stopped her swaying, and her eyes rolled down again, so that the purple irises were again visible. Her calm face became a scowl etched in stone, and the beautiful woman now looked more a feral animal. The marionette did not move; the watcher could not move. Mother Roots head-butted Nyva in the face, the cracking force of the assault so shocking that it nearly merged the watcher and the marionette back into one. It nearly snapped Nyva back into her rage and her fear and called up whatever corrosive devil was in her blood that she had used to boil that boar.

"It is not all right," said Mother Roots. Calm again, eyes in the back of her skull again, head swaying like a slithering snake again.

The watcher Nyva watched the blood drip from the marionette's nose over her lips and off her chin. The droplets fell and spattered onto the golden cup that had held the cursed wine, so that the blood now slid down like crimson tears from the cup's faceless emerald eyes.

"It is never all right for a man to use that word in the presence of a goddess," said Mother Roots.

Nyva nodded.

"Welfric has been warned, time and time again. And yet the cycle continues." The goddess in the headdress let out a long, dreamy sigh. "To end this cycle, there must be a punishment—an eye must be taken." Mother Roots walked to the bed and sat down at the foot of it. She placed the emerald silk garment on the sheets, and Nyva could now see the garment was a dress. "And it will be taken."

Mother Roots patted the bed with her now-free hand for Nyva to come sit with her.

The marionette obliged, even as blood still ran down her nose.

Nyva centered herself, the watcher and the marionette becoming one. She hesitated before reaching the bed, and pinched her nose to try and stem the bleeding. She refused to play the game any longer.

I will fight off the effect; I will take back control.

"Let it bleed," said Mother Roots.

Nyva's strength and determination fractured again at the command. The marionette obeyed, and the watcher fell silent, paralyzed, seeing all, doing nothing.

She sat next to Mother Roots.

Mother Roots placed the water pipe between her thighs then lowered her mouth to it. In the bowl were tiny crystals that looked like blue chunks of salt. Mother Roots elevated her hand a few inches above the bowl, and then her fingers started to dance. A thin stream of flame blazed from the air in front of her dancing fingers down to the blue crystals in the bowl. They heated until they glowed a beaming yellow gold then faded to ash. Smoke pulled through the bowl and into the wide, aqua-filled chamber of the water pipe.

With a delicate hand, Mother Roots gripped the glowing-hot bowl between her thumb and forefinger and inhaled air and smoke. She stared into Nyva's eyes without exhaling, the drone of the processions' music slinking through the cracks in the closed windows and doors. Seconds passed, maybe minutes, maybe an eternity, then Mother Roots exhaled.

As the thick golden smoke billowed out of her mouth like a dragon's fire, the very flesh on her face started to melt. Blood and skin and muscle turned to sludge and cascaded off a glistening white skull. Her eyes popped and viscous, boiling goop trailed down the skull's cheekbones. The horror that filled Nyva was trapped inside, a frantic bird in a cage.

The skull kept staring at her as it swayed, snakelike, its teeth chattering.

The cloud of golden smoke hovered, then pushed into Nyva's nostrils and mouth. She breathed it, tasted it, ate it.

With each breath, her vision became more and more strange. At first it haloed, and then it became kaleidoscopic. There was no up or down, no foreground or background, just a mad jumble of shapes and colors and the easily decipherable skull of Mother Roots, which even now had skin and muscle re-forming back overtop of white bone. The charred goop of her eyes crawled back up her cheeks and became the orbs they had been before, under lids of flesh and blood.

"Undresssssss."

Nyva again came back together for a moment, long enough to be horrified anew, long enough to fight against the command.

"Undress."

Nyva fractured.

The marionette stood and undressed, while Nyva screamed in tortured silence and railed against the will that was not her own.

Mother Roots leaned over to place the pipe on the floor, then she got on her knees in front of the naked marionette. She grabbed hold of Nyva's buttocks and pulled her close so that Mother Roots' had her left ear pressed up against Nyva's lower abdomen. The tips of the headdress's feathers tickled the marionette's nose, and she tilted her head back, about to sneeze.

"Hold it," said Mother Roots.

The marionette obeyed and held the pressure in.

"I'm listening," said Mother Roots.

For what? the watcher Nyva tried to ask. Of course, she could not be heard. She was too far away, on some other plane.

"Ah, very good," Mother Roots exclaimed after a pregnant moment. Then she stood and took a diagonal step backward away from the marionette. "You may sneeze now."

The marionette let the pressure go.

"Put on the emerald dress..." Mother Roots' voice trailed as she walked away from Nyva.

The marionette lifted the emerald gown. It was a thin material and had not a single button. The style was nothing a lady would wear—too short, too scant, sleeveless, and unadorned—but the material was undeniably royal. It glowed like the emeralds in the eyes on the golden cup that had held the wine.

Nyva donned the dress, as easy to get on as it was simplistic in its thin, flowing design. Mother Roots was at the door now. She opened it and, looking back, said, "Tonight it is you who will take your mother's place in playing the Emerald Lady." She nodded, as if in thanks, then stepped off the stage and closed the door.

Nyva laughed as she sagged against the wall, for it was either laugh or cry, and she had no tears left.

Something else laughed. "Hehe."

Nyva pushed off the wall and spun, her gaze flicking to the dim corners of the room.

"Nyva, what are you laughing about?" whispered Black Brenna from somewhere in the room. *Somewhere in her skull.*

She was about to ask the rodent she had once feared—the rat sorcerer she had thought she stomped out in the ravine—how he had survived, but he spoke first.

"Don't speak aloud, just think. Turn around… No, to your right, more to your left… Look down…"

On the ground, black ink squeezed out of a crack in the floorboards. Materializing into the form of Black Brenna, the floating black ink was soon entirely rat and fur.

"Look into my eyes." Brenna's mouth did not move as he spoke. He thought his words to her. "Just think."

"Who are you, really?" Nyva thought to Brenna.

He shook his head, and Nyva could not be certain due to the dim candlelight and the fact that Brenna's head was the size of an egg, but she thought he may have rolled his eyes in disgust.

"Wise up, hehe. Wise up." The volume of his thought-speak was at a shout. "We went over that in the ravine. You know who I am. I am your real keeper. I am your real Nan, sent here by your real mother to get you back. Your mother and Diana, they hate each other, absolutely, positively despise each other."

"Then why am I here? Why was I raised near the village of Wardbrook? Near Diana, on her lands? Why did you and my mother not raise me, *Nan*? And what of my father?" Nyva demanded of the sorcerer, words without sound. Her pulse pounded in her temples as she clenched her jaw in a growing fury.

"I think you might not truly wish to know your father's identity, hehe. And it matters not in this moment."

"What matters, then? What matters more than understanding the story that brought me to this madhouse? The plot that strung the trail of my life?"

"Getting out. That is what matters more, eh?"

Nyva's pulsing blood became hot. Painfully so. Her skin burned, not like it was on fire. It burned like she was corroding. Like acid and plague were boiling her from the inside out. She had felt this way before...with the boar.

But she said nothing, not even in thought. Instead, she listened, because she had not listened to Brenna before when he warned her away from this place, these people, and she had proven herself a fool.

"You have to fight," the rat sorcerer said. "You must fight every step of the way. They won't kill you. They will beat you down and try to break you, but they won't kill you. No, not until the end. Even if you kill some of them, they will keep you alive, right until the very end."

The end of what? And why keep me alive? The fear that Nyva thought had been drowned by the magic wine and Mother Roots' golden smoke returned now like ants scouring the pantries of her mind for things to bite and shred and eat. And eat. And eat.

"In a few moments, they are going to knock again at the door. They are going to ask if you have donned the dress. The door will open, and Mother Roots will not be there, but Welfric and ten more men will be. I saw them coming up the stairs while I snuck in through the walls and floors. Well, in truth, there are seven men...three of them I would not call men. I'd call them lycans, hehe. You have to fight them."

"Are you going to help me fight them, rat?" Nyva asked, and somehow, she already knew an excuse was coming.

"No. You need to thin their numbers, to fight alone while I go for Diana. I will kill her, and I will kill her husband and slave, the moon wolf, if he does not move aside. Hehe."

"Are you capable of that? Of killing Diana and Alexander Ward both, in their house, surrounded by her allies?" Nyva very much doubted the little man-rat before her, who stood jolting his head side to side and moving his fingers like he strummed imaginary lute strings, was capable of such a feat.

Brenna smiled a horrible smile, and his tiny eyes in his egg head went wide. "I doubt it, even with the two allies I have recruited. I truly doubt it. Hehe."

Even in the face of likely failure, capture, death, he was willing to try. She would do no less.

There came a knock at the door.

"Have you donned the emerald dress?" asked Welfric.

Nyva's pulse raced. Brenna nodded at her.

"I have," Nyva called.

The knock came again.

"Might we come in, my lady?" said Welfric.

If I say no, will you stay out?

The door flung open.

Brenna dripped into the cracks in the floor like black ink.

Welfric and his companions filed into the room. In was a large bedchamber, but it did not well fit the seven men and—as Brenna had said—three lycans, who panted with slack, open jaws, their glowing yellow eyes fixed upon her like they were simply awaiting the snap of Welfric's fingers to lunge forward and sink their fangs into fresh meat.

"You'll have to work for it," Nyva said, and in that moment, she realized she was her own self again. So had it been the bitter wine, or had it been the presence of Mother Roots that had made her so acquiescent earlier? And why had Mother Roots released her vile hold now? Why not keep Nyva the marionette? Nyva did not trust the foul games of these people.

The men laughed.

The wolves panted.

"Don't do this, Nyva," Welfric told her with a smile that said, *Please do this, Nyva.*

Nyva thought of the boar. She pictured it boiling under

her will. She called for that power, that sensation, and she felt the corrosion surfacing. Her spirits soared, then crashed as the sensation died. It would not come to her beck and call. It felt locked up, like it was going to boil *her* like the boar and not these monsters who now assailed her.

She had held the bow Diana had given her on the boar hunt. She had summoned an arrow from her blood. She had corroded the boar. While holding the bow.

A catalyst, you fool.

Had she learned nothing from Nan? She needed a catalyst.

She glanced around the room, her gaze sliding to the emerald-eyed goblet she had tossed to the floor. It lay between the feet of a wolf-man, far out of reach.

What else had power? What else could channel the emerald magic inside of her?

Frantic, she looked about, looked past the bed, only to have her eyes return. At the foot sat the water pipe, the one Mother Roots had left behind. The one, Nyva had no doubt, had been left for *her*.

*I*n all my years of knowing Diana Ward—nearly the entirety of my life—she spoke to me only once of her past. Her distant past, ages ago, empires ago, worlds ago. So distant were those times that one could even say they were ages, empires, and worlds that were yet to be.

It was the morning after the Deadmen's party. Diana, Alexander, and I wandered through the estate grounds. Truly picturesque, I remember. Sun, birds, white clouds, niceties any traveler could ever expect to see in the fields and ravines of Brynth. It was an ironic juxtaposition to how I recall I felt that late morning.

I did not want to think on it any more, that most horrible of all the Deadmen's parties. I don't want to think on it now. But I must. I think on it for a time every day. I have since the events of that party, and I think they will flicker in my mind as I die. Treachery, betrayal, dishonor, and so many other wicked things done, and all in the name of love. Love for something I could not yet fully understand.

I recall Diana was deathly pale as we walked that morning; her bronzed skin from her time away in sunny, evil places had lost its color overnight. She was as white as bone, and dark circles hung under her eyes. The spells she had used in the night had taken their toll.

Alexander too looked haggard, as if he had aged a decade over the course of the night. His arms were wrapped around his wife, holding a black shawl over her shoulders. She still wore her white dress from the party. It was white no longer; it was a blood-red dress with spots of white now.

She was somber, red-eyed... She had been weeping, and I know it was the only time I ever saw regret on the sorceress' face. It lingered there longer than a moment, and she was either too tired to contain the expression or she trusted me enough by that point to *reveal it. Either way, it did not last. She soon looked forward and stood erect with pride. She shrugged her husband's hands away and gave him back the shawl. It was that pride, that certainty in all things, that I found most intriguing about Diana. A dominance of will that made up the violent beauty of her core.*

I feared her.

I revered her.

And in silence, I adored her.

"It had to be done," Diana said, her voice as hard as stone.

"Diana..." What Alexander was going to say, or if he was going to even say anything more than his wife's name, I know not.

She glanced at me. "I will tell you a tale, Darcy Weaver. I was twenty-five years as you and I know them now," she said. "For mortals, that is oft more than half a life. For my kind, twenty-five years does not even see the seedling of life sprout.

"My father sat atop his throne in his mountain hall. A wizard and a man, a warrior and a king, he was. And next to him sat my mother. My mother, the most beautiful giantess to ever live. Indeed, she was the last full-blooded giant of our world. The bulwark of the mountain, Bronhulga, Last Shield Maiden of the Giants, my mother," Diana said as she stared out over her sleeping lands.

"So tall was my mother that when she knelt, my father's eyes would be at her breast, and my father was tall and broad by any man's standards. How they managed to conceive three children without my father being pulverized, I know not." Diana threw her head back and laughed. When she finally stopped, she wiped away a tear. Alexander had stepped closer to her again with the shawl ready in case a potent blast of melancholia was to follow the mania. She raised a hand to him and stared him down. He retreated, and Diana continued her tale.

"Stiggis was getting tattooed by a druid in one of the corners of the hall. He was surrounded by the swarms of sycophants that always surrounded him. Satyrs and men, mostly. The dryads always took a liking to him too. They loved the way he could tell a

story; they loved the way he infused purpose into everything from great battles to the time of day one takes a shit. My brother Stiggis could explain to anyone the hidden signs in their lives, and he was still just a boy of fifty years.

"'Do you recall, daughter, your purpose on this day?' my father asked. My mother smiled. We looked near identical, her and I—but, of course, for the fact that she was near twenty feet tall.

"'I know my purpose,' I said.

"'Good. Your brother is waiting,' my father said. He was not speaking of Stiggis. He spoke of my other brother, my brother who was locked away in a vast subterranean chamber beneath the mountain palace. From behind my father's massive throne of gold-embossed stone stepped forth one of the many-eyed monks of the Shahidi in his black robes and black turban. His eyes grew over his cheeks and jaws, and even down to his chin. He must have been very high up in the order to have had such sight. He held a rope, and at the end of it was a stag of white-moon fur. It was as big as any horse and had fourteen prongs upon its antlers, an even seven on each.

"My mother stood from her throne and lifted my father down from his.

"'Thank you, my love,' Father said to Mother, then he turned to the Shahidi and, taking the stag's leash from him, walked the creature to me. He handed it over and clasped my hands as I took it.

"'I am proud of you, proud of your bravery. This is the day you accept what we are. What you are.'

"I knew so little in those days. I knew not what my blood meant. I knew not what my older brother would become. I knew not the reason I was chosen to take the stag. I knew nothing. But I was about to learn everything."

≈

CHAPTER SIXTEEN

RAISED BY WOLVES

*N*yva's eyes shifted back and forth, assessing the sizes and threats and sneers and scowls of men and wolf-men.

Use the catalyst! The memory of Diana's shout when they had hunted the boar echoed in Nyva's ears.

She took her eyes from her foes, and even as she turned her head, she was lunging for Mother Roots' ensorcelled water pipe.

An eye must be taken, Mother Roots had said. *And it will be taken.* The woman—the *witch*—had not forgotten the pipe. She had left it for Nyva. Perhaps in sisterhood and solidarity. Perhaps because she hated Welfric's crass words. Perhaps simply because she hated Welfric. Nyva and no way to know. Reasons did not matter.

Welfric lunged for the catalyst too, seeing too late what Nyva went for. The others were yet to attack. They thought she was no threat, though surely Diana had warned them. Or perhaps she had not.

Nyva gripped the obsidian pipe and swung it like a mace with all her strength. She was surprised by the weight of it, and she was thankful for it. The bulb of the pipe smashed into Welfric's eye, and he stumbled back, screaming and howling.

The other men and wolves laughed.

"Wild, bitch!" shouted one of the wolves in a horrible, inhuman voice, hardly possible to understand as the words struggled down the long snout and past the fangs. But Nyva understood them, and though she knew the words were meant as a curse, she took them with pride. She had felled Welfric. She would fell them all.

Welfric slid down the wall, his back to it, both hands over the gift she had given him.

"Welfric, you got bloody blinded by a whelp witch holding a water pipe!" The man who spoke stepped forward in the group and went to Welfric's side. He too—Nyva only now realized—was not entirely a man, for he had the legs of a goat, and beneath his cowl were lumps of filed-down horns protruding from his forehead. The others laughed, but the three lycanthropes were more cautious, and although they growled their own laughter, they began to circle Nyva.

They did not understand what was happening. They did not understand what the water pipe was. *Baser animals.* They thought she merely used it as a club.

Welfric let out a piteous moan, and all eyes went from Nyva to him. She eyed the open doorway, wishing she could simply run free, but the throng blocked her path. She was well and truly trapped.

Nyva put her lips to the water pipe, and although she did not know the reasoning behind why she did what she did next, she knew it was the right thing to do. Most of the filthy water used as filter for the smoke of Mother Root's crystals had spilled out when she hit Welfric in the eye, but some remained. And all the thick filth that remained in the bottom like a congealing black abyss in the belly of the obsidian water pipe, Nyva imbibed with a vengeance.

The laughter of the men and man-things in the chamber became even louder at this, loud enough to blot out Welfric's wailing.

The taste was toxic… It was evil, if a taste could be evil, like she was drinking the fumes of burning sulfur in liquid form, and it slunk down the back of her throat all congealed, like an ancient molasses.

Nyva felt something stir inside her, the something that had stirred when she summoned the arrow and when she made the boar's flesh melt.

Welfric's mouth opened and closed in motions of silent screams as strings of decaying flesh pulled off his cheekbone and eyebrow, clinging to his palm as he let it drop away from his eye. His eyeball had popped, and from the remains, scores of little mayflies hatched from miniscule eggs. They flew out of the socket and danced above the destroyed man's head like black embers.

The satyr and the men winced.

"This is one hell of a start to the party," said one.

"I'm not drunk enough yet to be looking at that," said another.

A third levelled his malevolent gaze on Nyva and said, "Oh, we're going to enjoy having you at this party, bitch. We are going to enjoy."

Eyes narrowed, the satyr's gaze slid from Welfric to Nyva to the pipe clutched against her belly. "It's a catalyst. By Dammar's eye-covered antlers, Mother Roots left her a catalyst!"

The lycanthropes growled. Then they lunged for Nyva, and she scuttled back, putting the bed between them.

The sulfur bog she had swallowed rose back up from her belly, and she struggled to hold it down.

The satyr stared at her, and whatever he saw made him shout, "Get the fuck out of the way!"

Nyva lost her battle, and the first twitches and convulsions of the coming retching began. Her stomach coiled, and the agony nearly dropped her.

Time slowed as her head spun faster than the world moved.

The first of the wolves grabbed her wrist.

The satyr hoisted Welfric on his shoulder and went for the door.

Nyva began to spew.

The snarling wolf face before her was consumed by black and green death.

Venom, poison, acid, *corrosion.*

A mixture of skeleton and molten fur and flesh, blackened like tar and reeking like sulfur, pooled at her feet and burned the floor. Most of the enemies retreated through the door, the still-screaming Welfric in their grasps.

The remaining two wolves fell upon her. Four claws grabbed her now, two on each arm.

They grabbed at the catalyst, smooth volcanic glass still clutched in her hands, and they pulled. Their claws sank into her shoulders, slowly penetrating, and she felt the strands and fibers of her muscle squelching and tearing.

Somehow, with unnatural strength—perhaps brought on by the catalyst itself—Nyva held fast to the pipe.

She stared at the pile of muscle and gore and death that had been the first wolf.

Yes. She had done that.

I made you that. I am the monster. I am the predator.

"Let go of the catalyst, bitch!" snarled the wolf on her left as he leaned his stinking snout to her ear.

"Fuck you," she said.

The wolf sank his fangs into her ear.

The cartilage crunched, and Nyva screamed as she pulled away. The ear tore.

"Let go!" snarled the other wolf, yanking on the pipe.

"No!" Nyva still held tight. The wolf on her ear shook his head twice as the other held her in place.

Her ear came off, but the catalyst remained clutched against her belly.

She saw their bestial faces, their fangs, the spittle dripping from their mouths as she screamed. But all she heard were the sounds of the otherworldly instruments being played by the parades on the way to the house.

≈

Cullum's head bobbed and his fingers snapped, then in unison, every few beats, Damos and Cullum both went, *clap, clap, clap.*

This cannot be real. I feel not the Bloodburn. *I feel... I feel nothing, nothing at all. Nothing except fear. Not in my hand. Not in my heart or in my mind.*

He was repulsed by the dance, by the music. His thoughts willed him to stop, but his body refused to obey no matter how much mental effort he exerted in stopping his feet from walking and tapping to the beat of the drums and horns and stringed instruments of devils' kin. They played their mad, idiot songs as they too danced their way toward the great black house of Wardbrook.

He was halfway there now, making his way up the tree-covered hill. And still Cullum could do no more than control the direction in which his eyes looked, and even this caused him to feel like he would collapse from exhaustion. They walked on a path that had not been there the day before. Ash beneath his feet. Walls of charred branches to his sides, as if a forest fire had burned the woods to ash, but only to make this path, and then the flames were gone.

A bronze-skinned man wearing the bone mask of a giant bird with long gold and black feathers protruding from a headdress did some kind of acrobatic feat next to Cullum. He caught the movement only from the corner of his eye, for his head was forced straight ahead by the power of the song.

With a shriek, the man in the bone mask stumbled into Cullum, knocking them both to the ground.

Cullum hit the ash-covered trail... *My knees crash against hard, cold stone.*

The woods were gone. The ash trail no more. The procession evaporated from being. There was no sky. Only a towering stone ceiling lit by strange arcane lights and markings he could not understand. Living roots wrapped around his ankles and wrists, digging into the back of his skull, his blood flowing from many wounds. But he felt no pain.

This is a dream. A dream of a dream. A dream from which I cannot wake.

The sisters scream in their pool far away, or are they laughing at me?

Flashes of green. A dress. Flashes of brown. Her hair.

The music, the woods, the ash trail, the trumpeting call of the tusked behemoth that tailed the procession. A hundred evil dancing forms, costumed humans impossible to decipher from hairy, fanged, clawed beasts.

It all came bleeding back into view.

The man in the bone mask hoisted Cullum up. Mad purple eyes stared out from the shadowed sockets of the giant bird skull.

"You're not dreamin' bruddah. You're just dead. You're just a dead man now. One of the Deadmen now." A feral white smile gleamed out from the open beak. "Hahaha!" Even before the echo of his laughter faded away, the masked man disappeared, as did the procession and the music.

Cullum's eyes flicked right, left, right as all around him the trees grew, reaching like hands. *No...not* like *hands...they* are *hands.*

Hands and arms split through the trunks and branches and grew up, up, up into a yellow sky that was no longer night, nor was it day. And staring down was a black sun-moon.

"Stop dancing." A girl's voice.

He stopped dancing. Just like that, the spell was lifted.

"You have forgotten again, haven't you?" asked the girl.

Cullum turned to look at her now, his will his own again, control of his body returned to him. She stood in the middle of the ash path.

It was *her.* The girl in the emerald dress from his vision in the pool. It was the girl he and Damos and Brenna had pledged to save.

"It's you!" Cullum said, his heart racing with hope and something more, something sweet and wild. The dancing procession and the mad music faded from his memories. They were part of a different life now. A different world.

The girl smiled patiently and said "It is me."

"I have to save you," Cullum said, and ran toward her. "It was what I was sent here to do. I have to save you from *them.*"

"Oh, sweet Cullum," she said with affection and familiarity, like she knew him, like she had known him for many years.

That gave rise to a fear and a dread that burned so brightly in his gut that Cullum thought he might just catch fire. The burn made him run all the faster. Ahead of him, the girl started running too. She ran for the house and called back to him, "You can't save me. Not now. Not yet. You are too late, and too early. Perhaps it is I who save you."

Smoke filled Cullum's nostrils, and he looked down to see the trail of ash catching flame. The girl's emerald dress caught fire, but she made no a sound as she ran through the doors of the black house of Wardbrook, leaving an imprint of white ash upon the oak.

Cullum placed his flaming hands on the door and shoved it open.

Glowing in the center of a pitch-black foyer was a giant man, with long hair and a beard of white-gold, his skin marked with blue runic tattoos.

The man who gave Lazarus the book. The traveler of dreams.

In a voice as deep as the room was dark, the man-giant said, "Welcome, Deadman."

~

"*Darcy, my love. I've brought you something to eat,*" *said Darcy's wife.*

To Darcy's surprise, he was thankful for the interruption.

When had he last eaten? Yesterday...he hadn't eaten since yesterday, by the gods.

"My dear, my dear, you are too good to me. I don't deserve you, and you deserve better than me," Darcy said, surprising himself, for he did not spill out affection to his wife often. She truly was undeserving of his neglect, but no one got what they deserved. That was just the irrevocable nature of things.

His wife's delicate hand stroked the back of his head and neck, and she placed down the meal before him.

It was uncooked. Lightly salted. Dark brown. Stinking now that it was beneath his nose. Little white things burrowing in and out of the edges of the slab. Maggot-riddled venison.

Darcy smiled and started to laugh.

"Oh, well done, my peach, well done! What a beautiful meal," he said, and wasted not a moment in grabbing the bloody, stinking slab and lifting it above the candle flame.

"You have not gone hunting in some time, Darcy, and you have not hired the huntsman. You refuse me leave to do it myself. You have not gone in to Aldwick for months to see traders, and you have sent no man to do it. How is it possible to be so wealthy and have a son who eats so little, who looks like a beggar child?"

"Eating like the poor is a good thing. It builds character," Darcy said in a hollow tone. He did not want to say that. He wanted to scream out for Aldous. He wanted to go running and find the boy, to make sure his wife was only speaking in exaggerations. But he did not move; he did not do what he wanted. He just stood there dangling the rotten meat above the candle flame.

He knew he had gone mad. He knew his time with the Dead-men, his time with Diana...it was seeping in, bleeding into the now, from the past, from the future... There was no difference between the three. So often now he was not sure when he was writing, or just thinking about his time with the Deadmen and Diana. Diana. Diana. Was he with them now, only thinking about the cellar and his poor wife and his neglected son? The boy, so young and chipper he hardly noticed, and if he did, he did not whimper.

Darcy's wife did not seem to notice as Darcy willed the candle flame to grow. She just kept on assailing him. He was not listening to her; he was listening to the maggots burn and explode in the now preposterously large candle flame.

"Darcy! Darcy, by the sun, the meat is on fire! Put down your hand! It's burning!" She screamed and backed away.

Darcy kept looking at her. His hand was *burning, as was the meat. His skin sizzled and melted into the charring meat in his hand. He held his wife's gaze a moment longer, then he slapped the meat back down onto the plate. He smacked it again, then again. The black ash crackled, the fire and smoke billowed and died, and the uncooked center of the meat squelched.*

Darcy drew his oak-hilted knife with his unburned hand. The knife was his first ever catalyst; he had made it himself not two years past. Diana had helped him.

Diana...

He sliced into the meat and flayed off a strand.

"Darcy..." His wife gasped as she kept on backing toward the stairs that went up from the cellar, up from Darcy's woven hell back to the mundane world above.

Darcy put the rotten, charred venison in his mouth and chewed. And the sour juices dripped from his lips and down his throat.

"Thank you for dinner, wife."

She was up the stairs.

"You are what you eat, as they say," he said.

The cellar door slammed shut.

"Charred. Bitter. And rotten," he whispered to himself and the shadows while his soul wept for his son.

~

CHAPTER SEVENTEEN

THE WICKER MAN AND THE MOON WOLF

*N*yva's blood ran in warm streams down the side of her head and arms where the wolves' claws and fangs had made their holes and left her earless.

The mad music was too loud for her to make out what the lycans now growled at her. The processions were no longer on their way to the great black house of Wardbrook. They were inside the belly of it, and the clamor of their commingling songs was near deafening.

"Obey!" one of the wolf-men roared over the cry of the insane instruments, its blood-wet snout touching the chasm in the side of her head where her ear used to be.

Nyva's blood ran in a focused stream, as if it were moved by a thinking mind—*moved by her own mind*—to the pile of slaughter that was the corroded lycan at her feet. By her will, her blood took the form of hundreds of beetles and centipedes that scurried into the corpse. The mess of bone, hunks of fur, and partially dissolved meat squirmed and stewed in the evil yellow-green discharge with which Nyva had felled the beast.

Rise, Nyva willed it. *Rise.*

And the beetles and centipedes moved through the dead flesh, writhing and twitching. The lycanthropes' ears perked up as they heard sounds no human could hear, and now they looked to the corpse as it rose from the floor in scores of bubbles that grew and swelled and finally burst.

Rats.

Undead rats, fashioned of melted meat and fur and bone, born from the decay, spawning and snapping into motion as fast as flies in a swamp.

"By Bodan's axe of dread!" snarled one of the wolves.

The other was already whimpering and yapping as three of the rats fell upon one of his legs, quickly turning it bloody with tooth and claw. The first lycan let go of both Nyva and his grip on the water pipe to defend against the rats. The other waited too long, and one of the rats leapt into the air and sank its buck teeth—formed of the dead lycan's bones—into the neck of Nyva's assailant.

The second wolf let go of the obsidian water pipe, leaving it now solely in Nyva's grasp. But with his other claw, he retained his grip on Nyva's shoulder. Then he leaned in and sank his teeth into her upper arm even as one of Nyva's summoned rats tried to rip out his throat.

There was no sharp sensation to the bite. Instead, it felt as if her upper arm was caught between two anvils. She could hear her bones crunching, and it sounded too much like the rattles of the music players who reveled in the house.

Then came the pain. Nyva let out a guttural exhale that shoved bile from her belly and made her foam at the mouth.

It hurt—even with the ensorcelled wine and the effects of Mother Roots' smoke upon her, it hurt terribly.

But she was not done fighting.

She was not even close to done fighting.

"Kill them!" she screamed at her rat things. Like a furred, clawed wave, they surged over Nyva's assailants, tearing cloth and skin and muscle, gnawing through to expose white bone. One of the rats bit out the eyeball of the Lycan still on Nyva's arm. With a howl, the wolf let go of her to use both its claws to defend against the creatures that rent it.

The other Lycan was on all fours biting off one rat's head as the others flayed its flesh. Yellow acid spilled out of the decapitated rat, and the wolf yowled, a bloodcurdling sound, as its tongue and the front portion of its lower jaw began to melt off and drip to the floor.

Nyva's rats overwhelmed the wolves. They chewed through the tendons in the backs of their legs, leaving them bleeding on all fours.

One went for Nyva, heaving itself forward with one arm and swiping with the other. Red droplets sprayed off its shaggy black mane as it lunged.

Its legs were too heavy, and Nyva had no trouble getting out of the way. It flopped on the bloody ground like a fish, panting as blood pooled around its head.

She walked over the wolf and raised the water pipe above her head.

"Are you enjoying the party?" she asked between panting breaths.

She brought her makeshift mace down. The impact made a hollow thud that reverberated in the chamber of the water pipe.

The wolf grunted, and a tear of blood formed in its eye.

The wolf's skull did not explode.

The catalyst did not explode.

Nyva leaned back, stretching.

"Eh, mister wolf? Are you having fun now?" She swung again.

Clunk. Grunt. More blood. The other Lycan is silent now; the rats are burrowing inside it now.

"Are you happy you came?" She swung again.

Clunk-crack. No grunt.

She could see the brains.

Her own blood fell from her chin and hit the lycan's exposed gray matter. It sizzled and steamed. Blisters formed and then popped, and from them spawned black bees with green stingers. They scuttled out of the chasm in the wolf's skull then took flight, and soon they swirled around Nyva, a cyclone of carapace and wing. More rat things were growing from the other corpse, and soon the corpses were no more, and her rats and swarm of acid-stinger insects were many.

She could hear shouting and footsteps as more men made their way up the stairs and down the hall toward the chamber. There was no way out for her. There was only the fight that had been and the one yet to come.

Through the open chamber door, she watched the advancing next wave: walking skeletons—all over seven feet tall—garbed in black robes and black turbans fastened with obsidian. The one in the lead was no skeleton. He stood a little over six feet; his beard and moon-bright mane of hair made him look as animal as the lycans and the satyr.

"Alexander Ward," Nyva screamed.

The rats and the bees prepared to swarm.

"I don't want this. I never wanted this," Alexander said, his voice deep and caring. "But what a man wants, and what a man must do…they rarely coincide." His gaze met hers. Tired lids drooped over a sharp stare. His were the woeful eyes of a man who, through dark deals and darker deeds, had become king in the abyss.

There was something in the way he looked at her…

"You don't want this?" Nyva shouted. The army of her little hell rats twitched with anticipation; the buzz of the bees echoed through her ear and the bloody hole where the other one had been. "Then stop it. End it. Let me go free."

Alexander adjusted the claymore that rested on his

shoulder and drained the cup he held in his free hand before throwing it to the ground. His expression hardened. "Get her. But no more wounds."

"Yes, my liege," all the tall skeletons said at once, the words like death sighs, and their black eye sockets glowed crimson like Nan's candle flame as the syllables passed through their clacking teeth. They advanced at a casual walk, and something told Nyva it was not because these things underestimated her like her last foes had. It was because they were dead certain that they were going to get her regardless of whatever defense she offered.

But a defense she would offer, even in the face of the impossible. Because there was yet hope. There were still Black Brenna and his allies. She only needed to hold on a little longer.

With a shout, Nyva threw both her hands out before her like she was shoving an invisible attacker. Her tide of rats and insects poured out of the chamber and down the hall at the tall living skeletons and Alexander.

The robed skeletons at the front lifted their arms in the same motion as Nyva, their crimson eyes igniting with blasts of deep red flame. Instinct told her to get the hell out of the doorway even before she saw what the skeletal minions of Wardbrook summoned.

She put her back to the wall on the right side of the door and flinched as she heard her rat things scream. Then she felt the heat.

Molten crimson flame and viscous fluids blasted through the door. An ember—*droplet?*—of the magic spilled onto her shoulder, and the burn started off feeling like she was being flayed by a blade of ice. Then there was the heat, and her screams.

Her rat army was left in ashes.

She wasted no time feeling sorry for herself. They would

not kill her. That was what Brenna had said. They would try to break her, but they'd keep her alive until the end. So she wasn't done yet.

Her circumstance was dire. The corpses had provided materials for her rats and insects, but they were gone, burned by the flame. She looked around the room, desperate, her gaze landing on the window.

"Don't bother going for the window. It's bound shut with unbreakable spells," Alexander called from the hallway.

Nyva clutched the water pipe, her blood dripping down into it, over it. The weight of the pipe grew heavier while she simultaneously felt both stronger and dizzier. She drew back her arm and, with everything she could dredge from the depths of her will, threw the gift from Mother Roots at the window.

Light blinded, hot and white.

All-engulfing light, drowning in the sun, drink the fire, bring the night.

Air swelled Nyva's chest. She heard sounds of voices and distant music, but everything sounded as though coming at her through water. Shards of broken glass cut into her hands as she pushed herself to her knees and then her feet. She shook her head, disoriented.

"What—" And then her muzzy thought cleared and she turned to the window, which was a window no more. It was an open portal to the night and a chance to run. She did not care where, she would just run, and she would draw enough attention for Brenna and the allies he spoke of to launch their assassination upon Diana.

The glass cut the bottoms of her feet, and the remnants of the crimson tar summoned by the skeleton men burned her. Heart pounding, she reached for the shattered sill, ready to leap. Then she slid on bloody soles and grabbed the sides of the window frozen at the edge. Night so dark she could not see the lawn below yawned beyond the shattered pane. She knew how high this window was. She had looked out during the day, and memory told her it was high enough to break her leg, perhaps high enough to break her back.

She looked back at Alexander and his minions. They, too, had been momentarily blinded by the light of the explosion, and it appeared the undead were more easily dazed by such things, for they were now stumbling over their own black robes and tripping on each other's feet.

One of them slammed into Alexander's shoulder. He stumbled and smacked his face on the boney back of another.

His head jerked back, his nose bleeding, and in his pale eyes was a hatred and madness that Nyva thought must mirror the emotion in her own stare. He scowled beneath his beard and furrowed his brow, casting a deep shadow over his eyes and cheeks in the torchlight of the hall.

Nyva stood at the window. Alexander's claymore flashed into action, and with a downward swing, he battered open the skull and spine of the nearest fiend, his own ally. Bone, fabric, and dark crimson goop spattered the hallway. "I fucking told her I would come up here alone!" Alexander roared, then he swung again and eradicated another, hacking through arm, ribs, and spine, only to split the arm on the other side as well, felling the minion like a tree of bones in a single angry stroke. "Go back to her! Go back to my wife!" Alexander yelled.

"Yes, my liege," droned the things, and they went stumbling back from the direction they had just come.

Nyva stared at him. She almost dared hope that he had sent them away because he meant to free her. Hadn't there been a hint of regret in his tone, in his expression?

"You'll break your leg," Alexander said. If she were an idiot, she would think the worry in his voice was genuine.

But it wasn't. And he didn't mean to free her. Only a fool

would think it. Nyva laughed.

"How about I leap and break my fucking neck?" Nyva asked, then laughed again like a madwoman. "How would your devil whore wife like that?"

"She wouldn't like it all," Alexander said.

"What do I care? You are going to kill me no matter what, so what do I care what Diana wants?" Nyva asked, shifting her feet so her toes hung over the edge. *What if I break my neck but I do not die? What will they do to me then?*

"That's not true. You don't need to die!" Alexander shouted with emotion that surprised her. Then he said, his voice calmer, "It is not certain that they will kill you after the...ordeal you must undergo is complete."

"The ordeal I must undergo?" Having no wish to undergo any ordeal greater than those she had already known this day, Nyva surged forward and leapt.

"Dammit!" Alexander shouted from above, his voice fading as she fell toward the ground.

Nyva cried out as the pain from her ankle charged up her leg like a bolt of lightning. The world spun and went black, then white, then black again.

She rolled facedown and slammed her fists on the ground then tried to push herself to her feet.

She got up, but with the first step, her ankle rolled and she went back down, waves of pain surging through her.

"I have to get to the stable," she whispered to herself between labored breaths. "I have to get to Ishtarra. I will ride her away from here. I will ride her away. I will bring Seekers to this place. Diana and all of hers will burn on the pyres." Nyva knew every promised threat that she now gasped was a lie. But she kept saying them over and over as she dragged herself through the grass toward the stables. One arm useless. Her ankle useless. Still she moved forward, inch by agonizing inch.

The music of the hundreds of revelers inside the great black house seethed out of the smashed open window above. Its mad sounds spurred her forward as much as her fear and the mantra of vengeance that she spat through her teeth in foamy words only she understood.

She could not see the village from on her belly, only a stretch of shadowed lawn, then a stretch of moonlit lawn, then the tree line that she knew signified the beginning of the hill down to the town.

In the distance, a light burned in the house on the outskirts of the village.

The house of the coroner-surgeon.

The house where the man in the hat had been riding the other night. He *was* a Seeker; he had to be. She remembered some dream, some memory, of a vision of blue eyes staring at her and cold, strong hands grabbing her. She had to get to the Seeker. If she were lucky, he would apprehend her and then he would ride off with her, take her to be interrogated, and she would tell them all. They would hang her, or burn her, or cut off her head...because she was a witch now, after all. There was no denying that, not after what she had done to the boar and what she had just done back in the house.

At least she would die knowing that, when they were done with her, all the fury of the king and Church alike would descend upon Wardbrook, and Diana and Alexander and all the demon revelers that now drank and smoked and danced and sang would be slaughtered.

Nyva dragged herself over the lawn like she was climbing a wall of grass, thoughts of retribution, thoughts of Seekers on horses and knights of Brynth riding through Wardbrook and killing all those filthy villagers who had chased her through the woods, killing Diana and her cohorts alike— those thoughts spurred her forward like a whip to her back.

She made it past the shadow of the house, her heartbeat

too fast, the shards of glass in her palms and soles cutting too deep. Her broken bones, the holes the lycans had left in her, the chasm where her ear used to be… It was all…all too much now.

Nyva closed her eyes. She could lie here. She could sleep. She could dream. She could die here.

"No, I will not!"

She opened her eyes. She started crawling again, fingers digging into the earth—reach, pull, reach, pull.

The blades of grass began to squish through her fingers as she slid easier now across the lawn, her movements causing the soft and slimy ground beneath her to squelch.

Reach.

Before she pulled again, the realization dawned that she was on grass no longer. She lay on a bed of writhing white worms. White worms…there had been worms in her dreams…

"No…no, no, no, no!" Nyva screamed. Refusing to look back at the house, she kept her eyes forward, to where she was going, to the trees and the night sky.

But the night sky had changed from its blueish blackness to a miasmic yellow, like the whole world was engulfed in a foggy, sulfuric vapor. In the center of it all, like a void beyond space, the black sun-moon swelled.

Nyva's throat felt tight, her limbs weak, her thoughts muddled. *Do I sleep? Do I dream?*

The earth rumbled, and the trees split and fell as enormous hands and arms the size of battlements rose from the ground. The mad music from the house had fallen silent, and Nyva could only hear the world splitting now.

And something else, too. Was it moaning?

Just ahead of her from the breaking tree line, falling timbers around it, something was emerging.

A man? Is that the head of a man I am seeing?

Yes, it was a man, and he was moaning.

How did he get so high up? Is he riding some beast?

Forms of the falling trees and growing towers of arms and hands continued their slow, grinding erection from the earth as something monstrous emerged from the shadows.

A forest of hands. An orchard of brains with fruit of black tumors. Nyva closed her eyes tightly against the memory of that dream, then opened them again.

"Wake up," she whispered. "Wakeupwakeupwakeup…" She was not certain what terrified her more: the possibility that she was dreaming this moment or the possibility that she was not.

Another face appeared between the branches, this one a woman's face. She, too, was moaning, her eyes and visage mad with exhausted agony. Another face, this one a lycan's, appeared near the others, and although the head was that of a wolf, Nyva could see from the distortion of its features and the dreary whimper it made that whatever was happening to it was the same fate as the others. The thing that held the three moaning souls fully emerged then. And it took Nyva moments to understand what she was seeing.

There were more faces, all moaning, all sobbing. Men, women, lycans, satyrs, little winged fairies, and other sentient humanoid things that Nyva had never seen.

Her eyes darted from face to face, and when she could no longer bear looking at the tormented visages, she contemplated the bodies to which they were attached.

The bodies which were all impaled on sword-length thorns, through their chests, legs, arms, necks. There must have been over a score of bodies, speared there on the spines of a giant so large it looked as if it could have lifted Nan's hovel from the ground and thrown it through the sky. It stood on two legs like a man, legs made from the trunks of trees, its long arms and hands formed of thick, twisted roots.

In the center of the thing's chest was its head.

Nyva huddled on the ground; she could not go forward, nor could she return from whence she had come. She screamed as much in rage as in fear as she stared at the thing's face—a massive, unmoving, unbreathing, eyeless wicker sculpture of an owl's head made to look menacingly human by the vines of red maple leaves that formed the creature's mane of beard and hair.

"I..." said the wicker giant in a whisper that pounded on the drum of Nyva's severed ear like a raging wind. "Will... see...you...soon." It reached up its massive arm as if to wave. Then it turned its back, sword spines pinning to it a cape of tortured souls.

As the wicker giant stepped back into the forest of monolithic hands and cracking trees, the evil woods made way, warping and bending the trunks and branches and giant arm bones so that a great hallway was formed back down the hill.

Nyva breathed deep. Her wounds bled and her broken bones screamed as she did. She was about to follow it. She truly was steeling her mind to follow that devil under that night-day sky of the nightmare that was her life.

Someone, *something*, grabbed her by her injured ankle.

She screamed, but no sound came out as whatever held her flipped her over with enough force to push the air from her lungs.

Alexander.

No...

The moon wolf.

The change to Alexander's face was subtler than the transformation of the other lycans. His snout had elongated, too long to be a human face, and an underbite exposed predator-white fangs. His fingers and hands were bigger, longer, and had claws at the ends. But his legs remained human. His hair and beard glowed the color of a silver moon.

In his hand he held a twitching rat...

"No!" Nyva screamed. "No!"

It was Brenna that dangled, twitching, from the moon wolf's claws. His entrails were exposed, hanging from his open gut, and they hung over his face and dragged on the lawn.

Brenna, held in the clutches of her enemy.

Seeing his body, watching his blood drip to the ground, locked her breath in her throat and severed the last tendril of her hope. What was she fighting for? Her life? Control of her destiny? What did anything matter in the face of such power and sorcery?

As if in answer to her thoughts, behind her captor, Wardbrook rose from the earth, mounted atop a stepped ziggurat built of black stone.

The moon wolf dropped her ankle with a painful thud and then drew a long, curved knife from his black belt. He leaned over Nyva.

"Sorry for this, my girl," he said, and he almost sounded as though he meant it. He lifted the knife.

She tried to wriggle away, the hard stone at her back cold and smooth. Stone? She pressed her fingers to the ground, expecting worms, feeling a solid slab.

Alexander disappeared, leaving a hooded figure in his place. Then he slit her open.

It hardly hurt, but she knew she was spilling away. And somewhere in her mind, she knew she ought to be terrified, horrified, in agony. But she was not.

The hooded figure was gone. It was Alexander who sheathed his knife. He grabbed Nyva by the hair and then started dragging her back to the house. "A happy wife is a happy life," he grumbled through his fangs.

No...wait... She pleaded with the people she passed, revelers, leering faces, wide eyes. But no one saw her.

*T*he stag of white-moon fur huffed and darted its eyes wildly as I went into the subterranean chambers of the ancestral tombs 'neath the mountain palace, the air thin and stale. I used the first becalming spell I had ever learned, experiencing a sensation of overwhelming power as I charmed such a great beast to my will. The creature settled and followed me then.

I walked past the tombs of giants, their ancient corpses in upright stone sarcophagi, carved with the faces of angry beasts, all fang and tongue and mad stares. Oval lanterns that blazed with purple fire separated the caskets from each other. A sea of black adders and black rats parted before me as I went forth.

I was dizzy by the time I got to the steps that made the final descent to my brother. I remember thinking that if the air got any thicker deep in those cavernous catacombs of long-dead giants, I'd surely no longer be able to breathe.

The air did get thicker.

And I did breathe, and so did the stag of white-moon fur.

I counted the steps: nine hundred and ninety-nine.

I reached the bottom and stared down the hall to the vast subterranean chamber where my other brother dwelt—the brother I knew of but had never seen. The brother everyone feared, including me. The atrium was as black as shut eyes in the night, an all-consuming dark that crawled outward down the hall and dimmed the glow of the purple lanterns that lined the walls of the hallway, and all the way back up the nine hundred and ninety-nine steps.

"Sissster." My brother's hiss echoed in those caverns of stone and in the caverns of my soul. The incredible depth of his voice made my belly churn.

I remember...I will always remember the fear and revulsion that first time I looked into his eyes. Those insidious, indomitable, irreverent hundreds of glowing pink eyes.

Hundreds of pink dots in the darkness like an assembly of lone stars in an otherwise black cosmos taking on the form of megalithic snake's skull.

"Dammar." His name escaped my lips in an involuntary gasp.

"Diana." All at once, the colossal chamber became alight, the purple flames in the oval lanterns on the gray stone walls igniting with mystic unison.

Dammar's head swayed as his purple tongue darted from his scale-less snake head. His body slithered and undulated even as he remained in one spot.

I remember shaking.

I remember his laughter.

And then his question.

"Have you brought me a gift?" He slid toward us, the white moon stag and me, and slithered around us in figure eights. The white-moon stag's fear was strong enough to break my charm, and it was docile no longer.

It tugged on the rope lead and reared back on its hind legs. I pulled back with all my strength to keep it from leaping away and goring Dammar in the body or running back up the stairs into the mountain hall, to my embarrassment.

"Is this pretty white thing a child of Mother's and Father's as well?" Dammar hissed the S at the end of Father for a long time, as if my monstrous brother were disgusted by his parents and the thing before him. "Or does this child"—Dammar slithered out of his figure-eight pattern and circled only the stag now; he batted me away with his body, and as the air left my lungs, I let go of the rope and fell back on the stone—"belong to someone else?" Before the sound of the question finished hissing through my ears, Dammar lunged—so quickly, I did not see him move—and latched on to the white-moon stag's throat.

The stag screamed, and then Dammar was wrapping and constricting. The stag kicked over the stone floor, clopping as if it were dancing. I remember the way the bones popped. But more than anything, I remember what happened after the kill, when Dammar ate the quadruped rump first. Its antlers snapped as I stared into its eyesin those last moments before the black hood that was Dammar's jaws engulfed it entirely.

After the feeding, I watched my brother Dammar change. Long black fur erupted on his body, a thousand pink eyes watching me. Black antlers sprouted from his head, reaching for me like the twisted branches of a colossal dead tree. Scores of arms emerged from his back, long claws tipping the fingers. A long tail, the only remaining serpentine element, slashed back and forth against the ground. And then my brother looked at me and smiled.

$$\sim$$

CHAPTER EIGHTEEN

❧

THE LIFE OF THE PARTY

From the writings of Darcy Weaver:

I do not know from whence came ink and quill and parchment. Perhaps my wife bribed the guard—no, she too is imprisoned. Perhaps it was Diana. It matters not. I sit in a beam of moonlight from a full moon broken by the bars that cover the window set high in the wall. Tomorrow, they will take me to the pyre, they will set the wood alight, and I will burn. There is no chance for reprieve. My only hope now is that they do not force my son, my Aldous, to watch.

Before I die, I write these recollections, though they will likely not survive me. I hope they do. I hope these memories make their way into my son's hands someday. Here is a tale dark and terrifying. Beautiful, too. A tale of the Deadmen, a strange club to which I was initiated—regrettably—on account of my writings, which were read by the Lady Diana and her husband, and the man-giant, Stiggis. They were so enamored of my work, they shared it far and wide. Sitting here, I think it would have been better had they never read a single word.

The night of the Deadmen's party, I stood in the foyer of

Wardbrook with Diana's brother, Stiggis, whom I had walked with in the northern procession. The southern and eastern processions came inside Wardbrook before us. The slight, delicate wizards and witches of the Dragon Dynasties arrived alongside shamans of the Steppe. The former wore silk and gold robes, the latter armor, and with them they had gifts. Weapons—swords, bows, wands, staffs, clubs fit for the mightiest of men, and knives, many knives. Animals—little green-furred foxes with black eyes and white bellies and ears so large I thought they might use them to fly. They came with jade lizards and bronze-furred donkeys that trotted next to a white bull with red eyes, its pupils slit like a snake's. Jewelry and trinkets. Exotic foods and drinks. And they were all for Diana Ward, the hostess, who was strangely absent, as was her husband.

"Where are they?" I asked Stiggis.

"Alexander is indisposed," said Stiggis.

I frowned. "And Diana?" I tasted her name on my tongue, but I held my tone even, betraying none of my eagerness to see her.

"Diana is in the catacombs," said Stiggis. "The Shahidi are preparing her."

I envied the Shahidi. Their smug looks, their many eyes seeing nowhere and everywhere and nothing and something and everything all at once. The way they always told strange jokes and remained in a pleasant mood in the face of adversity. I have seen their kind tortured and executed, and the sound of their laughter always accompanied their deaths. Be you a man, be you a dragon, they only smile at you and treat you as what you are: one microcosmic element of the macrocosmic joke.

I thought they knew a secret none of the rest of us were privy to. I wanted to know that secret.

"Preparing her for what?" I asked, and felt my throat tighten.

"To be transformed, she is...becoming," said Stiggis. One of his buxom dryads with hair as green as forest pine handed him a drink. He smiled at her and ran a hand through her hair. They

spoke in a northern tongue, and Stiggis offered me no more information.

So I asked, impatient, "She is becoming what?"

The dryad twirled a finger through her hair. Brave creature she was, strange creature she was, for Stiggis Halfjotun, despite being the brother of the immeasurably beautiful Diana Ward, was easily the most frightening-looking man-thing I have ever met. His skull alone was near the size of the dryad's torso. He had a savage underbite and a square, flat face. Flattened from a thousand wars, with demons and devil-gods, wars with his sister...and his brother. I had been told of their feuds.

Stiggis stopped speaking to the dryad and turned slowly to face me.

I immediately regretted poking him, but I stood my ground the way you must stand your ground when confronted by a bear after pissing on its tree. Something about the way he furrowed his tattooed brow and scowled at me until I could see his lower teeth peering out from his white-gold beard told me to ask Stiggis no more questions about his sister.

"She is becoming, Darcy. She is becoming that which she has always wanted to be," said Stiggis, and he turned back to the Dryad, who was staring daggers at me for my interruption. If I had a spine, I would have told her that she was the one who interrupted my conversation with the man-giant, and not the other way around.

But I had no spine. Not then. And not now. I once thought I did, I thought I had a spine when I wrote the Indisputable Science of Goodness. If I knew a goddamn thing about goodness, my wife would not hate me, and my son would not wreak havoc upon her, only for attention. Perhaps writing this will remedy that.

No, writing it will do nothing. Likely, they will burn this parchment with me on the pyre.

But it must be published; it must be read.

The Deadmen must be stopped.

They will hunt me for it. Across the world, across time and space, they will hunt me. But I write nonetheless. So perhaps there is a tiny bit of spine in this doomed body.

I wandered away from the crowd that surrounded Stiggis and found a quiet corner, though quiet is a relative term. Music, raucous and wild, danced through the air, through my veins. Over the music I thought I could hear agonized screams from somewhere in the house. I ignored them; this was the Deadmen's party. Agonized screams were a matter of course.

I later found out those had been Welfric's screams. That was the day he became One-Eyed Welfric, but I knew nothing of what was happening at the time. I knew nothing of what they planned to do with the Emerald Witch's daughter. I didn't even know the Emerald Witch had a daughter, nor did I know who had fathered that daughter.

If I was a man who cared for sleeping, I'd tell myself the following words in bed at night in hopes that they would calm me, in hopes that the lies would make me feel better about who I am and allow slumber to take me without fear. I would say: "If I had known the purpose of that night, then I'd have tried to stop the bastards. I would have tried to kill Diana Ward with my very hands. For that would be the indisputably good thing to do."

I would say those words, but I doubt I would truly believe them. For I was a coward. In many ways and on most days, I am still a coward. I fear properly loving my wife and son.

I fear sobriety.

I fear that all I have ever done, every step I have taken, every word I have spoken was all for naught. All just shadows and embers and dust, to fade in the sun, to dissipate on the wind. Like ashes.

The front doors swung open, and in marched the skeletal sage Vulgare. At his boney back came a Seeker and a well-dressed Dahkah. I knew their vocations immediately, for the Seeker's eyes glowed with blue fire and the Dahkah's eyes were black orbs that rested in his sockets, the same shimmering darkness as the obsidian brooch that fastened Vulgare's turban. A Seeker at the Deadmen's party.

Behind the eye-catching trio came the whole western procession, their songs blaring, their Mamadon trumpeting through its trunk. Gooseflesh rose on my arms as I anticipated the moment the mangiant would slaughter the rare behemoth from worlds away and turn it into the party's dinner. The thought sickened me.

The procession carried in a sweep of wizards and witches from the northwestern regions of the continent of Azria. They wore headdresses of every color and had with them pets and demons most exotic. Golden snakes that spoke to their masters in hissing tongues and giant frogs, the size of hounds, with no eyes in their heads but instead a single massive eye on their backs that gleamed with a brilliant glow reminiscent of a firefly's thorax.

The Azrians puffed on pipes of glowing crystals, and I watched as their flesh and muscle and eyes melted off their skulls when they pulled in the smoke, only to re-form over the bare bone upon the exhale. A disturbing sight, that.

Behind the Azrians came the Lordanians, greater Upirs, and red-fleshed succubae with useless, undersized bat wings growing from their backs, their black horns the same shade as their shimmering hair. One of them winked a golden eye at me and blew a kiss, tossed back her jet-black hair and tapped a little jig with her demon's hooves.

My eyes were not for her, though, not for her or any of the others.

My gaze returned to the Seeker.

He was dancing, rolling his arms and tapping his feet as good as any river dancer I'd ever seen. But it was not this that fascinated me. His lips were twitching like they were fighting the smile on his face, and underneath the placid stare, drunk on the hypnosis of the night's magic, his Seeker's eyes still carried a blue blaze.

They blazed with hate and shame and wrath.

Somewhere inside his befuddled, ensorcelled mind, he was aware.

Only when I found myself standing next to Stiggis again did I realize that I had abandoned my quiet corner and wandered back into the fray. The Deadmen began "the most dangerous game"—a game where a prominent party member would be chosen on lottery to be hunted down by the partygoers. If the chosen one survived until morning, they would live and be given great riches, and all the weapons and catalysts and the binding collars of the demons used to hunt them. If they didn't survive until morning, they were eaten.

"Wonderful, isn't it?" asked Stiggis, knocking both his huge fists together in a display of aggressive joy.

"Look there," said I, pointing to the man that would soon be revealed to me as Cullum Shrike. "Look at that Seeker. Look at his eyes."

"What about them?" Stiggis asked.

"He is not fully under the spell of the night," I said.

"Ah," Stiggis said with a grin.

And his casual reply sprouted a suspicion in my thoughts. "You have seen Seekers here before?" The possibility surprised me.

"Yes. Not often. But he is not the first," said Stiggis. "They walk placidly about the party, smiling like drunken children, never speaking, and in the morning, they do not remember they were ever here. Just the embers of a strange and fantastic dream remain in them."

I looked again at the Seeker, at his blazing blue eyes, and a chill of premonition washed through me. I had a mad urge to leave, to run, to get as far from this place as I could. Instead, I said, "That man will not forget. He does not want to be here, not at all. And yet he is dancing, so the music is working on him."

"No, he will not forget. That you have right. But on the other, you are wrong. He does want to be here. It is exactly where he wants to be." Stiggis patted me on the shoulder, then stroked his

beard and said, "That Seeker, his name is Cullum Shrike. He is my guest. I sent the invitation to the man he called Father. I sent the invitation through the man's mind. That man, the father, is gone, and so the son has come. He has come here as a gift to my brother, and there will be two more."

"Dammar?" I whispered, and at my own mention of that cursed name, I broke into a cold sweat and snatched a drink off the tray as a dryad serving wench walked past. I drank it down before tossing the cup blindly over my shoulder. "I thought the gifts were for Diana tonight. That was what it said on the invitation...to bring gifts for hostess Diana Ward, Mother Diana Ward..." Mother. Diana was no one's mother. She was not because she could not, though she wished otherwise with all her being... I did not know this last as fact, only hearsay. But it was hearsay I suspected was true.

"The night is Diana's," Stiggis said eventually. "And though the gifts are for her, I never forget my brother. He will be free of the prison in which he is now locked. He will be free again, just as he always finds a way to be free again. And he will come here to claim his gifts."

"Tonight?" I asked, and wiped the cold sweat from the back of my neck.

"No." Stiggis grinned, smelling my fear. "Half a human life from now. A god's blink from now. He will be free and he will claim his gifts, for I must honor a deal not yet struck."

I quavered a moment at the knees, the abject strangeness of the druid's words nearly overwhelming me. What a thing, to be surrounded by madness and horror, by sounds and smells and sights of the primordial wild that is the living soul—and in the maelstrom of all that, to be brought to shaking by the utterance of mere words. A deal not yet struck.

I had never met Dammar. I hope I never do. For I have not the words to describe my reverence, fear, and at times worship of Stiggis and Diana, and when those two mighty mages—dare I say demigods—speak of their older brother, they speak of him with the very same reverence I feel toward them.

I can handle the presence of much. I can carry on after encounters with things from the very bottom of strangeness. But I know that the dark Dammar comes from has no bottom, and if encountered, it would be a dark that I, Darcy Weaver, would never be able to find my way back out of.

Stiggis and I followed the skeletal sage Vulgare as he led Cullum and the Dahkah with the curly mustache through the party. I recognized the Dahkah then. I had seen him once before at a party much like this one. We had never spoken. But I remember thinking he looked particularly benign for one of his order.

Cullum and the Dahkah danced and swayed as they walked, and I could not say I saw anything in the Dahkah's expression or demeanor that was any different than any of the other revelers.

Cullum's lips had worked their way out of a smile by now, and I was quite certain he was beginning to mouth words.

"Can you listen and hear what he is saying?" I asked Stiggis, wondering at the capacity of the druid's ears.

"I'm not a rabbit." Stiggis laughed, and the turn of lips only made his tattooed visage all the more threatening. "I can read his lips, though."

"Well, what is he whispering there with that look in his eyes?"

"I do swear," Stiggis said, then he squinted, focusing on the Seeker. "By the light of the sun...I will kill you all," Stiggis finished. His lips peeled away from his teeth in a smile, and he turned to me so fast that his hair and beard of white gold swayed. There was such childish excitement in his eyes that I could not help but laugh.

"I'm not sure I see what you find so pleasing about that," I said, then looked around for something intoxicating to imbibe, or smoke, or snort.

"Of course you do," Stiggis said.

Two nude fairies—or rather fae, as I think is the nomenclature the race of immortal impish flying children prefer—flew around

Stiggis' head on translucent wings. Wings that when crushed and snorted cause the brain to painlessly bleed, and what strange and beautiful visions do come from those cascades of crimson swirling with the gray goo of brain matter within the confines of one's own skull.

Stiggis lashed out with one of his tattooed arms and took hold of a fae's foot. It squeaked like a mouse, and the other one flew off, gone before it was made to witness what happened next. Stiggis swung the fae like a club and obliterated its skull on the small maple table next to him. As the table rocked from the impact, a floral arrangement of black roses and white death lillies in a gray clay vase clattered on the floor. None of the guests paid attention. Neither the vase nor the murdered fae raised any concern.

Stiggis tore off its wings and ground them to dust in his massive hands, rubbing them together like he was trying to warm them at a fire.

I felt sick watching it. It was the first time I had seen it done. Yet how many times prior had I joyfully snorted the stuff, uncaring of the unseen process that allowed the powder to reach my desk, or my knife, or the little vial and then my nose?

"Stiggis, you son of a giant bitch!" boomed the voice of a nearby guest. A Kehldeshi, by his accent.

A form as short as a young child and burly with muscle as any blacksmith in his prime leapt onto the table that had been used to prepare the fae dust. The dwarf-man had skin as pale as snow, a trait common of the race of people who lived in the northeastern mountains of the vast desert of Kehldesh—a great juxtaposition to the hundreds of tribes that made up the mountain people's dark-skinned countrymen to the south and west in the plains, deserts, and savannahs.

"Ah," Stiggis exclaimed. "If it isn't Shemyte Haroddoth, my favorite little man. My favorite little Dahkah." Stiggis took the dwarf-man's hand in his own. Shemyte had monstrous hands, so large they almost managed to not be entirely engulfed by the man-giant's grip.

"Darcy Weaver," said Shemyte, as he turned from Stiggis and stared at me with his black-orb eyes. His long white beard was tied with golden braids that hung down over the light mail armor of his chest plate. His skull was shaven, and on it were tattoos of eyes. He had once told me it was his tribute to the Shahidi, for it was the Shahidi, after all, that guided his hand, as they guided the hands of all the Dahkah.

"Haroddoth," I said with a smile.

"Are you still wasting your time writing things that no one will read, and if they do, will lead to your certain death? All because you think every man has a right to the hidden truths?" Shemyte asked with an all-knowing grin. The type of grin that causes every insecurity in even the strongest-willed and most intelligent of people to rise and break free of the box they thought they had so securely locked them away in. It was the smile that said, I've been here longer than you. I've seen more than you. And most of all, oh, most of all, I have done more than you.

"And every woman," I said.

"What's that?" asked Shemyte as he stepped down from the table. He drew a scimitar from his hip and scooped some of the fae dust from the maple.

"I am wasting my time writing things that no one will read, and if they do read, will lead to my certain death," I said. "All so that every man and every woman may have the opportunity to experience the hidden truths that I myself have seen."

"Good man, Darcy. You're a damn good one," said Stiggis, clapping my shoulder for the third time that night with a satisfied look on his face, like a pleased father.

"Yes, very good man," said Shemyte. He chuckled, but he held his sword steady, careful not to drop any of the fae dust from it. "Kneel, good man Darcy Weaver. Kneel so I may knight thee."

I played the game and knelt. I put my hands to my sides, palms *up in mock prayer to the Luminescent. Although I thought Shemyte did think at times like a troglodyte, I forgave him because he was a troglodyte. A troglodyte who was the last of a bloodline of the last remaining human ancestors that first left the caves and the societies of subterranean chambers, as they battled back the hordes of the beast to see the sun rise again.*

But never mind the history of Shemyte's people, good reader. He is of little importance in this story. He is more a viewer, like you and I.

After I sniffed the fae dust from the tip of the blade that he extended before my nose, I stood again, reborn into the life of the party. My senses bent through waves of disarray and honed perception. All was jumbled color and bending shapes for several moments, then I became more aware of the madness around me, of the minstrels out of time, of living skeletons in black coats playing horns and banging brass drums as others twanged on lutes that were ensorcelled with lightning so that blue bolts ran up and down the strings and their deepest notes rumbled like thunder. The dog-sized frogs with glowing eyeballs on their backs that had come in with the western procession climbed up the walls and onto the ceiling overtop of the minstrels. They stared down on them so that the firefly-like glow of their back-eyes made a cylinder of brightness around the musicians.

Then all I could perceive was wild colors and breaking shapes again.

This alone should have been enough, more than enough to command my attention for hours to come. The music, the creatures, the effects of the fae dust. But even with my mind warping, I kept thinking back on the Seeker with the wrathful eyes, who mouthed the promise of all the partygoers' deaths.

The one named Cullum Shrike.

The one Stiggis said was a gift for his brother Dammar. It was this narrative that I wished to follow, this "against all odds" story that I wanted to see play out, so I shifted my stare that melted and honed, and I searched the room for my protagonist.

Cullum was easy to spot again, with his wide blue pilgrim's hat and his impossibly angry face among a sea of revelers. There was immense magic in the air, magic to make him revel and forget. It would reach as far as the music could be heard, even to the village. While we reveled in the manse, they reveled down there in their town. And when they woke with the dawn, the night would be no more than a quickly fading dream that would leave them with two very clear feelings: dread and shame. And they'd have not a damned clue as to why they felt either of them.

Some of us, a select few, were given amulets. Amulets to protect us from the music and leave us only to the debauchery of our own choosing. Of course, Cullum was given no such amulet. He just had that much fight in him.

I watched in surprise as, like a marionette fighting the strings that pulled him, Cullum turned away from the minstrels. He turned away and walked in an absurd, slow, jagged gait and, with sluggish but still-great force, shoved revelers out of his way.

"Where are you going?" I wondered aloud.

"Look there, that is where he is going," said Stiggis, pointing to something in the madness, to a hallway, or a table, or group of other revelers—it could have been anything.

"What am I looking at?" I asked.

"The greater Upirs. Those filthy fucking leeches, they are taking his friend, that Dahkah, Damos," said Stiggis. The man-giant never tried to hide his disgust of all things vampire, Upir, Dampier, Haughui—the word used in the Northern Isles for those blue-skinned, bat-faced risers from the grave who drink human blood. Hannya, as they called their version of bloodsuckers in the Dragon Dynasties and the eastern part of the Great Steppe. I am aware of hundreds of subspecies and races of their kind, and I am certain there are hundreds, if not thousands, more. One must only crawl deeper, deeper into the catacombs of time to find them.

But it was only the greater Upirs of Lordan and Romaria that were welcome into the Deadmen. And in recent years, tensions had begun to rise between the vampires and other members. There were worries that the blood drinkers were playing double agents for Leviathan cults.

My eyes sought and found the group of tall, thin, pale-skinned, and meticulously garbed guests that made up the Lordanian and Romarian covens of greater Upirs. There was a score of them at least, and they moved in unison through the crowd of man and monster, guiding Cullum's friend Damos by the hand. The Dahkah looked as helpless, happy, and confused as a lost child at the fair before it realizes it is all alone in a terrible place.

This was where Cullum was forcing himself to walk.

"Where are they taking his friend?" I asked.

"To the Chamber of Want," said Stiggis.

"Should we follow?" I asked.

"I must follow," said Stiggis. "You may do as you will, but I warn you now, word weaver, what you are about to see may be too much for a desk dweller such as yourself to bear."

Fuck you, Stiggis. Not everyone can be a ten-foot magical man-giant, *I wanted to say. Instead, I gulped and said,* "Onward then, to the Chamber of Want."

It took us time to catch up to Cullum, Damos, and the vampires, because we had to first pass through the crowd, and either Stiggis, myself, or Shemyte was stopped every ten paces or so and spoken to by some other prominent guest who recognized us and wished to compliment our work.

"Great book, Darcy. That last one you wrote. Really had me thinking," said one.

"Wonderful assassination of the queen of south Lordan, that bitch, and her son. I know it was you, Haroddoth. I know it was you," said another to the man-dwarf with a wink.

"I hear it was you, Stiggis, who got Diana back from that world

we lost to Calteca and the Murlur. I hear you snapped the neck of Xolotos," said a third.

"You hear correctly. I killed the man-dragon with my hands. But the world was not lost by the Deadmen. It was given. A tactical retreat. Scorched earth," Stiggis explained. Then explained again when another made a similar comment. And again. Again. By the time we caught up with our protagonist, the orgy was well underway.

The Chamber of Want was filled to the very brim with naked flesh and fur, muscle and manes, perfect breasts small and large, fat cocks and small cocks, every variety of mound between pale vampire thighs. Males and females sucking and fucking, male and male and female and female. Nothing was off-limits. Moans of ecstasy. Cries of pain. Cries of terror. Laughter. Sobs. Sweat, I could smell it. Blood, ejaculate, urine... So much debauchery; so much filth.

A true feast for the flesh. And they all fed on each other's lust and passion and pain. They fed on it like winged insects make a feast of shit.

I was not there for the fucking and the sucking. Indeed, I never had an interest in visiting the Chamber of Want.

Nor did Cullum Shrike. He tugged and pulled and punched out with fists that did not fully obey him at the pale, naked, well-muscled bloodsuckers that were striking him and grappling him to strip him naked.

"Damos, fight. Fight, damn you!" Cullum screamed as he watched the vampires, male and female alike, hold down his friend the Dahkah and start to make use of him. Century-old demon or no, Damos was not Cullum, and he did not protest. He moaned in ecstasy. The vampires moaned, and all ignored us.

Until Stiggis said, "Blue boy...paint this chamber red."

There will come a time in every weak and comfortable person's life when they wish they had spent a bit more time making themselves uncomfortable, a bit more time making themselves hard. Because I haven't been to a world yet where the storms don't rage just as hard as the sun does shine bright.

I haven't seen a skeleton without a broken bone.

No, I haven't seen a country that didn't go from peace to war, and war to peace, only to one day go back to war again.

Let me tell you this, that comfortable bed, that cozy house... One day, they're going to burn.

Your healthy son, he will get sick. Your beautiful, innocent daughter, she will be harmed.

Your wife and your husband, their graves you will need to visit.

Your honest king, he will die and the prince will be a tyrant.

The dog goes mad and bites your soft hand.

The starving wolf you fed comes scratching at your door. He wants more and he's strong now, because he never knew comfort; he never had a soft bed or a cozy home. The only embrace he's ever known is the cold clutches of Mother Nature's arms.

You've tamed yourself, domesticated yourself, softened yourself.

So what will you do? How do you stay strong for your son? How do you punish your daughter's offender? How do you put down the mad dog you once loved, whose eyes are now red for your blood? How do you kill the wolf at your door, knocking and howling, "Give me more...give me more"?

You cannot. You can only wish that you had seen the prison walls of comfort for what they were before they closed in on you. You can only wish that you were like your ancestors, men and women who loved and lived and killed with hearts of ice and stone.

~Excerpt from *A Treatise to Cowards,*

by Mongrel Murdo

≈

CHAPTER NINETEEN

❧

PAINTED RED

*C*ullum had not stopped fighting the music's hold since the moment he first heard the mad, cacophonic symphony at Damos' house. He could still hear it, but he was almost free of it now.

As the greater Upirs detained him, ripping away his clothes, he watched Damos' face contort with pleasure and pain. The Dahkah thrust into one of the beautiful Upirs while a pale, muscled vampire with a sculpted face sodomized Damos from behind. Cullum renewed his struggles against the hold of the music and the bloodsuckers' hands.

He wanted to close his eyes; he wanted to look away. But what he wanted mattered not. What he *needed* was to see. He needed to watch and he needed to feel the shame, the rage, and the vindication that made him Vicar Cullum Shrike.

He would judge them.

He would execute them all.

With arcane chains around their forsaken necks, he would drag them to hell.

"Such fire in you," whispered a male in Cullum's ear from

behind. The vampire ran the tip of his nose over the back of Cullum's neck. Cullum roared and threw his head back. He was held steady by a male on each arm and two females around his legs and waist, so he could not get much power. But he still felt the devil's nose crunch.

His hat came off from the impact, and a nearby female walked over, picked it up, and put it on, then she knelt in front of Cullum. A hand grabbed the back of his skull and a forearm wrapped around his neck. He could feel an erection pulsing on his back.

"I'll kill you," Cullum said, and the arm around his throat tightened so that his teeth ground. Cullum's gut turned with bile and fear and hate. He had a fleeting thought of the girls he had failed, the girls taken and forced to accept attentions unwanted and vile. Tears formed in his eyes. But he would not break. This would not happen. *This will not happen.*

The vampire wearing his hat freed his cock from his trousers and began to stroke it.

"You bitches, you fucking bastards." Cullum's mouth foamed.

"Bend him over," said one of them.

Cullum's vision blurred, horror overcoming all his rage.

"Get on your fucking knees," said the Upir that gripped his skull. "I will impale you." His voice was tight with hate. "I will impale you like your order impaled my sister, like they later impaled my first lover, like they impaled my father."

"I hope you had to watch," Cullum managed to say. He writhed and struggled, horror giving way to panic.

Then words spoken in a voice of thunder echoed in the chamber. "Blue boy, paint this chamber red!"

All eyes turned to the speaker and the two strange companions who stood with him: a black-eyed dwarf-man that Cullum was sure to be a Dahkah, and a thin, well-dressed, wide-shouldered man, with long black curls tied into a knot at the back of his head and a neatly trimmed beard.

But it was the tattooed man-giant in the center of the room who held Cullum's gaze. He was the figure from Archdeacon Lazarus's dream.

He was here. He was real.

And his words set Cullum free. Cullum was the blue boy. And he would indeed paint this chamber red.

It was not gradual. It was an explosion of understanding and honing of the caged magic that always lived inside of him. The magic that he had been taught to shackle, to shun, to conceal with shame.

The grip around Cullum's neck now felt as weak as a child's, as did the holds of the other Upirs. He rammed his head back again, skull cracking on face, this time much, much harder. Cullum kicked out at the devil harlots who fettered his legs, and ripped free his arms as he swung fists and elbows. He made contact with air as much as skull and body, but he thrashed his holders enough to force them to step off. The ones who held Damos paused, but they did not move away. There were more of them huddled over the Dahkah than before.

When the first head tilted up and Cullum saw black blood —Damos' blood—dripping from a vampire's mouth, webs of blackened veins stretching over its pale face, dark fumes rising from its lips, Cullum called forth the chains.

The darkness that always accompanied his use of his gifts did not come. The veil did not fall across his sight. He saw all that he had been seeing, and when he saw the tethers that grew from his hands and whipped out at the bloodsuckers who consumed his friend, they were not blue chains. They were lashing gray vines, and sprouting from them in the thousands were flesh-ripping crimson thorns.

Cullum could not pause to wonder why, to try to fathom the transformation of his magic.

The vines wrapped around the neck of the vampire who was looking up from Damos' twitching body, and as the crimson thorns bit and tasted blood, Cullum felt stronger. And angrier.

"I am Cullum Shrike. I am the light. I am your judgment!" Cullum roared, and pulled hard on the vines. The vampire's head ripped off and flew against another's shoulder. Blood fountained from the severed neck, painting the hair and faces and bodies of the others.

Cullum turned on the one who had nearly sodomized him. The vampire had armed himself with a lance. He charged at Cullum, lance lowered, attempting again for penetration. With a heretofore unknown control over the chains, Cullum swung and tossed out the vines at his assailant. They wrapped around the vampire's wrists and as Cullum recalled the vines, they severed the vampires hands as easily as plucking the legs off a fly.

The vampire's expression twisted as he looked down at his spurting stumps. Before he could look up again, Cullum was upon him, throwing fists like his hands were unbreakable slabs of stone. The Upir's left cheek crunched.

"I hope"—*swing;* the jaw unhinged—"you watched"—*swing;* the right cheekbone cracked—"them die!" A final blow and the greater Upir went down.

Cullum stayed on him, punching, and punching, and punching. No music drove him to this madness. It was not the spell that the man-giant had cast to empower him that made his fists keep striking after every facial feature was pulverized into a red and purple mess of fleshy pulp. Only Cullum was controlling Cullum now.

The rest of the chamber faded away, and he was hardly

aware as the man-giant took off one of his arm rings, morphed it into a rune-covered axe, and set to hacking into the vampires.

Cullum kept punching as the dwarf-man with the tattooed head drew his curved sword and faded in and out of the shadow realm, dematerializing then materializing again to slice into pale, naked flesh.

Cullum kept punching as the man with the fancy clothes and well-trimmed beard and long, curly hair lifted a foot-long marble phallus from a table and exclaimed, "Suck on this, you leech," before clobbering a vampire sneaking up on the man-giant with a dagger.

"And take this!" yelled the man as he brought down the marble phallus again.

"You have betrayed us, chosen the wrong side," yelled the man-giant at the Upirs. "The Shahidi are with us. You think we knew nothing of your plots and agreements with Leviathan cults? You've gotten weak! And the weak will fall."

A Upir cried, "We didn't—"

Though Cullum could not see through the mass of bodies, he heard the swoosh of a swinging weapon, the impact of cleaving meat and bone, and the scream of the immortal thing.

"You didn't conspire? You didn't betray? Your brethren did and all of you will pay," the man-giant yelled.

"Stiggis! No!" came the agonized plea of one of the Romarian Upirs.

"A thousand years ago, you would not have begged, Vladdarran!"

"Stigg—" The scream was cut short by the sound of a boot —worn by a five-hundred-pound man-giant—crushing skull and squishing brains over stone tile.

Cullum kept on pummeling the meat in front of him until

an inhumanly strong female leapt upon his back. Only then did he take his focus from the obliterated face of the fiend that had nearly raped him.

The vampire on his back shrieked and sank her fangs into his neck, and although the *Ordeal* had made it impossible for Cullum to contract any form of vampirism or lycanthropy, it had not made it impossible for him to die from having the side of his neck bitten out.

Cullum summoned the vines from his palms. He felt no pain. He felt no symptoms of the *Bloodburn* on the back of his left hand. The magic honed by the *Ordeal* had become something foreign, something other, a new and frightening part of himself. He willed the vines to wrap around his fists and forearms so they were gauntlets of unbreakable briars. He reached back and grabbed hold of the vampire by her hair, contorting in an effort to punch her in the skull with his bladed fist. Three strikes before she lost an eye and let go of Cullum's neck. They stumbled away from each other, then in unison, blood streaming from their gaping wounds, they lunged back at one another.

The vampire went for the wound in Cullum's neck. His reach was longer, and thanks to the spell granted him by the man-giant, he was faster than he had ever been. He grabbed the Upir by the throat, sank his fingers through skin and muscle, and ripped out her gullet.

He dropped her convulsing body and turned.

"Damos," he called, clapping a hand against the wound in his neck. His vision spun as he searched for his friend. "Damos!"

Nothing ever changes. This is the same play on a different stage. Every mission I was sent on, every partner I lost, I did not let myself mourn. That made it so much easier to sacrifice the next. I did not allow myself to call them friend.

But Damos is a friend. And Damos is a Dahkah. He is not dead. He can't be dead. He needs to help me. He needs to help me and the rat sorcerer save the emerald-eyed girl. That is why I am here: to save an innocent life. I can still save her. Something good can come of this. Something good can come of me.

For a moment, he did not know if his thoughts were his own, his dying friend's, or the both of their thoughts combined.

Another vampire ran toward Cullum, a broadsword in its hand. The thing had managed to don a chest plate and get its trousers back up and fastened.

The creature of the night slashed out with nearly unperceivable speed. Cullum flinched in time to get his arm up and stop the strike from opening his throat. He accepted instantaneously that his arm was as good as lost. But when the blade struck the tightly woven gauntlet of crimson briars, it was the sword that split in two.

There was a lingering moment before the vampire could adjust to its shock and dismay over the sword's destruction. Cullum seized the moment and punched, hitting the vampire square between the eyes. The briars rent flesh and skull and punctured brain.

Vampires fought and died around him at the hands of the man-giant, the Dahkah dwarf, and the well-dressed man. Cullum's path to the ones feeding on Damos became clear as the entwined bodies shifted and offered a clear view for an instant. About twelve strides ahead and a little to the left was an overturned table and the splintered remains of regal oak-and-velvet chairs. Behind the wreckage, the coroner-surgeon's arm stuck out from the throng, twitching against the floor as black Dahkah blood pooled at the feet of the naked fiends atop him. Cullum did not know if the limb was stirred to move by the Dahkah's somehow still-beating heart,

DYLAN DOOSE

or if it was simply shaking from the force with which the vampires ripped into him.

In times of surmounting pressure and terror and pain and loneliness, Cullum had often silently prayed, prayed for intervention.

He did not pray now. For the god who had just liberated him from his captors, the god who had just unlocked a power in him that did not cause the darkness of the chains to come when they were summoned but rather the very wrath of Cullum's nature, that god was not the Luminescent. Rather it was the god who was a devil too, the giant who was here unleashing havoc upon his enemies.

"Turn and face me, you fanged cowards. Turn and face your death." So much blood spilled from Cullum's mouth as he yelled that the words were gurgled and he sputtered.

Cullum willed his vine gauntlets to lash again like crimson-barbed whips. He lashed at Damos' murderers, and each time he contacted flesh and the vines wrapped around limbs and necks, he would rapidly shorten the vine and retract it into his palm so that the indestructible crimson thorns became hundreds of sawing razor teeth that chewed through meat and bone like a scythe through corn stalks.

He managed to kill one and turn three others into mutilated, crawling things. The others cleared out and sprinted for the door. Most of them still naked.

"After them!" Stiggis shouted, his voice laced with glee. The man-giant's maniacal laugh bounced around Cullum's skull and made his ears ring.

His focus was on Damos. The Dahkah's head had been torn off, his cheeks eaten, eyes torn out. The Upirs had defiled his corpse in every way.

Cullum could offer no burial, no words, nothing that the dead Dahkah deserved. He could not even take the time to ponder how it was possible for a Dahkah to die, even at the hands of such fiends. Perhaps Damos' order was filled with as many lies as his own. Hot tears rolled down his cheeks.

"I'm going to find that girl," Cullum said to the corpse. "I know your ghost is haunting this room right now, Dahkah. I know you tried. I know you tried your damn hardest to fight that pull in your mind tonight." Blood sloshed out of Cullum's mouth as he spoke. He did not care. And though he spoke to a dead man, he did not feel the words were wasted. "I'll save the girl. I'll kill the rest of them." Cullum nodded. "And you'll have been the one who helped me do it, my friend... I hope you find peace now in your second death."

Just as Cullum turned to the door to make his way from the chamber, he saw his objective—the girl in a green dress, the same green dress she had worn during the vision he had in the pool with the Sisters—being dragged by the hair down the hall. She was hardly conscious, and her belly was bleeding profusely, perhaps as badly as Cullum's neck. The man dragging her was not a man, and he was not like any lycanthrope Cullum had ever seen, either. His face was elongated and had a jutting underbite of fangs and a mane of beard and wild hair the same color as the strand Cullum and Damos had found at the scene of the dead villagers and the dog in the woods. The moon wolf. His features were still far more human than wolf, and it was this that made his appearance so monstrous.

"Alexander Ward!" Cullum tried to shout, but he just coughed blood.

Alexander did not turn. He passed by the doorway, dragging the girl behind.

Cullum made it into the hallway. There was shouting and crashing and screaming and clapping. The musicians still played as Stiggis, the Dahkah dwarf, and the dapperly dressed man went after the fleeing Upirs. Other guests joined the hunt as well, while still others continued to drink and snort and smoke and revel.

Cullum saw Alexander move past a trio of succubae and then turn right down another hall.

If Cullum had any stomach left, he could feel it sinking. Alexander was dragging the girl in the emerald dress by the hair in his left hand, and now, because of the direction he turned, Cullum could see what he carried in his right hand. The disemboweled corpse of the rat sorcerer, Cullum's only remaining ally in this living nightmare.

Black Brenna was dead.

"It doesn't matter," Cullum gurgled to himself. "You still have to try." He stumbled forward.

"Bravo, Seeker," said a satyr who leaned on the wall while smoking on a pipe, a dryad squatting in front of him sucking him off.

Cullum spat blood on them.

"Such purpose, such drive," said one of the succubae on his left, where Alexander had turned down the other hall.

"Burn in hell," Cullum said, and they laughed and clapped as he turned his back on them and went after Alexander.

His legs felt like softening noodles in a boiling pot, and he had to stop a moment to balance himself on a suit of armor.

"Easy there, champion of the sun," said the suit of armor as it hooked an arm under Cullum's armpit and hoisted him upright. The knight's iron helmet turned to look Cullum in the eyes, and in the empty shadow of the helm, two eyes glowed gold like two little suns.

"Crack on," said the suit of armor, and Cullum nodded his appreciation at the being he was not certain was real. He had lost enough blood now to hallucinate, but in this place, a helpful, living, holy suit of armor did not seem implausible. Either way, it mattered little, and Cullum cracked on.

"Go get 'em," said a gaunt man of Cullum's height, bearing

an accent Cullum had never before heard. He wore a long black coat and had a black pilgrim hat like a Seeker's, but the wide brim was turned up on the sides. Cullum thought of bull horns looking at it. Around his waist, the man had two strange...knives? No, they were small...hammers?...with thick iron handles and wooden heads, and some sort of rotating metal piece in the center? No, that did not make sense at all.

Cullum did not know what the weapons were, and he stopped thinking on them. Apart from the strange weapons the black-hatted man wore at his hips, he was entirely human, and perhaps...familiar?

Then he tilted his head up and spoke again, revealing his eyes. They were two silver coins, one with the relief of a vulture upon it and the other with the image of some lord or king of another place and time. "The initiation, it ain't ever easy, brother. But once you're in...you are in," said the man with two coins for eyes.

"I am joining nothing."

"Yeah, sure you ain't. And I don't hang rogue warlocks and witches in the bayou above the gators... Tell yourself what you want, man. But by the time you wake...you're gonna be one of us, blue boy."

"Fuck you," Cullum said, and kept moving.

"When you see the wicker man, tell him the Lawdog sends his regards," the coin-eyed man called to Cullum's back, then he started laughing.

The next one hundred steps—or was it a thousand? Three thousand? *How big is this fucking house?*—were a blur of hallucinated daze and confusion. Cullum focused only on the red path of blood that had been left by the girl in the emerald dress. He ignored the gawks, laughs, insults, and compliments made by the other guests. He just kept following the path, until it took him down steps and darker empty halls, to more steps, through subterranean chambers with old tomes and books and liquids in vials and skeletons of dead things, human, humanoid, and beast alike. There were fetuses of many creatures in jars of green liquid on shelves, and evil paintings on the walls of old gods and slaughter. Cullum was too far gone to be afraid now; he was too far gone to be curious about any of it. He just kept following his course deeper and deeper, until he reached his destination.

"Hell," Cullum said when he entered the final chamber.

He stood at the top of the steps that went down ten more meters into an atrium larger than the one in Wardbrook's house by far. It was larger than the chapel in the House of Deacons. It was the vastest interior Cullum had ever seen. A strange, luminous glow permeated the air from the surface of the rock walls. From floor to towering ceiling, the walls were marked with runes, sigils, and signs, nearly all of which were unrecognizable to Cullum. Not in form but in meaning. He could see shapes like a three-legged wolf, skeleton hands, snakes and birds, rams and stags, and waves next to shapes that made no sense at all. As a whole, it was mad and meaningless, megalithic, and it made Cullum feel smaller and and more insignificant than ever before. It was not just the ominous symbols in some evil tomb beneath the earth, or that he was bleeding to death, outmatched and alone, that brought on this feeling of complete and utter worthlessness, it was the scene before him.

In the center of the chamber floor was a massive wicker sculpture of an owl-faced beast, with a mane of red maple leaves. From its arms, back, and shoulders poked massive spikes. From the hands that were held stiff at its sides grew fingers of long roots. These roots extended across the floor to the nine stone altars that surrounded it in a circle.

On one altar lay the girl in the emerald dress. One of the wicker beast's roots was attached to her skull at the left temple. Rings of light pulsed from the wicker beast's hand all the way through the long root finger and into the skull of the girl. Her whole body glowed for a moment, then she became pale again, only to have the routine repeat.

Over her stood two Shahidi, all their many eyes focused on the girl as they stitched up her belly through the torn dress. *Save her. You must save her.* Cullum wasn't certain if he spoke aloud. He wasn't certain if the words were for himself or the Shahidi working on her.

On the altar to her left was another woman, blond and tanned, breasts and neck glistening with sweat. Diana Ward. There was the witch he had come here to kill.

Diana, too, was unconscious, but no root clung to her head as two Shahidi stood over her stitching her up in the same place they stitched the girl. On the next altar, this one to the left of Diana in the circle of stone slabs that surrounded the wicker beast, was Black Brenna.

He was gutted; the orange boils that gave him his unholy powers were all popped. The roots gouged Brenna to the altar through his eyes and mouth. He too glowed with light when the circles of illumination pulsed into him, and each time they did, his little limbs twitched and flailed. Five of the remaining six stone altars had skeletons rooted to them, some with armor, some in the robes of witches and wizards. One clutched a bow and was wearing the green cloak of a ranger. Their bones rattled on the stone when the light pulsed into them.

Cullum started down the steps to the center of the subterranean chamber.

He removed his hand from the bloody bite wound on his neck.

"The gifts of the *Ordeal* will keep me. The man-giant, devil-god's empowerment will keep me," Cullum muttered to himself as his blood pulsed from his neck in time to his heartbeat. Cullum summoned the vines of crimson thorns and let them drag on the steps. Their sharp tips clicked on the stone like the feet of an army of iron insects.

One of the Shahidi stitching up the girl waved a hand in Cullum's direction, but did not glance his way. In a sleepy, disinterested tone, he said, "Alexander?"

"You go get him, you bug-eyed fuck," said Alexander as he stood up and stepped out from behind the wicker beast. His sword was sheathed and he was drinking from a wineskin, and he yet wore the form of the moon wolf.

"I am performing surgery on Nyva," said the Shahidi, and then he laughed. "I cannot subdue the vicar and perform surgery. Do your job, Alexander."

Do your job, Cullum.

Nyva. That was the girl's name.

"My job?" Alexander yelled, and he fell to a knee from his drunkenness. He threw down his wineskin and drew his sword. "My job!" he roared as he got back to his feet.

The mad hum of the music from the house buzzed around the massive chamber and lingered even after the echoes of Alexander's shout died.

"You think I'm nothing, eh?" asked the moon wolf as he stumbled toward the many-eyed monk that had insulted him. The monk was already backing away from Nyva, and the other simply continued working alone, as if the change from two to one mattered not at all.

"Alexander, be civil," said one of the monks attending Diana.

"No such thing as that," said Alexander as he strode toward the Shahidi. As if he had in an instant sobered up, he walked sure-footedly as he had been walking when Cullum first saw him dragging Nyva and Brenna moments ago.

No, it had been hours ago. Cullum had been stumbling

deeper into this hell beneath the evil shadow home for hours. He had been dying for hours.

"No such thing as civility here, you fucking insect." Alexander leapt through the air with speed and distance unachievable by any human and split the Shahidi monk's skull in two, popping eyes along the way. "No such thing as civilization here." Alexander spat on the dead monk's corpse. "You should have seen that coming, eh? You should have prophesied that."

Alexander sheathed his sword and began walking toward Cullum, but he was looking past Cullum and up the stairs, and he staggered toward them, intent on leaving. That was fine with Cullum. All that mattered was getting to Nyva.

"Diana will be very angry if you are not here when she wakes," said the Shahidi who worked on the girl. "And she will be waking soon. She will be in pain and want her husband."

"Diana? Curse her!" Alexander spun back and pointed to the altar where the girl lay. "That is my daughter! That is my child. You cut out my child's womb. I helped you do it!" He pressed his hands to his face then let them drop away. "None of this is her fault. I made the mistake. Elyra made the mistake. Why is Nyva punished? I should be punished. Elyra should be punished!"

His daughter? How? Why…? Cullum's gaze flicked back and forth between the moon wolf and the girl. He meant to step forward, but his strength waned and he found himself sinking to the floor.

"Elyra will be punished," said one of the Shahidi working on Diana. "And do *you* not feel punished?"

Alexander walked up to the Shahidi, and he screamed and roared and howled into the monk's ear. The monk did not so much as pause his work for an instant.

"Go, then," said the monk. "Go and mope in the woods.

But know that other men would be joyous at the news that they will soon be having a son."

Alexander turned away again, and he ran up the steps and past Cullum, not sparing the Seeker a glance. Cullum tried to rise, but the room spun and the floor chased him, and he could not seem to lift his arms.

An image from the pool flashed in Cullum's mind: Alexander running, weeping, through the woods.

Another image came: white tentacles slithering through eyes and nose and mouth.

They are not here. I have seen every manner of heretic and monster and fiend, mutant and demon and devil in this place tonight. I did not see those things. And I will never know any of it— who was behind the attack on Aldwick, on the church. What those tentacle fiends are... I will never know, for I die here tonight.

He thought of the girls he had failed. He thought of the bat in the cave bursting from that child's belly. He had been too late then; he was too late and too weak now. He was nothing but a man who failed. He had seen his fate in the pool, had seen his failures with the Sisters, and still, he always walked into them. He made the choice every time to see the truth of his own destruction and walk to it anyway. It wasn't about the Luminescent. It wasn't about the Church or Lazarus. It was about wanting to die.

Lazarus's voice danced at the edges of his thoughts. *Take your own life, or live and slay the beast and the witch, and the heretic and the mutant, until you can slay no more.*

Cullum could slay no more.

He looked to the girl on the altar. *I have failed you. I have failed myself.*

Nyva's eyes opened, blazing into Cullum's soul an imprint of emerald green.

Her lips moved, and like a spell, her whisper washed through him. "Cullum." He knew her voice. She had whispered to him on the wind outside the coroner-surgeon's house. "It's all right. Sleep now. It's all right. Wake up now. You did not fail. In death is birth."

Cullum coughed and gasped as his lungs filled with too much blood, and he drowned in dreams of the past.

Diana looked into her husband's eyes now, high in that hidden tower over the sea in the clouds. She spoke through her stare, and he listened with his soul, listened in his chains. She still loved him. But she did not trust him, did not trust he would not kill her the first chance he got.

Do you remember when he was born? *she asked without words.*

I wasn't there, *he answered in silence.*

You were, no matter how far you tried to run. You were still there, *she said.*

I remember, *he admitted as tears welled in his eyes. They welled in Diana's eyes too, and their thought speaking continued.*

In the end, *she thought.*

When this began again, *he thought.*

When all my pushing and screaming and bleeding were done.

When my lungs caught flame, no further through the woods could I run.

When I held him in my arms and stared into my living child's blue eyes.

When I told myself I was done with the pain, all the fucking lies.

I thought, *Such a gift to have, the right is not mine.* He blinked and smiled. I wept. He made no sound.

I screamed like a man, and howled like a dog. I broke both my fists just slugging them on the ground.

When I knew what I had done, when I finally understood what I had made you do, it was far too late.

I thank you. I truly do, my magnificent wife, for admitting now it was you who doomed us both, you who sealed our fate.

Diana strode across the floor, grabbed her sweet husband by the hair, and made him kneel. Her next words were not thought but spoken aloud like a spell.

"Of course it was I. You're just a dog. You think and live as a dog does, and all your spite will never shatter your loyalty to me. Because in your collar, in your chains...you'll always understand that you are the mundane and I am the profane."

Alexander stood and said in a low voice, "And you must always remember that without worship, you are just a cheap stone idol. Dead and hollow."

Diana stepped back and slapped Alexander across the mouth. Only as hard as a woman would slap a man, not as a goddess would smite a heretic.

"I looked into Theron's eyes that day, the day he was born. And they were not my eyes, they were yours, yours when we first met, all the hope, all the fury, all the passion that is only found in men and not gods. Only found in men and not their dogs. In his eyes was everything I loved about your race. And I knew then that one day my babe would grow into a boy, he would grow to a man, a man who questions, a man who is always hungry, always hunting for the answers behind the doors of his pain and passion. The fire I tamed in you, I would never tame in him. And one day, one terrible and magnificent day, my baby will become a man and we will have a war."

"You're mad, you and all your kind," *Alexander said.*

"You are my kind now," *Diana said. She turned her back on him and walked to the obsidian mirror in the center of the otherwise entirely empty chamber in the tower where Alexander was locked away.*

In the mirror, Theron Ward and his companions were passing through the portal in the land that had once been Dentin.

"I told him then, even as a babe, as I rocked him and he suckled on my breast. I told him, 'When that day comes, the day you find *out what you are, the day you understand you are the son of a god and you come for my head and my throne, I will do all I can to bury you, my child.'"*

~

CHAPTER TWENTY

HALF A LIFETIME

"Wake up," said his emerald-eyed wife from far off. *My emerald-eyed queen.*

Cullum rolled over on the stone slab. *My bed.* He rolled over on his bed. The stone slab had been a long time ago, and a world away. *Or am I still lying there?*

"Wake up. You make for a bad king, hehe," said his court sorcerer from close by. "You make for a sad king." The voice grew nearer still.

"You are a great king. You are my king. The Blue King," his wife whispered right in his ear.

Cullum's eyes opened and he sat up, not on the stone slab, but yes, in his bed. His bed in the lord's chambers of the great black house of Wardbrook. Without disgust or disdain, he rolled back his favorite soggy, black, maggot-riddled sheets. He did not shiver or flinch as the squirming things squelched between his naked toes when his feet touched the floor. He smiled as he watched his sweet Nyva feed chunks of rotten flesh to her little pets—big brown, black, and gray rats with growths upon their backs like spider egg sacs.

Brenna lay curled up at the foot of the bed in his rat form

like a faithful dog. Cullum—*I'm not Cullum anymore*—the Blue King was happy for that loyal pet. He was thankful for him. He was thankful for his queen and their great black house. He was thankful for life after life in this place behind space and time.

"You're awake," said the Emerald Queen.

"I'm awake," confirmed the Blue King.

"Are you having trouble remembering again?" she asked, a saintly patience to her tone that made him sure he had trouble remembering often.

"No, my dreams reminded me of much… Thank you."

"Thank me? Whatever for?" A rat hopped up into her lap, and she patted its head with two fingers as it squeaked gleefully.

"For not hating me, for not hating me for failing to save you from…this place." The Blue King tried to say *this place* with revulsion, but he could only muster awe.

The Emerald Queen laughed. "You did not save me. It is true. And I did not save you. And Brenna, too, failed in his task." The sorcerer lifted his head at the mention of his name and silently listened on. "Instead, the three of us took this place and made it *ours*. Or do you forget the day we danced around the burning wicker man, just us three?"

"I remember it," said the Blue King, and he felt the warmth of that fire even now. "He burned."

"Hehe, and he has risen again. And he belongs to us now," said Brenna.

The Blue King nodded and added, "And we have his minions at our beck and call."

He walked to the window and looked out over the lands. The forests of dead trees with colossal pale arms and hands reaching up into the yellow miasma sky. Orchards of brain trees with black, tumorous fruits being harvested by black-clothed skeletal forms. Rivers of rotted brown filth webbing through the grounds like toxic veins.

The Emerald Queen walked beside him and put her arm around his waist. He put his around her shoulder and pulled her close.

"It may be hell, but it is *our* hell," she said. "So, it was a gift that Diana and my father gave us when they made us the victims of a war that was not ours. But they took from me my *right*." Nyva put her hand to the scar on her belly over the space where her womb had been. "And for that, I will take their lives. We will find a way free of this place, and we will hunt them, and we will hunt their blood and all in their line until it is no more."

"We will do it together," Cullum promised, burning with purpose and righteous fire. "However long it takes, however far it takes us, we will find them, and they will burn."

EPILOGUE

Farno and his brother Faillin looked quite a bit alike, but Faillin was shorter and broader. They both had the same dark brown hair and hazel eyes as their late parents. Refugees from a massacred Enlightened settlement on the savage northern isle of Blodjord, they had resettled in Brynth a generation ago. First in Norburg, then in Aldwick. They had been herbalists—good ones—and Farno and Faillin were failures and thugs. Farno often thought their parents had died six years ago of disappointment.

After their parents' demise, Farno and Faillin remained as they were: pagans, bloodletters, and, above all, criminals. They did not believe in the Luminescent as their parents had, for all the sun had got them was a home turned to ash and a basement hovel in a big, uncaring city to live in.

Farno and Faillin believed in Dammar, the change god, and so they tattooed themselves with images of the skulls of many beasts and old runes, images they found in books they had stolen while sneaking into the forbidden sections of church libraries, after taking the key from some hapless abbot. The brothers regretted nothing in how they lived.

They had only lived in New Wardbrook for a short time. Most settlers had only been there a short time. All the settlers but for that man with memorable dark eyes, a perfect bowl cut, and a curled mustache. He said he had been in these lands for decades, but he barely looked to be the age of Farno or Faillin. So either he was a demon, or he lied.

He called himself coroner-surgeon.

Farno had not liked the look of the man. He had not liked the smirk of the man. And he knew that inside that man's large house there would be many riches.

"We should leave in the morning," Faillin said now as they crept through the ravine, following the tracks of a massive buck. "When the authorities catch on to the fact that we are the Wardbrook Ravine poachers, the village cutthroats who left a man robbed and dead down by the stream to the south-east, the ones who set the church aflame, and killed that woman and her husband praying inside—"

"You do sound proud of our accomplishments," said Farno

"—they are going to skin us and cut off our dicks before they impale us and burn us on the pyres like the fucking Romarians do," finished Faillin as if there had been no interruption.

"Don't worry, Faillin. We leave in the morning. But first I want to kill that man, the coroner-surgeon, and see what he has in his house—deal?" Farno asked, in the tone of a command.

"Why?"

"Because I don't like the way he looked at me, Faillin. I don't like it at all. I feel like he is still looking at me," said Farno in a whisper as he looked side to side in the woods.

"You're a lunatic, Farno," said Faillin.

"And the only way he is going to stop looking at me," Farno continued, and gritted his teeth, ignoring his brother's words, "is if I cut out his fucking eyes, flay his lips for wearing that stupid smirk, and take his goods... Then we can leave Wardbrook, on the coroner-surgeon's horses. With poached meat and stolen gold, we leave."

"*New* Wardbrook—we can leave *New* Wardbrook," Faillin corrected him in jest.

It was only a few years ago that the Brynthian army reclaimed the lands, burned all titles, and took all the holdings of the heretic, traitor, conspirator, murderer, and war criminal Theron Ward, the known ringleader of the *Plague of Three*, as the town criers and wanted posters called them.

The cohorts of Theron Ward were the heretic monk, church burner and mass murderer Aldous Weaver and the ruthless fugitive, prison escapist, dishonored and deserting crusader Kendrick the Cold. Some said that these three men were naught but legends and myths made up by the monarchy to stir strife and hatred for all enemies foreign and domestic of the lands of Brynth. Three unreal figures and names to carve upon every single outsider and free thinker in order to make it more palatable for the public when they watched any and all enemies of the state do the gallows dance.

Others said that Theron Ward, Aldous Weaver, and Kendrick the Cold had not only carried out a string of crimes across Brynth, but some travelers insisted that the trio had been in Romaria and that they were at Brasov when the Patriarch fell beneath the crumbling Basilica. Worse still, it was said the trio was present during the invasion of the islanders from the cold lands of Ygdrasst and Blodjord, who even now pillaged, sieged, and assaulted towns and keeps in Brynth.

New Wardbrook was yet to see the northern invasion, but Farno and Faillin knew it was only a matter of time.

Their cousin had died in the butchery of Baytown only three months past.

"Do you think he is truly as evil as they say? Do you think he'd welcome us to his merry band of murderers?" Farno whispered to his brother as they followed the stag tracks in the ravine, their bows at the ready.

"Who?" asked Faillin.

"Theron Ward, the man who used to hold these lands," said Farno.

"Maybe," said Faillin. "But he is probably a better man than they say, as well. For people are split in twain, evil and good, and I don't trust any man or woman who ever claims to be pure good—don't trust them as far as I can throw a cow."

"If he is real," said Farno.

"Of course he is real," said Faillin. "Don't be starting with your strange theories this early on a fine day, Farno. I just want to shoot a buck through the heart as the birds chirp and the crisp wind blows. Is that too much to ask?"

"Of course that is too much to ask," Farno said. He punched his brother in the arm, and they both laughed.

"Look at the size of his bloody hooves," said Faillin as he twirled one of his mustache braids and examined the hoof marks etched in the ground.

"Big," said Farno, and then he twirled one of his own mustache braids in an identical motion to his brother.

Farno leaned down to look closer at the track.

Grains of dirt in the print were still stirring, fallen leaves and blades of grass springing back after being trampled.

Farno's heart pounded. It was somewhere only strides away from them, it had to be, but he could not see it as he scanned the ravine while motioning to his older brother to be silent.

He saw trees and branches and rays of the sun making the morning fog glow gold.

Where are you?

Farno stared directly at a tree with low black branches, two of them, each one protruding from an identical height about seven feet up the trunk, from the left and right sides. Then, without blinking, Farno watched the two black branches appear to slide down the tree's trunk.

"Antlers," whispered Faillin.

Farno felt like an incompetent idiot. He was not staring at branches; he was staring at antlers. It was the stag, only a score of strides away, directly in front of them, in front of a tree. It had just lowered its head to graze.

As silent as the sandmen they were, one brother circled a few feet to the right, whilst the other brother circled a few feet to the left.

The stag's coat was as black as a shadow stallion.

Farno lifted his bow; his arrow was already nocked.

He breathed deeply as he drew the bowstring.

He silently prayed to Dammar that he and his brother would be able to abscond with the meat before any of the administrators that now ruled over New Wardbrook found them poaching.

Then the stag raised his head and turned to face Farno. He looked right at him, with all of his hundreds of glowing pink eyes.

Farno lowered his bow at once and fell to his knees.

"Dammar," he gasped.

The stag screamed.

Faillin had just shot it from the other side.

The pink eyes shut. There were only two now, two black eyes. The stag sprinted a short distance, stopped, then, as if deciding to take a nap, lay down.

Farno put his arrow back in the quiver and shouldered

his bow. He drew his knife and approached the stag, not fully comprehending what he had just seen, or thought he had seen.

"Did you see its eyes, Faillin?" Farno asked, his voice shaking even as he managed to keep his hand steady.

"What do you mean?" asked Faillin. Clearly he had not seen the hundreds of pink eyes. He was a few paces away as he closed in on the other side of the stag, who lay, still breathing heavily, in the leaves. "How the hell is it still breathing? That arrow is in its fucking heart." Faillin laughed a dumbfounded sort of laugh, shouldered his bow, and drew his knife.

"I'll finish it," said Farno. He did not want to let his fear of this strange happening get the better of him. Perhaps the heart of this stag was somewhere else, a birth defect, and the eyes, they were a good omen, not a bad. Yes. "A good omen," Farno said, then he kneeled over the stag. Blood pooled out of its mouth from the arrow in its chest; if it was in pain, it showed no sign of it.

Farno raised the knife.

He plunged.

Dammar's eyes opened. Hundreds of glowing pink orbs stared into Farno.

It was too late to stop, and the blade rent fur and flesh.

Blood sprayed up, with an unexpected force and trajectory, like there was some dark intention that caused it to do this. It was as if the blood had a mind of its own. It covered Farno's face. So much of it that he had to shut his eyes. It did not feel like the blood was dripping, but it felt like the blood was crawling, like a swarm of wet insects.

They crawled into his mouth and pried open his lids just enough to glaze his eyes.

A black cathedral on a banished mountain.

Lightning is striking in a clear night sky above, the country of forests and crags.

A pact is made, a child is possessed and transformed.

Years pass in the blink of an eye, and then sights of a white stone city, a festival underway.

An army of demons falls over the white city. They charge through streets and butcher men in bronze and gold masks who fight to the bitter end with sword, bow, and spear. The demons rape and slaughter and burn white-robed civilians, under incandescent lights that line the street blazing with the glow of magic. Rivers of blood now run over stone streets, and the horde of demons assail the great white structure.

The doors open.

The vision changes again.

The interior is not the white structure.

It is the interior of a nameless hell, structured like a church, where the walls and floors are made of moaning, tortured souls, and an army of soulless dregs wander the aisles between the pews made of bone.

A deep and monstrous voice echoes inside of this place.

"Join me now, become me now as I become you. Oh, child of mine."

It is the voice of Dammar.

It is the mind, and heartbeat, and blood of Dammar.

"Farno! Brother...snap out of it." Faillin was shaking Farno and yelling in his face. The blood had not fully cleared from Farno's vision. "Are you all right, Farno? The stag's blood went into your face, and you fell down and started twitching and moaning and rolling your eyes back in your head."

He was not Farno anymore, not just Farno. He was Dammar now too, and Dammar was stronger...much stronger. So even when Farno tried to stop his arm and leap back, away from his brother, he could not.

317

As if he were no more than Dammar's puppet, Farno rammed the blade of his knife through Faillin's lower jaw; steel split through tongue, palate, brain, and bone like nothing. Farno had not been so strong in all his life. And even as tears rolled down his cheeks as horror and grief assailed him, he grabbed Faillin in an embrace with one arm and pried the knife free with the other hand. It squelched and skull fragments crunched as blood and brain juice spilled from the gaping gash.

Faillin! Farno tried to scream. He tried to fall to his knees next to his brother's corpse, but Dammar the puppet master would not allow it.

"A brother spills a brother's blood, to rebirth a feud as old as mud. This is my spell; that is this curse. I rise out of hell to quench the old vendetta's thirst," Farno said, but it was not he who spoke. It was Dammar. And before the last word left his possessed lips, as the blood of Faillin fed the ground and seeped into the earth, the first of the tears began to open.

Tears in the very fabric of the space and air before him.

Gray-fleshed human hands manifested as if reaching out of an invisible curtain. Then the curtain parted more, and a humanoid thing with the torso and arms of a man and the head and hind legs of ram pulled its way through the tear and entered this world. This creature was the first to do so, but not nearly the last.

All around Farno, holes in reality opened up, and from them came the hordes of horned demons. Some with gray skin, others red; others still had skin the complexion of Farno, but the parts that were goats and rams and stags were all covered in black fur.

There must have been a hundred, with more still coming when the host of horned monster men kneeled before Farno.

"Hail, Dammar. Hail the God of Destruction. Hail the

Devil of Change!" said the first to appear, and it kneeled closest to Farno. Then the others echoed the first.

Their exaltation was empowering. It was so bolstering and emboldening that Farno nearly forgot he had just murdered his own brother. He nearly forgot he was Farno at all.

The blood has been in you mere minutes, and already you are prepared to submit.

This is why I chose you. This is why, after being freed from imprisonment inside of Theron Ward, a mind that no devil or god would ever tame, that no spell or curse could ever bind, I knew life as a devil-god would be far easier while possessing a less resilient soul. A soul that does not try to cling to its humanity, but instead wishes to expunge itself of it.

That soul is yours, villain Farno.

I watched you in New Wardbrook. I knew are the man and now is the time to strike. Now is the time to journey deep into the subterranean chambers beneath the great black house of Wardbrook and claim the three souls promised me by the mighty Stiggis. They are there, waiting. Three magical souls. Powerful souls. Power that is mine to claim.

"Thank you, brother," Farno whispered, Dammar whispered, as visions of the smiling man-giant entered their mind. Then Dammar turned his puppet's attention to the horde.

"Guldareck, take your warriors and hew trees. After we take New Wardbrook, we will turn it back into old Wardbrook. A Wardbrook from another age, a dark age of endless war. We fortify and hold this place as our lands now. And any and all of those from the world of men that would attempt trespass will learn our true nature... Bane Dunnah, Ragharn, you and your forces with me!" Farno strode through the woods in the direction of the estate. "With me!"

The horns of war blew, and when the king's men that

stood guard outside the house's front doors saw Farno, bare-chested, tattooed and covered in gore, his eyes white and black orbs staring out of a crimson mask, with a horde of horned demons at his back, swords and axes and spears in their hands, the guards threw open the doors and ran inside.

Deep from Farno's belly, Dammar's laughter bellowed.

"Bane Dunnah, come to me and have a word," Dammar said to the demon general, with a black stag's head and a man's muscled torso, parts of it rotting with green, festering sores.

Bane Dunnah hurried to Dammar's side.

"Master of Malice," said Bane as he bowed his head.

"Kill everyone inside, but bring me the emissary of the Void. He will be hiding in the skin of an old man, dressed as an archdeacon of the Order of Seekers. When all in the estate are dead, go to the village. Kill everyone. Go to the nearest roads and lie in wait for three days. Kill anyone who passes. Then return and help Guldareck fortify this place. When all this is done, send runners north, northeast, northwest, until you find my brother Stiggis."

Bane Dunnah snarled at the mention of Dammar's brother.

"Easy, Bane. He and I are on good terms now. Very good terms. For he has given me a precious gift, one that lies beneath the house, locked away in the catacombs of time. Stiggis knows how to open the door. He knows how to bring forlorn souls back from the land of the endless night-day, where dawn comes from the west and evening ends in the east, where no one dies and no one lives. Pain and fear rule all, and there is sleep but no rest. There is only the nightmare of the black sun-moon. They are there, my three. The three promised to me."

The End

If you enjoy Black Sun Moon **please leave a review** to help other readers decide on this book. Word of mouth is an author's best friend.

∽

Read book 7—Embers on the Wind—Now!

Keep reading for a sample of *Embers on the Wind*!

Want to be the first to know about new releases, excerpts, giveaways, and more? Join Dylan's Reader Group! www.DylanDooseAuthor.com

∽

Never miss a freebie, sale, or new release announcement. Follow Dylan on Bookbub!

EMBERS ON THE WIND

*T*heron knelt on the wooden deck of the Arasmas.

His father's sword was in its scabbard, point to the ground, the bottom of the blade and hilt resting over his shoulder.

Your father's sword is gone. You lost it in Dammar's Black Cathedral, atop the banished mountain. Remember, Theron?

"I remember," Theron said aloud and the sword became an axe. The head rested on the ground, the shaft over his shoulder.

Chayse, Theron's beautiful, brave, and brutal sister sat across the longboat's deck, staring at him. She was here, alive, and he knew this was a dream. But he was deeply glad to see her, even if she was not real, just a conjuring of memories and regret.

Their eyes locked and they smiled at each other as the same soft wind that stirred the ship's sail caressed their hair so that their golden locks flowed like the easy waves 'neath the hull.

"I love you, sister. I love you and I am sorry that I am no

leader. I am sorry that I am blind, and that I am lame," Theron said, his voice deep and clear like it used to be before the events of Brasov and the Black Cathedral.

"And I love you, brother. Do not be sorry. Do not ever be sorry for the fights you fought. Do not be sorry for those you have inspired to fight alongside you." Chayse shook her head and tears welled in her eyes, then trickled down her cheeks and melted away into the sea breeze. "You are not blind, Theron. You are looking in the wrong direction. You are not lame. You are climbing the wrong mountain."

"Tell me, then," Theron pleaded. When had she become wiser than him? "Where am I to be looking? Which mountain must I climb? I am lost, sister. I am lost. And I am weary of this waiting. I am wary of some coming war of a magnitude that I cannot comprehend. I hear its drums echoing up from the darkest halls of premonition. What is my part to be in this? What is my destiny in the coming chaos?"

"You know what it is. You know what you are. You are the wolf."

He heard her words through a sudden, stabbing pain in his eye. The agony toppled him forward so that he was on all fours, screaming.

You only have one eye now, remember Theron?

Dark red blood spilled from Theron's empty eye socket onto the deck of the Arasmas. His screaming turned to wolfish howling as invisible fire began burning the wound shut.

"You are the thing that culls," Chayse said. "You are the creature that haunts the dark woods of worlds. You are a killer of monsters in whatever form they come, from whatever portal or pit they are spawned. You hunt them down and you take their heads." Chayse's voice pulsed with fervor as she yelled her words over the sound of the now growling wind and the rising waves, over the sounds of Theron and the wolf inside of him howling.

Chayse got to her feet, put her arms to her sides and tipped her face to the sky. The wind swirled and she ascended from the deck. Theron stretched his hand toward her but she was already too far away. He recoiled as her face altered, melting and reforming until she was Chayse no longer.

Now, she was Mother in a flowing white gown.

"You take their heads, as they once tried to take yours. Remember? Remember, my son!" The veins in Diana's neck pulsed and swelled as she wailed the words.

More blood spilled onto the deck, this time from a slash freshly formed across Theron's neck. His howling halted as he coughed and choked on his own blood. He was certain he would die, that even in this dream, even in this vision, he could afford to lose no more blood.

The prick of invisible stitches made him grit his teeth and the burn of invisible flame made him pant as they set to work repairing his sliced throat. Invisible drums set his heart to pounding and his soul to raging. He stumbled to his feet… Nay, he rose with strength and ease, once more the man he knew himself to be.

"You are not the servant of the king or the peasants for whom you carry out your gruesome work. You are the servant of death," Mother said.

As she spoke, the ocean beneath the ship drained away, and the Arasmas remained sailing now through open sky. A sky that changed color from a light blue spotted with white clouds to a sick and miasmic yellow blotched with drifting bodies of black smoke.

"You are a servant of conflict," Mother roared, over the sounds of burning cities far, far below. "You are the servant of *yourself*! And so, you shall remain until the fire takes you and you are no more than embers on the wind. Until a sun dies, and a new one rises and you hunt again." Her body grew translucent, then disappeared altogether and her head fell tumbling back toward the deck.

Theron blinked. Mother was gone. In her place were Celta and Aldous and Ken. Butcher. The doctor. The child and her dog. Were they here in truth? This was a dream, was it not? He could not say. He felt certain of nothing.

To Theron's left stood his man, always his left-hand, Kendrick the Cold, the Dahkah now, with tattoos of black snakes running down his cheeks from the lower lids of his sharp, beady eyes. He held a curved knife that looked much like the curved tooth of some great saber-fanged beast. Ken's left hand remained a stump, for the Dahkah's darkness was not yet summoned.

To Theron's right was Celta, his wife, the woman he had been promised to when she was just a girl. Theron had thought himself a man then, but he had been just a boy. That boy had run away from her, broken his oaths to her. But she was here now, by his right hand, and he by her left. She held a small axe and a shield.

Across the deck from her stood a tall and lanky man, facial features sharp and intelligent like some sinister bird.

A raven, I think. Yes, Gaige is one of Aldous' ravens made into human flesh.

His eyes were an unnatural crimson and his hair was of the same color. In each of his hands he held a gleaming scalpel, the tools of his trade.

Beside the doctor stood the center of their adventure: Aldous Weaver, Theron's ward, the boy Theron had saved those few years ago…those *many, many* years ago.

Time is relative to the space that one finds oneself in.

Aldous who had loved Chayse. Aldous who had been torn

asunder by Dahlia the Dog Eater. Aldous who had watched his own father burn alive, who had been locked away in a church basement when he received news of his mother's suicide. The boy born to a twisted fate, Aldous who was now the young Red King.

He was a boy no longer. He was a killer of demons and a wielder of magic most terrible and magnificent. His long black hair was slicked back into a tight topknot, his shoulders wider than they had been. He smiled at Theron, a friendly smile, a brotherly smile, a loving smile. And Theron felt the muscles of his own face pull into the exact same expression.

The echo of drums punched through the yellow sky, the sound reverberating from the black sun moon that cast its shadow over this nightmare realm.

As the beat pulsed so did that dark sphere in the sky, swelling and shrinking to the rhythm of those invisible and ethereal war drums.

Theron gripped tight onto the shaft of the long axe in his hands. He spat on the deck and looked to Aldous' left where stood the scarred, mutant of a man. Butcher. He had his meat cleaver in hand.

"Who are you, he who looks so much like a monster? He who brought us through the portal to this place?" Theron had only uttered the question in his thoughts, but Butcher answered anyway.

"I am but the Red King's most trusted Doorman is all," said he, and although his already exposed teeth could not make a wider smile, a glint in his eyes indicated that he held a kind of pride in his position.

In the circle's center was the little girl, Bruna, and her white dog. She was an orphan the group had taken in. She was clearly afraid, as was her dog, as they looked frantically between the monstrous mortals that made up her adoptive tribe. When he reached down and said, "I am no beast," the girl whimpered and crawled backward like a crab and cried, "Devil, monster…keep away!"

Her little dog yapped and nipped at Theron's hand. He pulled away and looked hopelessly to the others.

Is it even possible, I wonder? For the mighty to ever know how to nurture the meek? Again, Theron's words were confined to his thoughts. Again, responded to what was not said.

"The warrior's way is not a path upon which to raise a child, only warriors. And so, for better or worse, she is with us now and like us she shall become," said the crimson eyed doctor.

"It was how my father raised me. Like a man, like a beast, and three husbands lie dead behind me on this road," Celta said in mournful agreement.

"Aye," Kendrick said. "But a broken, lonely lad, an orphan filled with fear and hate was I when the conscription was signed and I marched until the marsh was the sand and the fog was dust storm, until west was east and a devil I became in a foreign land."

"Pay attention!" boomed a voice that did not belong to any in their group.

Theron turned and set eyes upon the man-giant , Stiggis. He had appeared from nothing, sitting now with his legs crossed and back upright against the ship's mast in a meditative posture. His hair and beard of white gold swayed in the wind as the ship soared through open sky.

Something moved in the periphery of Theron's vision. A white snake—

He spun.

The girl and her dog were there longer.

Theron's belly sank. The horror and guilt of losing the child so early in the quest nearly dropped him to his knees.

But anger kept him upright, anger at the things that had taken the girl and her dog.

Theron hacked through writhing white tentacles. The others were already in the fray. Celta swung at a bulbous white head, an explosion of yellow gore spraying out over the lot of them. Kendrick summoned his phantom limb, the serpent arm of the Dahkah punching a hole through the creature's squishy white chest.

"The Friends of the Void," Theron said through heavy, panting breaths, chunks of white slopping off the edge of his axe and onto the deck.

"They are here," said Stiggis. As he rose, a great deluge began to pour down from the sky, the black sun moon turning azure blue before blinking crimson. With a flash of purple lightning, it went back to azure and back and forth, red to blue and red again. The torrential downpour put out the flames of the burning world below and in a manner only possible within the mad confines of a dream, the ship once again sailed over a raging, stormy sea.

The longboat rocked and Theron spun round to face the left side as white tentacles reached out from the waters and into the ship. Green scaled claws by the scores gripped firm the rails and then heaved themselves over and onto the deck. They came, fiends of the sea: scaled Murlur with glowing yellow eyes, hulking with muscle, hopping forth on thick frog-like thighs. More of the bulbous-headed *Friends* mixed among the throng.

What if we never escaped Dentin? What if we still fight them there?

"What if we never escaped the church when it burned in Baytown? What if you and I still lie therein?" Celta asked through heavy breaths as she blocked an incoming spear thrust by one of the fish-men. She parried the blow and her own one-handed axe sunk through muscle and cracked through the green scaled things clavicle with sound like splitting wood.

"What if this is all just a dream?" Aldous asked.

"And what if the dream is mine?" said Butcher, his cleaver sinking into a foe sending blue and yellow blood spraying in all directions.

Lightning cracked the sky as Ken pointed his blade backward toward the ship's mast and the one that stood before it. "Worse yet, what if the dream is his?"

All eyes went to Stiggis. The blue runic tattoos that covered the man-giant's body pulsed with a blue glow along with the alternating colors of the moon.

"Not his," said a voice that came from the sea and the sky.

Stiggis squinted and, with a glower, raised his axe high. Snow fell from its ice-enchanted tip as he pointed. Turning once more, Theron looked up to where the sea was rising before the ship, rising up, up, up like a monolithic tower of black water. Standing atop it, with arms outstretched and palms upright like a monk praying to the Luminescent was man.

"Not a dream," he said. "A nightmare…"

More and more fiends of the sea crawled their way out of the waves and onto the Arasmas' deck. Stiggis joined the companions in hewing down the foes, but when one fell another slid into its place.

"It is the nightmare of the one who sleeps," said the man atop the tower of water. "It is that terrible terror that sits in the mind of the one who dwells so far in the fathomless deeps!"

Once more, lightning tore the sky asunder. For that horrible and doomed instant, Theron saw beneath the surface of the rising tower of water. He saw the one the deeps held within, the one he had seen before in Dammar's vision, too horrible to look upon, as tall as mountain, a mountain of scaled flesh and cold blood, of fin and tentacle and claw, of many hydra heads and a single visage the resembled the gigantic face of a humanoid babe with sharp fangs as tall as ancient oak trees. The dreamer of this nightmare.

It cried out, a sky-splitting, mountain-cracking call, like the whole world was folding in on itself. The sound clawed at Theron's mind and his head felt like it would explode. He fell to his knees and around him, his companions did the same. Blood ran from their eyes and noses and ears.

The tentacled and scaled creatures on the deck were unaffected, perhaps even spurred onward by the cataclysmic sound.

"Rise!" The man-giant's mouth moved as he shouted the command but Theron could not hear him over *the call.*

Theron was shoved down, monsters piling atop him. He called for Celta and Ken and Aldous. They could no more hear him than he could hear Stiggis. He could do naught but flail and fight a futile battle as all were overwhelmed, even the man-giant. All Theron's strength and fury, all his rage and skill, were not enough, not near enough to break free.

He fought for breath.

A scaled elbow rammed into his face and pressed against his jaw, pinning his head between monster and deck. That same elbow exerted pressure until Theron's jaw hinged open against his will. He tried to scream, to squirm, to get an inch of space but he could not move. He could only look on in horror as the white eel slithered across the gore-spattered deck toward his pried open mouth.

He prayed then to his mother, to Dammar, to any god or demon that could intervene. But alas no one and nothing did as the pale white thing wormed its way in and the wizard atop the tower of the sea that was Leviathan roared.

"This is *his* nightmare, oh great Leviathan, and I am his light. I am *the* light! I am the sun in the sea. I am the Father of the Arcane Church of the Great Dark! I come from the great below and the worlds of men shall reap what they have sown. I will take your souls. I will make you mine. I will break you all at the Tower of Aldrone!"

Read book 7—Embers on the Wind—Now!

ALSO BY DYLAN DOOSE

SWORD AND SORCERY SERIES:

Fire and Sword (Volume 1)

Catacombs of Time (Volume 2)

I Remember My First Time (A Sword and Sorcery short story; can
be read at any point in the series)

The Pyres (Volume 3)

Ice and Stone (Volume 4)

As They Burn (Volume 5)

Black Sun Moon (Volume 6)

Embers on the Wind (Volume 7)

RED HARVEST SERIES:

Crow Mountain (Volume 1)

～

For info, excerpts, contests and more, join Dylan's Reader Group!

Website: www.DylanDooseAuthor.com

ABOUT THE AUTHOR

Dylan Doose is the author of the ongoing Dark Fantasy saga, *Sword & Sorcery*.

Dylan also pens the new Dark Fantasy/Western Horror series, *Red Harvest*.

Fire and Sword was chosen as a Shelf Unbound Notable 100 for 2015 and received an honorable mention from Library Journal.

For info, excerpts, contests and more, join Dylan's Reader Group! www.DylanDooseAuthor.com

photo credit: Shanon Fujioka

For more information:

www.dylandooseauthor.com

Printed in Great Britain
by Amazon